CAROLYN DAVIDSON
CHERYL ST.JOHN
JENNA KERNAN

Wed Under Western Skies

For three special women, love will be found in the most unexpected of places!

ISBN 0-373-29399-2

Harlequin® Historical
is proud to present
WED UNDER WESTERN SKIES
a special collection from

CAROLYN DAVIDSON

"Davidson wonderfully captures gentleness in the midst of
heart-wrenching challenges, portraying the extraordinary
possibilities that exist within ordinary marital love."
—*Publishers Weekly*

"Carolyn Davidson creates such vivid images,
you'd think she was using paints instead of words."
—bestselling author Pamela Morsi

CHERYL ST.JOHN

"Ms. St.John knows what the readers want
and keeps on giving it."
—*Rendezvous*

"Ms. St.John holds a spot in my top five list of
must-read Harlequin Historical authors.
She is an amazingly gifted author."
—*Writers Unlimited*

JENNA KERNAN

"...engaging characters, a colorful backdrop and
[the heroine's] personal growth make this
classic western romance something special."
—*Romantic Times BOOKclub* on *The Trapper*

"With this strong debut, Jenna Kernan
puts her name on the list of writers to watch for."
—*The Romance Reader* on *Winter Woman*

Wed Under Western Skies
Harlequin Historical #799—May 2006

CAROLYN DAVIDSON

Carolyn Davidson is a product of the marriage of two strong, stubborn individuals, who taught her the values and precepts by which she lives—a love of God, home and family, an abiding respect for this great land we live in, and a grateful heart that truly appreciates all she has been given in this life. She has a loving husband, six children, over twenty grandchildren and three great-grands. Life is good.

CHERYL ST.JOHN

Cheryl says that knowing her stories bring hope and pleasure to readers is one of the best parts of being a writer. The other wonderful part is being able to set her own schedule and work around her family and church. Working in her jammies ain't half bad either! Cheryl loves to hear from readers. Write her at P.O. Box #24732, Omaha, NE 68124, or e-mail CherylStJohn@aol.com. Visit her Web site, www.tlt.com/authors/cstjohn.htm.

JENNA KERNAN

Multipublished author Jenna Kernan is every bit as adventurous as her heroines. Her hobbies include recreational gold prospecting, scuba diving and rock climbing. Indoor pursuits encompass jewelry making, writing, photography and quilting. Jenna lives in New York State with her husband and two gregarious little parrots. Visit Jenna at www.jennakernan.com for excerpts of her latest release, giveaways and monthly contests.

CAROLYN
DAVIDSON
CHERYL
ST.JOHN
JENNA
KERNAN
Wed Under
Western Skies

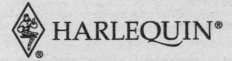

HARLEQUIN®

TORONTO • NEW YORK • LONDON
AMSTERDAM • PARIS • SYDNEY • HAMBURG
STOCKHOLM • ATHENS • TOKYO • MILAN • MADRID
PRAGUE • WARSAW • BUDAPEST • AUCKLAND

ISBN 0-373-29399-2

WED UNDER WESTERN SKIES
Copyright © 2006 by Harlequin Books S.A.

The publisher acknowledges the copyright holders
of the individual works as follows:

ABANDONED
Copyright © 2006 by Carolyn Davidson

ALMOST A BRIDE
Copyright © 2006 by Cheryl Ludwigs

HIS BROTHER'S BRIDE
Copyright © 2006 by Jeannette H. Monaco

CONTENTS

Dear Reader,

Although few, if any of us in this lifetime, will be afforded the dubious pleasure of traveling on a covered wagon across this great land of ours, the prospect of just such a trip sounds appealing to many—me included. I've thought longingly of this sort of venture, and wished for fleeting moments that I might be transported to the days long ago of wagon trains, and the adventure involved in seeking out new worlds to conquer.

But I have limits. I am of the persuasion that hot showers and modern facilities for my personal comfort are important. Thus, I'd make a lousy pioneer woman. However, I have found the perfect solution to my dithering between the reality of this modern world and the lure of the past. I simply write stories that might have taken place back then. My heroes and heroines are purely products of my imagination, but to me they are very real, and I'm privileged to place them in situations that I then maneuver to suit my own fantasies.

Writing historical novels is a delightful occupation, one that encompasses a certain amount of talent. And for that talent I am appreciative. Daily I give thanks for the Lord of Creation who has allowed me to enjoy the pleasure of telling my tales.

Wagon trains are a thing of the past, but the love between decent men and virtuous women is still alive in this modern world. And because of that love, expressed through the bonds of marriage and parenthood, I find myself blessed—having been gifted with dreams of yesteryear and the brave souls who peopled that world.

Best,

Carolyn Davidson

ABANDONED

Carolyn Davidson

Abandoned is dedicated with love and respect
to those of my ancestors who were pioneers
in another way: that of traveling to the
"new world" to make new lives for
themselves and their loved ones. To all those
stalwart men and women, I dedicate this story.

And, as ever, I offer it as a gift to my beloved.

Prologue

The flames were all around, and Elizabeth felt the heat as if the very fires of hell encompassed her. Although clothing protected her skin, the weight of cotton and linen against her body was almost too much to bear. Even through open eyes, she saw only the red glare of the wagon burning and blinked frantically to clear her vision.

Over her stood a figure. A man. Almost naked, holding a weapon. If this were to be her last memory of life, it would be only a preface to hell itself, for she could think of nothing worse than to be given her death blow by way of a monster waving a hatchet.

And yet, that was not the proper name for it, she thought. Her brain seemed to be operating in slow motion, for the man who crouched by her side moved almost languidly, one arm lifting the weapon high, his other hand reaching for her, grasping her hair and then hesitating, as his dark gaze fastened on the length of golden tresses he held. For a long moment she froze, her eyes staring as they met his.

His mouth opened and a guttural sound spewed forth, a word that to her mind sounded like a curse. He dropped her hair, stood abruptly, and then lifted her from the edge of the flames. As if he were undecided, he backed to where a horse stood, those dark eyes impaling her.

Elizabeth yearned to awaken, for surely this could not be reality, but she felt a shriek of despair rise from her throat as she realized she existed, alive in the midst of her nightmare. Another voice called out and the man who held her answered the summons, shouting out unintelligible words she strained to understand. With a last look of pity, she thought, or perhaps resignation, he placed her on the ground, and she closed her eyes.

If he were going to kill her, she had no desire to see the death blow, and yet, in some separate part of her consciousness, she knew that he would leave her there, alive. Her face hurt, her eyes felt scorched, and she curled into herself, more fearful now of enduring a hellish death than of facing the men who had surrounded her so recently. The wood of her wagon crackled in the silence, devouring itself with the fire that sought to destroy it. But the sounds of men, their voices, their movements, had vanished. Indeed, it seemed she was alone. No more sounds of chanting and shouting. No sense of being watched by eyes that devoured her.

She lifted a hand, the motion slow, for her arms and shoulders were surely afire, so great was the pain. Her fingers felt once again for the throbbing spot near her temple, and she winced at the smarting sting of open flesh. Rubbing her eyes, where smoke and fire had brought tears flowing, she glanced fitfully at her fingers and could not mistake the bloodstains there, blood that must surely be her own. The crimson glow she peered through was that of her own blood.

She breathed slowly, wondering if her wounds were fatal, and in that moment, knew she would survive. For her father had told her she was strong, strong enough to survive this trip to a new land where fortune awaited them. Strong enough to withstand the heat and the rutted trail that stretched into the West. For him, the man who had brought her thus far, who had cared for her and protected her as best he could, she must honor his faith in her, and survive.

And yet, he was not there, not beside her, and her heart cried out vainly for his presence, whispering his beloved name as she sank into unconsciousness.

"Father?" And then with a sob, she whispered again. "Where are you, Daddy?"

Chapter One

Kansas, July 1848

"Will you look at that! She ain't dead, but I'll warrant she's right close to it."

Joe Campbell, a hardened veteran of the Indian wars, bent low over the bruised and battered young woman curled on the ground at his feet. His exclamation held a trace of horror.

"What have you found?" A second man rode closer, skirting the still-smoking embers of the wagon that hid the female from his sight. Cameron Montgomery's horse picked his way through the litter strewn for yards in every direction, all of it shattered and ruined for any useful purpose. Yet each piece had once been part of a household, and now lay abandoned by whoever had attacked this wagon. And if the signs he'd already seen were anything to go by, Indians had had a heyday here, burning everything in sight, leaving carnage behind. How the girl had managed to crawl far enough from the wagon to save herself from the fire was a miracle, he decided. Perhaps she had been dumped from a horse when her captors decided she wouldn't live long enough to make hauling her along with them worthwhile. Joe was right. She appeared more dead than alive.

Cameron dismounted quickly as he reached the young woman's side, hoping to find more than a bare flicker of life within her battered body. It was unlikely that her attackers had left her with more than a spark of life, but it was a point of honor that the scouts either rescue the victims or bury the bodies they found in a situation such as this.

Scouts for a wagon train were privy to sights that chilled their blood and yet inured them to the presence of those who could not be helped, those whose broken and bloodied bodies they buried beneath the grassy plains. Cameron and Joe were only a few miles ahead of the train they worked with, scouting out the trail for the fifty or so wagons that followed them. They'd have to make a wide berth around this scene, Cameron thought. One look at the havoc created here would cause the womenfolk to gather their young'uns around them, and worry for the whole livelong days ahead about what would become of them.

Stray children were targeted by those who lived in this part of the country, those men who knew the value of a child, white and Indian alike. More than one had been spirited away, never to be seen again. And Cameron's wagon train would not be prey to such thieves if he could prevent it.

He knelt by the young woman, driven to straighten her arms and legs, making her appear more comfortable on her resting place of hard, crusted dirt. No meadow grass softened her bed, only the tracks of wagons, ground into place by the thousands of wheels that had rumbled past this place.

The slight movement of her breasts signified an attempt to suck in a breath, and Cam bent lower, holding his hand beneath her nostrils, hoping to feel her warm breath. Now she moved her bloody hand and inhaled, then released the air from her lungs with a sigh. He bent closer, his ear almost touching her mouth, hoping to catch the whispered words she spoke. It was only a soft mumble, but the broken syllables sent an unaccustomed chill down his spine.

"Don't. Please, don't." And then her voice faltered and her eyes opened, wide and staring, their blue depths filled with horror. "No!" It was a scream of pure terror and without thinking, Cameron placed his hand over her mouth, lest the sound carry to the tops of the hills surrounding them on three sides. God only knew who hid from sight, watching the small drama take place in the unsheltered area of carnage.

The sun beat down, not yet at its full strength as it would be at noontime. But in July he'd expected the heat of early morning, had known that sweat would accompany him daily on this journey from St. Louis to the placid rivers of Oregon.

"What do you think?" Joe asked. "How bad is she hurt?"

"Not as badly as I thought at first. We'll take her with us," Cameron told Joe quietly. "And if she dies, it won't be because no one cared enough to get her out of this mess." Cameron looked up to see the hopelessness of Joe's gaze on the girl, and knew that his partner held little hope for her life.

"I'll take her on my horse," Cameron said, rising and lifting the slight form with ease. He was a big man, used to hard work, and his muscles were barely challenged by the weight of the woman he held. His dark hair blew in his eyes and he tossed his head impatiently.

"Take her for a minute, Joe," he said shortly, handing his burden to the other man, and then easing himself into his saddle. His big gelding stood quietly, used to the weight of the man who had ridden him from Independence, Missouri, to this spot on the plains of Kansas.

Joe held the girl as ordered, and then reached up to give her into the hands of the man who waited. She fit nicely across his lap, Cameron thought, a good armful, definitely more woman than girl, now that he had a chance to feel her against his body. His horse shifted a bit, acknowledging the extra weight he was being called on to carry, and Cameron steadied him with a movement of his knees.

Then, gathering the woman closer, he turned his gelding away from the rubble surrounding him, his gaze filtering through the abandoned clothing and bits of furniture left behind by the marauders. Perhaps there was something there, some bit of her past that was important to the woman. A bit of lace-trimmed fabric caught his eye and then a single half-boot that smouldered in the remains of the fire.

They'd done all they could, their rescue operation consisting of just one woman; the rest of the small group either missing or buried in shallow graves.

Impatient with his own dilly-dallying, recognizing that nothing of value lay at his feet, he turned his horse around and rode in a wide circle past the smouldering remains of three more wagons, heading east toward the train whose wagonmaster would be expecting the return of his two scouts.

Joe moved more swiftly, his own horse seemingly anxious to leave the scene, and rode ahead of Cameron. He pulled his hat a bit lower and eyed the hills closely as they followed the trail of wagon wheels across the prairie, his gaze alert for movement, lest they fall victim to an attack before they reached the relative safety of the wagon train.

His hand lay easily over the butt of his rifle as he rode, for it was his lot to protect Cam and the girl, although Cam was well able to fire his pistol, no matter that his arms were currently occupied with the female he held.

The woman moaned, her eyelids fluttering a bit as she attempted to rejoin the land of the living, and Cameron wished silently for a wet rag to wipe the streaked blood from her face. His canteen was over half-full and in a careful movement, he shifted the woman on his lap, then jerked the kerchief from his neck and sloshed water on it.

He wiped the cloth gently across her cheek, and then against her forehead, where a gaping gash and an abundance of dried and clotting blood gave evidence of the blow she had sustained. Why they hadn't scalped her was a miracle for she possessed a long length of golden hair, one which would have been highly prized by any Indian brave. In fact, why they hadn't taken her along with them to their camp was another mystery. She'd have been a prime trophy at the least.

Around her throat, more bruises testified to her assailants' attempt to remove the necklace she wore. Hanging from it was a simple gold ring, a circle he would guarantee was a wedding band. Probably a keepsake of some sort, perhaps her own. But if that were hers, it should have been on her finger. That was a puzzle he'd think about later, he decided.

Her features were small and regular, the gash on her temple and the bruising surrounding her eye dark reminders of her pain. But not even that evidence, or the cut on her chin could disguise the natural beauty of the woman. She opened her eyes again and focused on his face, and he ached for the pain of her memories…for the utter hopelessness of her expression was silent testimony of what she had endured.

"You're safe now," he said quietly. "The Indians are gone, and we're on our way to the wagon train just east of here."

"How?" She seemed to search for the words she would speak, and Cameron shushed her with a finger on her lips.

"We're scouts for a train, ma'am. You must have been attacked yesterday from the looks of it, and we found your wagon an hour ago."

"I hurt," she whispered. "I didn't expect…I thought I would surely die."

"Well, I have a notion you're a strong woman," Cameron

said, holding her close to his chest. The urge to bind her to him, to protect the woman, was strong within him, a strangely possessive emotion, one he was not familiar with.

"Thank you." The sounds were barely discernible, but the smile she attempted to offer spoke to him as no words could. Her lips trembled as she lay back against his strength and her head turned away a bit, revealing the heretofore hidden side, where blood had dried earlier, but was even now seeping from a cut high on her cheek.

He wiped at it, cleaning most of the blood, noting her wince as he carefully swept his kerchief across her eyes. He wiped the rounding of her cheek, allowing him to see the wound, which welled up afresh with his touch. The cut was not deep, but might need a stitch or two, he thought, thankful for the presence of a doctor on the train. He could have sewn it himself, but the thought of driving a needle through her tender flesh didn't sit well. He'd help the doctor do his work, offering his help as she was examined for damages and then cleaned up.

She was sleeping now, her breath even and her eyes shadowed by pain. Cameron tucked his kerchief away.

Ahead of him he saw the smoke from campfires, where breakfast was being cooked and readied for the families who rode the wagons. He and Joe would be greeted at any of several fires, offered plates of food and welcomed by most all of the men and women who depended on them for safety.

His horse broke into a lope as if the lure of oats drew him to the circle of wagons. Cameron had a barrel of feed for his mount. A man who didn't take good care of his horse was a foolish man indeed, his pa had always told him.

Elizabeth had felt the rocking rhythm of the horse beneath her, and known the warmth of the masculine arms that held her. Now, recognizing the scent of bacon and the redolent aroma of coffee, she knew for certain that she was alive. She stirred, attempting to sit erect, but the arms that held her only tightened around her and the gruff, masculine voice she'd heard against her ear was once more speaking, this time impatiently.

"I'd rather you didn't end up on the ground, lady, after all the trouble we took to get you here alive."

Elizabeth opened her eyes, leaning her head against a wide shoulder and looked up into a dark gaze she seemed to recall. It was the man who had lifted her so recently from the ground. His were the hands that had wiped her face with a damp cloth, and his arms had been her security for the past…hour perhaps?

Time had seemed to come to a standstill once the painted figures had surrounded her wagon. She'd been hauled off the seat, thrown to the ground and mauled by two men who seemed to have been torn between stripping off her clothing or knocking her senseless.

They'd succeeded at one, as her aching head testified, but she was still clothed, so they must have been diverted by more pleasing prospects. Maybe the three women in her train, who were heading for a saloon at the end of this journey. Even on a trip such as this, they had dressed in satin and lace, crushed and soiled to be sure, but the men hadn't seemed to mind.

It could be that her own attackers had sought out the more attractive sights offered by the saloon girls. That they hadn't stripped her of her clothing was a good sign, she thought. Perhaps they'd decided to leave her for the buzzards. The memory of a hatchet aimed at her head would haunt her forever, but somehow, she knew she was safe now. The man holding her had said so, and for whatever reason, she believed him. Knew that his harsh voice and the strength of his body were to be trusted.

Strong hands gripped her, lifting her from the horse, and Elizabeth knew a moment of piercing pain, her head striking the shoulder of an unknown person. "Watch it," the familiar, gruff voice said from above her. "I'll guarantee she's got a dandy of a headache."

Doggone right, I have. The words were her last conscious thought as she slipped once more into the depths of darkness.

"What do you think, Doc?" Cameron watched the medical man as he examined the girl, checking her for broken bones, his blunt fingers gentle as he opened her eyes to peer into their depths. Her dress was no barrier to his instrument, and tucking the earpieces in place, he listened to the sounds of her heart and lungs.

"I expect she'll live," Doc Forrest said roughly, as if his throat ached at the sight before him. "Don't know what would make a man treat a woman thisaway. Makes me ashamed of my gender sometimes, when I'm sewing up the results of some man's brutality."

"I doubt the Indians look at it that way," Cameron said. "White men, and women, too, are their enemies. They treat 'em all alike. Except that the women get taken as slaves, or even wives, if they're real lucky. Can't figure out why they left this one behind."

"I reckon they thought she wasn't worth the trouble, figured she wouldn't live long enough to make it worth their while to haul her back to their camp."

"Is she that bad off?" Cameron resisted the urge to reach out to the girl, his fingers itching to touch her hair, the soft flesh of her arms. That they were marred by bruises from uncaring hands mattered little. He'd brought her back, held her close to his body, and had known a sense of responsibility for her well-being. Now he was freshly aware that his feelings had turned to a possessive need to shelter her from harm.

"She'll need some nursing, someone to watch her tonight anyway, make sure she doesn't pull at her bandages." He taped a soft, white cloth bandage over her chin, then another at her temple, his hands careful not to apply hurtful pressure. Turning her head a bit, he inspected the place on her cheek where the skin had split, probably from the force of a man's fist.

"I'll stitch this up right quick," he said, "and we should be about done. Witch hazel is the best thing we've got for the bruising, and that'll need to be used again every couple of hours." He met Cam's gaze squarely.

"Are you planning on watching her? Or shall one of the ladies stay with her?"

"I'll look after her," Cam said without hesitation. "I've already fixed her up a bed in my wagon."

"You'll cause tongues to wag, you know. They'll think it's not decent for you to be tending a female."

Cameron smiled wryly, yet anger lit his eyes. "If any of these folks think I'd take advantage of a woman in this condition, they're not worth the time of day."

"Guess you've made up your mind then." The doctor bent low over the girl, his needle threaded and ready. "Want to hold her down a little?" he asked Cameron. "I'd hate to have her jerk while I'm sewin' this up. It's pretty close to her eye."

Cameron felt his hands tremble as he placed them on either side of the woman's head, his fingers lost in the golden waves and curls. She was warm to the touch, and her hair was the texture of silk against his rough fingers. Her jaw clenched against his rough palm as Doc took the first stitch, and Cameron looked down into blue eyes that widened with pain, even as he watched. Eyes that held questions he felt compelled to answer.

"Hush now, sweetheart. Doc here is sewing up a cut on your face. He'll be done in no time, and I'm just holding you still so you don't jerk or jump and hurt yourself. Can you understand me?"

Her eyes blinked once and he nodded. "You're in the middle of a big wagon train, sweetheart, with about fifty guns ready to fire in case someone should decide to come looking for you. Does that make you feel any safer?"

She blinked again and winced, her mouth trembling as the needle pierced her flesh once more.

"Pour a little whiskey right here," Doc said, moving his hand back to make room for the potent liquid. Cameron's mouth flattened as he did as asked, knowing that the sting of alcohol in the raw wound would be the most painful part of this whole thing. The girl cried aloud and Cameron was quick to hold her still once again, allowing the doctor to complete his work. Tears slid from her eyes and made twin trails into her hairline where they were lost in the wealth of curls, and Cameron watched, his teeth gritting, his heart aching for her pain.

In mere minutes, Doc Forrest bandaged the cut, having carefully put five stitches in place. He nodded in Cameron's direction. "I'd suggest she oughta eat something, Cam. See if you can get a bit of bread or oatmeal down her before she settles down to sleep."

"You think she'll sleep now?" His voice sounded dubious, as Cameron picked up the slight weight of the girl and turned toward his wagon. He looked down at her, attempting to smile reassuringly. "You hungry, sweetheart?"

Her lips formed the negative reply and her eyes closed.

"Just a piece of biscuit maybe?" he coaxed. "Mrs. Perry sure knows how to make good ones. And it looks to me like she's got a few left over from breakfast. I'll bet they're still warm, sweetheart."

He detoured past the Perry wagon, and Dora Perry grinned at his approach.

"Got you an armful, haven't you, Cam? Where you taking her? If you want to leave her with me, I'll take care of her."

"Thank you, ma'am," Cam told her briefly. "I want to keep a close eye on her myself. Guess I feel responsible for her."

"I'll bring over some coffee and biscuits," Dora said obligingly. "There's even some jam to sweeten them up."

"That'd be appreciated, ma'am," Cameron told her. "This little gal might not eat one now, but I'll bet when she wakes up, she will."

"Well, I'll be puttin' on a kettle of stew for dinner at noontime. You come on by and get some for the both of you," Dora said. "It'll fix what ails her, at least part of what her problems are." Her gaze touched on the girl's face and traveled down her body, where her dress was torn and bruises covered her arms.

"You may be right," Cameron said. "I'll be waiting for that coffee, ma'am."

"Comin' right up." Dora set to work, filling two cups and wrapping biscuits in a dish towel before she followed Cameron to his wagon. He managed to climb inside and settle the girl on his feather tick and then turned to see Dora approaching, her hands full.

"You gonna let her sleep in the back while you drive?" She peered beneath the white covering of the wagon to where the woman was curled beneath a light quilt.

"She won't bother me any," Cameron said flatly, his eyes narrowing as if he dared the woman to suggest anything wrong with the arrangement. A blatant possessiveness toward the girl blinded him as his plans were put under Dora's scrutiny.

Dora backed off and a dark flush colored her features. "I didn't mean anything by it, Mr. Montgomery. I just wondered if she needed to have someone with her, maybe another woman." Her eyes told him she thought he was sadly lacking when it came to looking after a female.

"She'll be fine. I brought her to the train. I'll take care of her. And if I need any help, Joe Campbell will be glad to lend a hand."

"Well, I declare," Dora returned, her brows lowering as she shot a nasty look in Cameron's direction. "Doesn't seem quite right, is all. She's a woman, after all."

"I noted that, right off," Cameron said with a grin, one he knew would really tangle Dora's garters. He was right, for she walked directly from his wagon to where the wagon master stood.

"I'll bet he gets an earful," Cameron muttered to himself. His eyes swept over the team of oxen he drove, noting the yoke was not fitting his team perfectly. And that would never do. He jumped down and approached the team, rubbing their noses and speaking softly to them. And while he spoke, he straightened the yoke, sorted out the harness and checked the animals over.

Twin pails of water stood by the wagon, and Cameron took them to the head of his team and watched as they drank their fill. They'd been staked all night in the meadow grass, so food wasn't an issue, but he hung the empty pails beneath the wagon, hoping they would find a source of water during the day or perhaps tonight.

He'd not traveled with his own wagon before, but this scouting job might very well be his last. For the land he'd bought and for which he held a deed, lay ahead, and he'd brought along supplies and necessities for setting up a household should he decide to settle there after this trip, putting his scouting days behind him.

His was the second wagon in the train, Joe having cast his lot with a family who traveled last in line. Cam's own wagon contained only the barest of necessities; his clothing, a barrel of oats for his horse, and a large stack of hay in one corner and an assortment of items he knew would be necessary when he set up his home. A home he yearned for, on his own land. He let his eyes feast on the girl he'd claimed. If she was willing, he would build her a home, a haven for them to share.

And unless he had it figured wrong, they would be seeing the mountains ahead come morning, signifying an end to the lush prairie grasses.

He hadn't seen anything that promised a stream ahead during his predawn jaunt with Joe. But then he'd only concentrated on tracking the shoeless Indian horses and their riders, until they found the small group of wagons, burned and deserted.

He climbed swiftly to his seat now and spared a look into the shadowed space behind him. His dark gaze took note of the cool cloth he'd placed on her forehead, still in place. Her bandages had not darkened with seeping blood, and he was encouraged by its absence. She was on his feather tick, but since he slept most nights beneath the wagon, it hadn't had much use on this journey, and he was happy to see it providing comfort for her. She was lying as he'd placed her, her hair tangled on his pillow, and he allowed his gaze the privilege of resting on her for a moment. He'd never been so drawn by a female in his life. Not only the physical presence of her, although there was a lot to say for her hair that gleamed like sunlight and eyes like a summer sky. He sensed, more than that, courage and a will to survive. For she would survive, no matter that Joe held out little hope, given the cruelties dealt upon her. She would survive, for Cameron would see to it.

Chapter Two

⟨⟨⟨∽∾∾∽⟩⟩⟩

The bed she lay on was moving. Elizabeth shifted a bit, heard the involuntary groan that left her lips and opened her eyes. The light was dim, the pale canvas stretched above her shielding her from the sunshine, and she recognized the rolling rhythm of the wagon as it made its way at a slow pace.

"It must have been a dream, a nightmare," she whispered to herself. And yet, her mind did not recognize the bits and pieces of clothing and equipment surrounding her, nor the bed she lay on.

"You awake back there?"

The man's voice was deep, his eyes dark and searching as he turned on the seat at the front of the wagon and looked down at her. "Your head feeling any better?"

She lifted a hand to the bandage that adorned her brow and shook her head, a slight motion, but one that sent a sharp pain winging its way across her forehead and back.

"I hurt." It was an effort to say the words and she was amazed at how puny her voice sounded as she spoke them.

"I'll just bet you do, sweetheart." A twitch of his lips transformed his face and she felt his appraisal upon her shift from her head down the length of her body and then back. His eyes were dark, almost black it seemed, for the dim light of the wagon's interior did not lend itself to improving her eyesight. His hair, as dark as his eyes, brushed his collar, indeed covered the fabric. Thick and wavy, his hair seemed glossy in the sunlight that appeared at the front of the wagon, causing her to squint against the bright glow.

She sighed deeply, knowing a sense of security, yet why that should be so was a puzzle. The man's name was not known to her, nor the circumstances of her presence in his wagon, but an aura of safety enveloped her and his presence appeared to be the reason for it. She recollected the faint memory of hard arms holding her, of that deep, rough voice speaking to her, and then his gentle movements when he deposited her in this wagon. For unless she was mistaken, she lay on a feather tick, and a pillow lay beneath her head. The pillowcase smelled of fresh air and lye soap, and she inhaled the familiar scent, aware of its place in her memory.

"You want to tell me your name?" the man asked. "Or shall I just call you sweetheart?"

"Elizabeth." She spoke the syllables carefully, lest the effort to speak caused her head to throb from the attempt.

"You got a last name?" he asked quietly.

"Yes, of course," she said quickly, and then subsided as she realized that it was unknown to her. Her first name, Elizabeth, she was certain of, a faint memory of a man speaking her name still fresh in her mind. Beyond that she saw only a pale mist, with no knowledge of what lay beyond it.

"I'm Cameron Montgomery," he told her. "You can call me Cam if you want to."

"How did I…" She halted her question as the memory of a cruel face appeared before her in her mind. A hatchet held upright in his hand, the overwhelming smell of horses and blood, the knowledge that death awaited her momentarily—she shivered and felt tears running down her cheeks.

"He was going to scalp me," she whispered. "I don't know why he didn't."

"Just be thankful he changed his mind," Cameron told her. "Probably the rest of the warriors were leaving and he didn't want to stay behind. What surprises me is that he didn't take you along with him. The Indians set store by yellow hair, either in their tepees or hanging from their belts."

She shivered at his words, and felt more hot tears well up in her eyes and then knew their heat on her cheeks.

Cameron wrapped his reins around the upright post at his side, and the wagon moved on at a plodding pace. Turning back toward her, he reached a hand to touch the top of her head. "Your head will hurt worse if you cry," he murmured. "And I'll bet it's bangin' away like a sledgehammer right now."

She nodded reluctantly, feeling the stitches in her cheek pull against the pillow. "How badly am I hurt?" Her body felt to be in one piece, nothing appeared broken, only the bandages on her face seemed to be a problem. Beneath them were cuts of some kind, of that she was certain.

"You'll live," Cameron said, his voice flat now as if he remembered the place she'd come from. "You've got a couple of cuts and a lot of bruises, but you'll be feelin' better in a few days. Can't say that for the rest of your group." He paused and his voice lowered, became more concerned. "Were you with your family?"

She felt a huge, empty hole where there should have been a fountain of images in her mind. Only the faint memory of her name being called broke through the mist and she spoke but one word. She curled into herself, looking like a child.

"Daddy."

Cameron watched as fresh tears rolled from her eyes. "You were with your father?" She'd ceased crying a few minutes ago, but it looked now as if she were about to drown in her own tears, for the single drops became a deluge and her sobbing was almost more than he could bear.

He climbed over the seat, into the wagon bed, where she lay in a heap, her face buried in his pillow. His hands were careful as he lifted her, depositing her on his lap as he sat beside the feather tick. She was as he remembered, soft and warm in his arms, her tangled hair flowing to cover his shoulder and her own body. She leaned into him and made a valiant effort to stem the tears, whispering an apology beneath her breath.

"Don't worry about it," Cameron told her. "You're entitled to a good cry, even if it makes your headache worse. You've had a narrow escape, living through an Indian raid. You lost all your belongings in the fire they set in your wagon, and you're damned lucky you didn't burn up with it."

He pulled a clean handkerchief from his back pocket and mopped at her eyes, skirting around the bandages she wore. Her slender fingers took it from him and she straightened in his lap and blew her nose, folded the cloth over again and wiped the tears once more.

"I'm sorry, Cameron," she said softly. "I've gotten your shirt all wet and used your hankie and been a real pain in the neck, haven't I?"

He grinned, settling his chin on top of her head, inhaling the faint scent of talcum powder she wore. "Yeah, you're a pain, all right." He tipped her chin upward and smiled at the crestfallen look she offered. "You're the prettiest little pain in the neck I've ever encountered. And you're riding in my wagon. Miss Elizabeth, I'm the envy of every man on this wagon train. I just may give up my job as scout and devote myself to keeping you happy, right here."

"You're joking," she said flatly, yet unable to withhold the twitching of her lips.

"Yeah, I am, but it made you smile a little, didn't it?" He buried his hand in the length of golden hair and pulled it free from his clothing, where it had clung like a length of silken fabric. Pulling it to the back of her head, he murmured low words.

"Would you like me to braid this for you? I'm afraid it'll be snarled beyond redemption if we don't get it in order." He flexed his fingers in the waving strands and smiled, his nose flaring a bit, his eyes narrowing as if he relished the feel of her curls brushing his skin.

"If you'll find me a comb, I can do it myself," she said, sitting up straighter on his lap, aware that his interest had gone from friendly to something more fraught with danger. Not that his actions truly frightened her, but the dark beauty of the man was a temptation, one she did not recognize, yet knew she must resist. No one else had ever held her just so, no man had ever run his fingers through her hair or wiped her tears. Even though her memory had failed her, she knew with a woman's intuition she would have felt the familiarity in his touches had she been accustomed to such in her past.

There was a certain allure about a man who had saved your life, she thought. And Cameron Montgomery had done just that. With his dark hair and equally dark demeanor, he appealed to all that was within her, her woman's instincts. The hunger she felt for his presence frightened her. And yet, it was a comforting hunger, as though she knew he wanted only what was right and proper for her, feeling that dark gaze upon her and glorying in the thoughts behind his hooded eyes.

He leaned to one side, sorted through a box at the side of the wagon and handed her a sturdy, bone comb, one guaranteed to withstand any snarls she offered it. "Thank you," she whispered, pulling the wide comb through the sides of her hair. Then, snatching up the long tail that trailed down her back to curl on his lap, she pulled it over her shoulder and drew the comb through it. It waved and curled, defying the comb's ability to tame it, and she muttered a word of frustration.

"It's always been the bane of my existence," she said. "But my daddy was dead set against me cutting it." She stilled then, as if listening for a voice. "I can almost hear him saying…"

A bleak darkness filled her then. "I don't remember what he looked like," she said with another sob. "I just know that he was there, with me. And that he liked my long hair."

"I'm in agreement with your daddy, Elizabeth. My mama used to say that a woman's hair was her crowning glory, and I don't think I ever understood what she meant. Not till now." Cam paused, considering his words.

"Who else was with you? Your husband, maybe?"

She seemed bewildered by the query. "Husband? I don't think so. I'd remember that, wouldn't I?"

She seemed buried in thought, and shivered against his body. "I'm sure I would." She shivered as if shrugging away the thought. "My hair," she whispered, as if remembering her task. "I need to…" Her voice trailed off as her fingers worked quickly, gaining control over the golden mass, subduing it into a braid.

The plait was uneven, obviously less tempting to the man watching, definitely not to his liking, if his words were to be believed.

"I kinda thought it was pretty just the way it was," he said, running his hand down the braid, to where it ended just below her waist. She was still in his lap as his hand rested there, and her eyes widened and chanced a look at his face.

He was strangely sober, and his dark eyes searched her own, even as his fingers kneaded the sore muscles on her back, below her waist.

"What are you doing?" Elizabeth asked, knowing how foolish she must sound, but unable to allow his advances without a protest of sorts.

"Just appreciating you," he said, his mouth barely moving as he spoke. "In fact, I'm aching to show you how much I admire you, ma'am. If you'll let me."

"I'm not sure what you mean," she whispered, although her feminine instincts were denying her query. She knew what he meant, somehow knew the look a man possessed when he was interested in a woman. The memory of several men on the train she'd traveled with casting the same sort of admiring gaze on her during the past months, swept through her. And all of them warned off by her father. As quickly as it appeared, the memory slipped through her mind and then slid into oblivion.

"How old are you, Elizabeth?" Cameron asked. "Nineteen, twenty, maybe?"

"Maybe," she said, her cheeks flushing brightly, as the intensity of his eyes darkened. "Does it matter?"

"Yeah," he said slowly. "It matters. I don't make advances to a woman unless she's old enough to know her mind."

"And you're going to make advances to me?" she asked. She looked around the wagon, noting the unrelenting pace of the oxen that rocked their two bodies together. "I'd say you were well on your way already to doing just that, Mr. Montgomery."

"No." His smile was tender. "Not now, Elizabeth. For today I'll settle for just a touch. That's all I'm asking of you." He bent his head and his mouth caressed her forehead, a soft, undemanding pressure she accepted readily. Then his lips traveled down her cheek, brushing her mouth from side to side, a soft murmur giving proof of his pleasure.

"I won't hurt you, sweetheart," he whispered, his lips touching hers again. "I only want to be with you and take care of you." And then his hand moved to rest between her shoulder blades, holding her firmly in place. His lips were hard and firm, giving his visage a stern image, but the reality of his mouth against her face made a lie of his appearance, for he was gentle, as if he feared frightening her.

She relaxed against the security of his embrace, allowing his arms to enfold her, reveling in the knowledge that he would protect her. He was tall, strong and muscular, a man not afraid to risk himself to help a woman in distress. For surely, he and the other scout had been in danger when they'd found her, even though the Indians had already taken their loot and vanished. While lying on the ground, she'd seen shadowed figures, wearing the briefest of clothing, running hither and yon, then watched her father's wagon go up in flames and listened to the dying cries of those surrounding her.

She remembered the hatchet and her fear, and then—nothing. Until the two men had appeared who had picked her up and brought her away from the carnage to this place of safety. There was no guarantee they wouldn't meet up with more danger ahead, but for now, she felt secure.

"Have I frightened you?" Cameron's voice was soft against her ear, and she shook her head, a slight movement that stirred him to kiss the tender spot at her temple, a place that throbbed with the racing of her blood.

"No one has ever…" She could not finish the words, for her tongue felt thick and dry, cleaving to the roof of her mouth.

"For some reason, I've already figured that out," he murmured, rocking her in a soothing motion. "You're as innocent as a newborn baby." And then, as if reminding himself of her need for sustenance he asked a question. "What can I get for you? Are you hungry? Thirsty?"

At that offer of something to drink, she nodded. "Water, please. If you have any."

"A barrelful, as it happens. And my canteen still has a bit left. It's not cold, but it's wet."

"Thank you." She reached for it as he unhooked it from his belt, not waiting for him to open it. Her hands trembled on the lid, but it gave way to her desperation for the taste of water on her tongue. Bending her head back, she drained it, the last drops dripping down her chin, only to fall on his shirt. She lifted a slender finger to wipe the stain away, but it had soaked in quickly.

"Don't worry. With this heat, it'll dry in no time." He took her fingers in his hand, holding them in his palm, and she looked down at the contrast between his long, suntanned fingers and her own. He was gentle and his touch firm, but she knew if she pulled away, he would release her. And then his dark head bent, and his mouth kissed the back of her hand, a series of open-mouthed caresses that threatened to take her breath.

With a tender movement he turned her hand over and gently opened her fingers, examining her palm. "You've got calluses," he said softly. "You're used to hard work." His mouth touched the rough spots on her hands and she winced.

"What are you doing?" Her voice was trembling, as was her body. Should he want to, he could have her on her back, beneath him, in mere seconds. She was helpless in the face of his greater strength, her slender bones no match for the weight he could cover her with. And yet, she did not quail from his touch.

"I think I'd better get back on the wagon seat where I belong," he said, his voice suddenly dark and strained. "Why don't you lie back down and see if you can sleep a while longer. We'll be stopping for dinner pretty soon. That'll be time enough for you to get up."

"All right." It seemed she would obey him; indeed, she had no other option. She was in his wagon, and if he was willing to help her, feed her and keep her comfortable, she'd be a fool to protest.

The wagon master rode his horse beside the second wagon as Cameron climbed back to his seat and unhitched the reins from the upright post. The oxen had not varied their pace, only kept about fifteen feet behind the lead wagon. They were a good team, bred and born on Cameron's family ranch. This was their third trip to the West, and their strength hadn't faltered yet.

"Your lady friend awake now?" Dallas Smith asked politely. His glance touched the opening to the wagon bed, and a hand lifted as if he would wave at someone.

Cameron looked over his shoulder to find Elizabeth just behind him, and she shot a smile at Dallas. Her hand touched Cam's shirt and he wondered if it was there to give her balance or because she hid behind him.

"This lady is Elizabeth," Cameron told Dallas. "We haven't come up with her last name yet. She's still a bit confused about things."

"Well, I reckon I can understand that," Dallas said, tipping his hat politely. "I'm Dallas Smith, ma'am, and I'm in charge of this train. Sure am sorry you ran into trouble, but I'm awful glad my scouts found you before the Indians came back for a second look."

"Thank you, sir," Elizabeth said softly. "I've been sleeping away the morning. Just woke up a few minutes ago."

"Best medicine in the world for you," Dallas said. "We'll be stopping for our noon meal in about half an hour. Will you feel like joining us?"

"Yes, of course," she said quickly. "Perhaps I can lend a hand somewhere?"

Cameron frowned. "Do you think you're up to it?"

"I don't know. But I can try, can't I? It would be better than lying here trying to remember what I was doing on that wagon train, and where we were going and why I lived through the whole thing."

"Did you ever think that it just wasn't meant for you to die yesterday?" Cameron asked. "Maybe there's something more for you to do with your life."

"If only I could remember," Elizabeth said quietly. "I know that my father was with me, but I can't catch hold of more than that. How can I have any kind of a future, if I can't even remember what happened yesterday?"

"Could be it's better if you don't remember right now," Dallas said firmly. "Could be your mind can't handle those memories yet."

"I don't even know who I am," Elizabeth said, her voice trembling, her hand on Cameron's shoulder gripping with a strength he wouldn't have suspected she possessed.

Cameron turned his head a bit, his cheek pressing against her fingers. "You know you're safe here, Elizabeth, and I'm certain you'll soon remember the rest of it. Although, I suspect Dallas is right, and digging up your past isn't the best thing for you right now."

Dallas turned his horse to ride to the far end of the wagon train. "I'll be putting out the call for dinner. Once I get back to the first wagon, we'll stop," he told them. And then tipped his hat for Elizabeth's benefit. "Ma'am," he murmured, with a last glance at her.

A thoughtful glance, Cameron decided, as if he were considering staking his own claim on the lady.

Not if I can help it. The words spun in his head as he set his mind to the oxen that pulled his wagon.

All her brave words about helping out with noontime preparations were for naught, and Elizabeth huddled, trembling under the quilt Cameron provided. The temperature inside the wagon was high, but she was cold, chilled to the bone. She'd made it to the ground, and then almost collapsed against Cameron's chest as her head began to swim and her legs turned limp, her weight seeming to be too heavy for them to bear.

Without a word, he'd lifted her into the wagon bed, following her inside the white canvas to kneel beside her on the wooden floor. His presence was a comfort, yet she felt chagrined by her weakness, embarrassed by her collapse into his arms.

The ladies of the train, at least three of them, had looked her way in sympathy as Cameron tended her, but she knew her presence in his wagon was about as far from discretion as she could get. A young female, alone with a man, allowing his touch against various parts of her person, was ripe for condemnation, no matter the circumstances.

How she knew the rules of good behavior was a mystery, but discomfort at her situation made her wary. Cameron's hands were on her back and shoulders, his greater strength lifting her to a sitting position against the side of the wagon, his presence bringing a welcome bit of heat to her shivering frame.

He'd covered her with his quilt and rubbed her back through the heavy covering, bringing warmth to her flesh. His soft words of comfort did more than that, assuring her of his concern, letting her feel his strength, guaranteeing his presence so long as she needed him.

"You'll be all right," he said soothingly. "You've had a shock, and your body is reacting to it. You may not be able to gain your strength back right away."

She looked up at him, her vision blurred. "I'm sure I'm usually much stronger than this," she told him.

"I'm certain you are. I told you your hands show signs of hard work. I doubt you're used to spending much time being lazy. Not that you are now," he hastily amended as she frowned her displeasure.

From the opening at the rear, a female voice spoke his name. "Cameron, I brought some food for you and the lady. Are you hungry?"

Elizabeth shook her head, feeling her stomach roll as she considered putting a meal into her body. "I don't think I can eat."

"Well, you're going to try. Dora has been kind enough to bring us some stew," Cameron announced, reaching for the plate Dora held out toward him.

"She needs to eat, or she'll never get her strength back," Dora announced, the words sounding very much like disapproval in Elizabeth's ears.

"I'll try," she murmured, and was rewarded by Cameron's smile.

* * *

"We'll see what we can do," Cameron told Dora, settling the plate atop a trunk.

The plate held meat and gravy, probably rabbit, he thought, along with bits of potato, no doubt carried along from St. Louis. Greens had been cooked beyond recognition, and he eyed them disparagingly, his appetite not tempted by their limp presence on the plate.

Filling the fork with a bite of potato, he dipped it into the gravy and offered it to Elizabeth. Her mouth opened automatically and she chewed the food slowly.

"I hate to say it, but it's not very good," she whispered. "That lady doesn't know how to make tasty gravy, does she?"

Cameron laughed at her observation, pleased that she didn't have any qualms about speaking her mind.

"No, she's not the best cook on the train, aside from her biscuits, but she was here first. Maybe someone else will wander by and offer something better."

With that observation, he grimaced as he took his first bite of the food they'd been given. It sat in his mouth, not inviting him to swallow, but he recognized that good manners demanded he eat it anyway. It would be an effort, but if it were all they had available, he'd survive on it.

"Cameron?" From the rear of the wagon, another voice called his name and a woman poked her head into the interior of his wagon. Jennie Sloan smiled at Elizabeth and held out another plate of food. "I didn't know if you would be fond of the rabbit meat Dora cooked for dinner, so I brought over some johnnycake and bacon. My father likes it for his noon meal, and it's pretty tasty."

"It sounds wonderful right now," Elizabeth said beneath her breath, her nose twitching at the scent of the plate in Cameron's hand.

"Miss Elizabeth seems to take kindly to corn bread and bacon,

Jennie," Cameron said with a smile. "And you're right, she can't handle heavy food yet, as thoughtful as Dora was to bring it over."

He switched plates with Jennie, and she looked about her, scanning the area, probably for one of the dogs that traveled with the train, Cameron thought. He was proved right when she leaned over the tailboard and murmured softly for Elizabeth's benefit. "I'll get rid of this when I spot one of the mutts looking for a meal," she said quietly. "You can keep my plate and I'll pick it up at suppertime. I'll be by to visit later on, Miss Elizabeth."

The corn bread was still steaming, the bacon looked more than appetizing, and Cameron made a makeshift sandwich from the two ingredients. He offered it to Elizabeth and she took it from his hands, then bit into it without delay. Another piece of the corn bread was broken in half and two more strips of bacon enclosed between the yellow pone, finding its way to Cameron's mouth.

"This is good," Elizabeth said, her fingers agile as she picked several crumbs from her bodice. "I never ate it this way before, but I appreciate Jennie bringing it over." She took another bite, and chewed the crisp bacon before she spoke again. "Is Jennie married? Does she have a family?"

"No," Cameron said. "You have something in common with her. She's traveling with her father, and several of the young fellas on the train are mighty interested in her."

"Including you?" Elizabeth asked, her eyes flashing as if she teased him.

Cameron shook his head. "Jennie Sloan is a nice lady, and pretty to boot, but I haven't been inclined in that direction. In fact, you're the first woman I've had much to do with for the past couple of years. My wife died almost five years ago, and other women haven't appealed to me. Not thataway at least."

He thought Elizabeth might cry at that, her eyes filling, her mouth trembling.

"It's been a long time, Elizabeth, and I've pretty well adjusted to it. We weren't traveling the same road in life from the very first. She couldn't understand my yearning to go West with the first wagon train I scouted for. Wouldn't go with me, and was unhappy when I got back. Marriage wasn't suiting her, I suspect. I'd thought to tempt her with the promise of a nice place west of Denver to settle, and suggested we could settle down, raise a family there, but she dragged her feet at that. Said she couldn't abide the thought of living beyond civilization."

"Was she a city girl, born and bred?" Elizabeth asked.

Cameron nodded. "Yeah. She enjoyed the theater and concerts and parties, and we never could come to an understanding about how our life together should be. I married her because she was pretty and a lot of fun, and I was old enough to begin raising a family."

"I'd think Jennie was the sort of woman you'd be interested in," Elizabeth said idly, her eyes touching his gaze and then shifting to the limited view she had of the outdoors.

"She's wanting to teach school in Oregon, and I'll bet once she settles in there, she'll find someone who suits her to a tee." He offered Elizabeth the plate he held, three slices of bacon and two more squares of pone still left.

"Thanks," she said, reaching for the bacon. "I haven't had any of this for a month or so." Her eyes widened as she spoke. "Now, how did I know that?" And as if she recognized he would not attempt a reply, she laughed softly. "Maybe my memory is coming back." Her gaze met his. "I hope so, Cameron. I feel like a nobody, with no past and no future."

"You have both, sweetheart. One of these days your past will reveal itself to you, and by that time, you'll be living in your future."

"I don't have any money or anywhere to live. And empty as my mind is, I know that I can't survive without—"

His hand touched her lips, shushing her words. "I don't want you worrying about that today, Elizabeth. You've barely survived an Indian raid, and our main concern right now is to find you something to wear."

She looked down at herself. "I'm pretty tattered looking, aren't I?"

"You'll clean up just fine," he said firmly. "Once we get you another dress, you can wash this one and hang it to dry. Not fancy, but clean, and two dresses will get you by for a while."

"Where… Who…" The query was obvious.

He knew what she asked. "We'll see if Jennie has anything she can spare, or maybe she'll know one of the ladies who would be willing to sell some of her clothing."

"If we can even get a sheet from someone, I could sew something up," she said, and then her face froze, as if she'd had a glimpse into days gone by. "I've made my dresses in the past," she said slowly. "I know how to use a needle and thread."

"Well, that solves that. I've got a couple of sheets I've never used, and my sewing kit is pretty complete. Even a pair of scissors."

"You sew?" she asked disbelievingly.

"I'm a bachelor these days. I don't have anyone to sew on my buttons or mend my ripped seams. So I do the best I can."

"I can do all of that," Elizabeth said impulsively, and then blushed vividly as if she'd somehow intruded on his privacy. "I didn't mean anything by that," she told him.

"I'd more than appreciate your help, ma'am," he said, then rose to his feet and stood over her. He had to bend a considerable distance, the frame that supported the canvas overhead being less than six feet from the floorboards.

"I'll get the wagon ready to travel now. I need to water my oxen first and then check out the harness."

"Can I help?" she asked, stirring as if she would rise from the feather tick.

"You just stay here and keep warm."

"I'm all right now. Maybe eating warmed me up. Whatever,

I don't think I need the quilt any longer." She hesitated and then shot him a wary smile. "Will it be all right if I sit with you on the wagon seat while you drive?"

"You can have the whole seat to yourself. I'll walk this afternoon with my team. Most of the folks leave their wagons after noontime and walk for a few hours."

"Can I join you?" He thought she looked hopeful and could not deny her.

"Of course. But I don't want you to overdo any. Walk awhile and then rest on the seat. All right?" In fact, he looked forward to pacing his oxen with her at his side, and was aware for the first time in years that he was missing the companionship of a woman in his life. For the woman he had rescued just hours ago was well on her way to becoming important to him.

He searched her face. She was pretty, blue-eyed and with clear skin that was blessed by a scattering of freckles across her nose and somewhat marred by the bandages Doc had put in place. And yet, it was an appealing display, he decided. Her freckles made her somehow more approachable, causing her to look young and innocent. But if the ring she wore around her neck on the gold chain fit her finger, she was either married, or had been some man's wife in the past. And he prayed it wasn't so.

Chapter Three

Walking was preferable to sitting on the wagon seat Elizabeth decided before the afternoon was over. But the heat was debilitating, and she found herself lagging behind as the sun began its downward plunge.

"How about resting awhile before we circle for the night?" Cameron asked, his sharp gaze obviously noting her lack of stamina.

"It seems as though I've been sleeping all day as it is," Elizabeth said. "I thought if I got good and tired I'd be able to close my eyes and not lie awake tonight."

"You're tired," Cameron said, "and I feel as if I should be taking better care of you. I want you to eat well tonight, Elizabeth. And if you can't sleep, you can rap on the bottom of the wagon and I'll hear you."

"And then what?" she asked, knowing already that he would not be far from her during the nighttime hours.

"I'll roll out from beneath the wagon and sit with you. I don't want you to have bad dreams all alone. And you probably will, you know."

"If I could learn anything about myself in a dream, I'd welcome it, good dreams or bad. But I'm not counting on it." She trudged in his wake, one hand on the side of the wagon, balancing herself so that her weary legs would not give out.

He slowed his pace until he was at her side and, with an amazing amount of strength, he picked her up and lifted her to the moving wagon, settling her on the seat.

"You're lucky you didn't strain your back, handling me that way," she scolded. "I'm too heavy to be toted around."

"You're a little bit of a thing, and my back is strong. If you'd just given in to your tired body, I wouldn't have had to be so pushy."

He looked up at her and she met his gaze, seeking a message in the long, thorough examination he bestowed upon her. The darkness of night dwelt in his eyes and she felt a strange warmth exuded upon her. Narrowed and piercing, his gaze brought an unfamiliar heat to her body, and she thought for a moment that he gauged her very being and found her not wanting in any way. It was not a comfortable feeling, she decided, this notion that the man was measuring her, seeking out her secrets.

She squirmed on the seat and then swung her legs over into the wagon bed. "I think I'd better lie down," she told him, unwilling to continue the silent confrontation she felt taking place between them. Her heart had begun to act of its own accord, delivering a rapid beat that resounded throughout her body. She knew a flush rode the crest of her cheeks, and for a long moment she was aware of her tenuous position, riding in Cameron's wagon, dependent on him for her food and a place to sleep. It was not a comforting thought, she decided, to know that this man had pinned her in place with his dark eyes, had struck at the very heart of her, giving her the knowledge of his possession of her.

And yet, she would not have it any other way. He'd been kind, his touch had been gentle all the livelong day, even when he'd lifted her to the wagon seat. He'd been all that was protective of her and her welfare, and if she sensed an aura of ownership in his sharp features, she could not complain. His hair was ruffled by the breeze, his tanned forearms were muscled and bare to the sun, and he wore the look of a man who had his life in order.

All but for the woman he'd taken responsibility for, and perhaps even that had been slotted into a place in his mind. For unless she was mistaken, he was determined to lay claim to her.

"Are you frightened of me?" he asked, and Elizabeth shook her head.

"You've done nothing to alarm me thus far," she said quietly. "It's just that you look at me in a strange way, as if you're plotting something that includes me and my future."

"I am." The words were spoken firmly, his lips thinning as he looked ahead of his team to the wagon they followed.

"I won't let you plan my life for me. I know you rescued me and I appreciate the fact that you've been more than kind to me. But I'm a full-grown woman, Cameron, and I won't be handled like a child."

"Trust me," he said with a long look of amusement, "handling you as I would a child is the farthest thing from my mind. I'm well aware that you're a woman, Elizabeth. If I'm making plans that include you, it's in your best interest, believe me."

She felt a shiver at his words, a long chill that had her reaching for the quilt.

"You can't be cold," he said, frowning at her as she pulled the warmth of his bed covering over her shoulders. "It must be hotter than Hades in there, with the sun baking the canvas." His mouth twisted, and he almost smiled. "You're safe for now, sweetheart. It's broad daylight and I'm not about to force myself on you anyway. I feel almost honored that the fates decreed your place in my life. I'll tell you now, and hope the knowledge doesn't scare you away from me, but it seems my guardian angel has brought you to me. You've already filled a place in my life that has been empty for too long."

"I don't understand," she admitted, huddling on the wagon

bed, looking out at the man who walked beside his oxen, just half a dozen feet from her place of safety. "You don't even know me, Cameron. I don't even know my surname, or where I came from or where I'm going."

"I know where you're going," he said firmly. "With me. Wherever I decide to settle, you'll be there with me."

"You can't just decide to move me in with you," she protested. "I'll not do such a thing."

"I want to marry you, Elizabeth. And then it'll be your duty to do as I say," he said. A smile formed that belied his stern words. "But I've never been one to give a lot of orders to a woman. I've found other ways of persuasion work more effectively."

"Marry you?" She paled, her face ashen with the shock of hearing the words that plotted her future.

He was on the wagon seat in a moment, then turned, his feet inside the wagon bed. She backed from his touch as he would have reached for her, and his hands returned to rest on his thighs. "I didn't mean to spring it on you that way," he said quietly. "For now, let's just put it aside and concentrate on your healing. There's lots of time to look ahead and think about the days to come."

From beside the wagon, Dallas Smith's voice announced the circling of the wagons, surprising Cameron as he spoke of the presence of a small stream just ahead. Then he rode ahead to the front of the train, telling all and sundry that they would stop for the night beside a small grove of trees just a bit to the south, where the stream had brought life to the trees and bushes there.

Cameron turned from her and took up the reins, guiding his team with care. Within minutes, the first wagon had turned to the left and those following had begun the process of forming a tight circle.

When it seemed that he felt it was leaving them exposed to attack, Dallas instructed a dozen or so families to circle their teams inside the outer perimeter of the camp.

"This is a big train," Cameron said, following the vehicle ahead of him. "The folks with children feel safer inside the circle, rather than stringing out on the outer edge."

"I can understand that," Elizabeth said, on her knees now, watching as Cameron's wagon pulled up close to the one in front. "It seems that the train we traveled with was much smaller."

"I'll stake my oxen beneath the trees, and then come back and push the wagon a bit closer to the next one. We don't want to leave gaps large enough for someone to sneak through."

She knelt behind him, looking out across the prairie to where the sun was fast dropping from sight. "Are those mountains up ahead?" she asked, noting the sun's disappearance. "Are we coming closer to Denver?"

"We've got a long way to go. The mountains are farther from us than it looks. We'll be seeing them for several days before we reach them."

"And then where will we go? All the way west to Oregon?"

"The train is scheduled to do that, but we won't be traveling the last of the Oregon trail with them. I've got a plot of land just west and north of Fort Collins that has my name on it. If you like the area, we'll stay there."

"I don't have anything to do with where you live, Cameron. I set out to go west, and that's what I'll do."

"How far west were you going with your father?" he asked, already knowing she had no memory of their planned destination.

Her eyes filled with tears. "I don't know. There was someone else with us, I remember, but I don't know who he was."

"He?" Cameron turned his head and shot her a quick glance. "You were traveling with two men?"

She was hesitant, searching the blank places in her mind for an answer. "I'm not sure. I just know there was someone else there."

"Your husband, maybe? Maybe the wedding band on that

chain is yours after all. It was one of the first things I noticed. I couldn't figure out why it wasn't on your finger."

She touched the circle of gold with her index finger and lifted it from her skin. "I should try it on and see if it fits, shouldn't I? I'd know then if it was mine."

"I don't want it to be. I don't want to wait while you mourn a husband you can't even remember. A man whose face is unknown to you."

"You're impatient," she said softly.

"You're right." His words were harshly spoken, his jaw was set as though he'd determined on a course of action and would not be deterred from it.

Dallas came to the wagon, rapping on the wooden side and calling out for Cameron. "Supper is ready at Miss Jennie's campsite," he said. "She's made enough for Joe and all of us."

"Cameron is staking the oxen," Elizabeth said, moving to the back of the wagon where Dallas stood. "He shouldn't be long. He filled his buckets from the stream and carried water to the team a few minutes ago."

"Well, tell him to bring you with him when he gets back. Miss Jennie's a good cook. You'll enjoy both her company and her food."

"She brought us dinner at noon. I look forward to spending some time with her. She's a lovely woman."

"That she is. Pret' near the prettiest girl on the train."

"Not a chance. The prettiest one is in my wagon." Cameron walked up to where Dallas stood and peered just inside to where Elizabeth knelt. "You ready to eat, ma'am?" he asked.

She was flustered, blushing at his words, and unable to think straight. "Dallas said we were to eat with Miss Jennie tonight."

"She's awful good to us poor solitary men," Dallas said with a grin. "And looking at Miss Jennie while we eat is no hardship."

"You need to be courting her," Cameron said cautiously. "Before anyone else stakes a claim. She'd make you a dandy wife."

"And what would I do? Take her with me the next time I'm hired to take folks across the country? Being a wagon master is all I know, Cam. Been in the business for more years than I can count."

"Aw, you're not that old," Cameron said, grinning widely.

"Some days it seems like it. I've about decided I'll never have me a wife. I'd have to settle down in one place, anyway, and I'm not sure my wanderlust will let me do that."

"Well, if you change your mind, just look Miss Jennie's way. I think she kinda likes you, boss." Cameron grinned at Elizabeth, inviting her to join the bantering.

But Dallas had other ideas and, with a quick swipe of his arm, his hat was removed from his head and he bowed to Elizabeth and issued an invitation. "Will you join me for supper, ma'am? We'll let old Cam here fend for himself if he's gonna be so sassy."

Her eyes widened in surprise at the sudden switch and she looked quickly at Cameron, whose face resembled a thundercloud. "I think I'll let Cameron help me out of the wagon, and we can all walk over to Miss Jennie's wagon together."

At that, Cameron motioned for her to rise from the wagon's floor and as she did, he clasped her waist and lifted her to the ground. A bit dizzy from his handling and the rapid transfer, she swayed for a moment, and only his hands on her waist kept her on her feet.

"Are you all right, sweetheart?" His question was low, his eyes holding concern for her; and his hands were firm about her middle.

"Just woozy for a minute," she said. "I've been resting too much today. I need a long walk, but probably Miss Jennie's wagon is too close to qualify as exercise, isn't it?"

"After we eat, I'll take you in a circle around the wagons," Cameron said. "Let you get acquainted with some of the folks."

"As long as you're feeling a bit puny, why don't you make us look like two lucky gentlemen and take my arm, too, ma'am. If you hang on to both of us, you'll walk easy, I think." Dallas proffered his bent arm, and with a dark glance in his direction, Cameron did the same. Without dispute, Elizabeth placed her hands in the bend of their elbows and they set off across the wide circle of wagons.

Jennie's raven-black hair caught her eye, and Elizabeth almost laughed aloud. If Dallas were to lay claim to the young woman, he'd have a clutch of bachelors to fend off. For there were four young men gathered around her campfire, all doing their best to impress her and gain her favor.

Jennie looked up as the trio approached and a smile lit her face. "I've been waiting for you. I made plenty for all of us."

"I can't thank you enough for your kindness," Elizabeth said, limping a bit as she began to tire. And it wasn't even a long walk. How she'd make it around the outside of the circle tonight was more than she knew right now. Her grasp on the two men grew firmer with each step she took, and the sight of an overturned keg just ahead of them seemed like the answer to a prayer. Surely it was meant for her to sit upon, she thought, and Jennie did not disappoint her.

"Have a seat, Elizabeth," she invited, motioning to the makeshift chair. "These men can sit on the ground to eat, but ladies deserve something better than dirt beneath them when they accept an invitation to supper."

Cameron tugged at her and she released Dallas's arm, turning toward the keg. With a gracious bow, Cameron seated her and then dropped to the ground beside her.

"What was that you said about staking a claim?" Dallas asked in a low tone, settling on the other side of Elizabeth's position. He looked at Cameron and his laugh was laden with sarcasm. "Looks to me like you've already made your move, Cam. Watch your step unless you want the ladies on the train to take a hand in things. You know what they'll do if they think you're making hash of Miss Elizabeth's reputation, what with her sleeping in your wagon."

"Do you think I'd care?" Cameron asked with a cocky grin. "It would make me very happy to have the ladies after me to set things right with Miss Elizabeth."

Elizabeth spoke her mind, something she didn't feel comfortable with, but necessary if she were to keep her self-respect right now. "Miss Elizabeth is not about to be forced into a marriage, gentlemen. I lost my past just yesterday. I have no family, no future and no last name. Do you think that I'm the least bit interested in gaining a husband when I have so many other things to be concerned with?"

Dallas looked chagrined. "I'm sorry, ma'am. I spoke out of turn. If anyone casts a slur on your reputation because of the current sleeping arrangements, they'll answer to me personally."

"On the other hand," Cameron began, "marrying Miss Elizabeth would be no great sacrifice on my part. I'm in the market for a wife, and I've known arranged marriages or even forced marriages to work out better than those with long courtships behind them."

"Well, I'm not in the market for a husband," Elizabeth said stoutly. "I appreciate all you gentlemen have done for me, but I feel weary and battered by events I had no control over, and I fear my appetite for supper is gone. Please excuse me."

She rose from her seat and made her way back to Cameron's wagon, his tall figure right behind her. She sensed his presence there, but stubbornly refused to turn and acknowledge him in any way, simply continuing on her way without haste.

"Elizabeth." His voice halted her as she would have climbed to the back of the wagon. Her heart was beating at a rapid pace and her hands trembled, failing to grip on to the tailgate of the wagon. She felt quick tears burn behind her eyelids and she bent her head to the high wooden tailgate, lest her tears embarrass her before the man who stood so near.

"I've upset you, and I'm sorrier than I can say." Cameron spoke softly, the words reaching only to her ears, his hands resting without coercion on her shoulders. "I'll help you into the wagon, if you like. But I'd rather have you come back and eat something. Jennie is mad at both Dallas and me for upsetting you, and I fear my name will be mud with the rest of the ladies, too, if you don't accept my apology."

Elizabeth felt the warmth of his big hands, knew his words were sincere and again realized she was alone in the world with no choice but to accommodate the man who had already given her so much. Not just a place to sleep, a bed to rest on and the promise of transport to Denver at least, but his protection and the strength of his honor to protect her.

The tears flowed, no matter that she blinked furiously and clenched her teeth in a bid to force them to dry up on their own and leave her with some semblance of dignity. It was not to be, for Cameron turned her to face him, his hands gentle on her arms. Indeed, if he had applied any force to his gesture, she would have fought him, but the knowledge that his broad shoulders would shelter her was more temptation than she could resist.

Her head found a resting place on his chest and she heard the booming of his heart, a steady, reassuring beat that soon had her measuring her breath to keep time. The urge to cry was subdued as she shuddered, and then placed her hands on his upper arms. The muscles there flexed against her palms, and then relaxed, as though he would not allow her to fear the power contained in his body.

His hand held a clean kerchief and once more he used it with care, wiping her eyes and cheeks, then handing it to her. Again, blowing her nose seemed an intimate act to perform in front of a man, she thought, but it was fast becoming a necessity. She turned in his embrace and finished removing the signs of her tears, then spoke aloud the words that had been nagging at her for several minutes.

"I'm sorry, Cameron. I'm sorry I walked away and insulted Jennie, when she'd been so nice to me. And Dallas, too. He was kind and I appreciate it, but right then I felt surrounded, as if I were being forced into a decision I'm not ready to consider."

"Things are different out here, Elizabeth. I don't know where you came from, but I'll lay odds it was one of the cities back East. Men have the privilege of courting a lady there, of spending months preparing their bid for her hand in marriage. That doesn't apply on a wagon train. There's a whole different set of rules, and they've been put in place mainly for the protection of the women." His hands turned her again to face him.

"I don't think I understand," she whispered, aware of the male scent of the man who held her. His shirt held the wind in its very fabric, the smell fresh and clean. Wrinkled it might be, but the buttons almost strained to hold together in front, and the material was smooth against his chest. A scent of leather and another of horseflesh rose to tempt her and she burrowed her face against him.

"A woman isn't safe in this country without a man to protect her," he said firmly. "That's first and foremost, and a woman is beyond reach for the other men on a wagon train if she has a husband. For the most part, the bachelors will give her a wide berth, leave her alone, in other words. She's off-limits and they know it."

"And in my situation?"

"You're up for grabs right now," Cameron said harshly.

She felt the words reverberate in his chest, and sensed the anger he strove to contain. "Are you upset with me?" she asked, lifting her head to peer up at him.

"No. Not even a little bit. I'm just wanting to keep you safe, and I can't keep you in my wagon where I can watch over you when you're an available woman. If we're not careful, we're gonna ruin your reputation. Especially if you continue staying with me. And I don't intend to make any changes in that arrangement."

Elizabeth pressed her palms against his chest and released herself from his embrace. "Where else would I go? Is there another wagon with just women, somewhere I can ride until we reach a town?"

"Denver is the next city we'll see. And to answer your question, there isn't anywhere else for you to stay, unless you choose another man to look after you."

"I don't want another man," she protested.

"There's just one problem. You may already be married, you know. If that circle of gold you have around your neck is your wedding band, you may have a husband somewhere."

"Maybe I'm a widow," she said. And yet, she found no memory of another man in her past. And surely she would remember something so important. She knew she had a father; she'd almost been able to hear his voice speaking. And if she'd had a husband, surely his memory would override that of her parent. The gold band seemed to burn against her chest, tucked safely inside her bodice, out of sight. She felt as if she'd worn it all her life, and yet had no memory of a man's arms holding her, his hands touching her.

"You'll have to make up your mind, Elizabeth. Probably sooner than later. A couple of days is about all you'll have before the ladies make a big production out of this. They'll be after you to take a husband."

"Would you like me to go somewhere else to sleep?"

"Now you know better than that. I've already made that clear. I'll be underneath the wagon, and if you need me for anything, I'll be close at hand. I don't want you looking for another place to sleep."

His hands circled her waist and he lifted her from the ground, high enough for her to climb into the wagon. "Do you need to go for a walk first?" he asked, couching his offer in such a way so as not to embarrass her.

"Later, after dark. I just want to lie down now." She moved forward in the wagon, seeking out the feather tick she'd used as a bed. Shaking it to fluff the feathers, she placed it back on the floor and sought out the pillow he'd given her to use. She had no nightgown to wear, so her petticoat would have to do. But for now she decided to stay fully dressed until such time as she found privacy in the bushes beneath the trees.

"I'll be back," Cameron said quietly. "I'm going to bring you your supper."

She didn't have it in her heart to argue with him, so only nodded as he spoke. The thought of food had lost its appeal, but she would not insult Jennie further by turning down the meal she'd prepared.

Chapter Four

The days went swiftly, with Cameron rolling from beneath the wagon to ride out each morning with Joe, scouting out their path for the day. Joe kept both of the scouts' horses tied behind the wagon he rode in, and Cameron tended the gelding's needs, carrying food to him nightly, when the grazing seemed sparse.

Elizabeth slept lightly, and so did not miss his grumbles as he readied himself for the day, struggling to don his trousers just inches below her bed in the wagon. She watched from behind the white canvas covering as he splashed water on his face, ran long fingers through his hair and shook the excess from him as might a dog fresh from the creek.

Once he and Joe had vanished west of the circle of wagons, Elizabeth arose and donned the clothing she had available. Jennie, true to Cameron's assuring words, had donated a dress to Elizabeth, allowing her to change from and then wash the single dress she owned. Cameron's sewing kit and the sheet were rapidly coming together to form a dress for her, though it seemed that white was not a good choice for clothing on this trip. It would require almost daily dousing in water and the use of a scrub board, one of which Cameron had brought along for his own use.

Elizabeth looked down at herself and bit her lip in frustration. This was the sixth day she'd spent with the man and the other members of the group, and unless they found a stream deep enough for her to submerge her body, she might never feel clean again. The memory of sitting in a deep tub of warm water swam in her memory, along with the feel of a large towel that she used to scrub the dampness from her skin.

"Daddy." It was a whisper, sent into the unknown, an appeal perhaps that her missing parent would somehow hear her and answer her plea. She searched her mind again for some small glimpse of his face, wondering if he were handsome, or rugged and possessed of harsh features. If he weren't dead she might run into him in Denver, Elizabeth thought, and never even recognize his face, and that alone was enough to fill her with despair.

A faint rustle at the back of the wagon caught her attention, and she busily buttoned the bodice of her dress, the same one she'd worn yesterday. She'd wash it tonight when they found a place to circle the wagons. For now, she concentrated on looking decent and well covered, lest a visitor pop her head into the back of the wagon.

But it was no woman who appeared as Elizabeth buttoned the final mother of pearl fastening on her dress. Joe rapped sharply on the wagon bed and called her name, deliberately looking toward the south, away from the place where she had slept.

"Miss Elizabeth, Cam said to ask if you'd try to put together some breakfast for him if I lit a fire for you. Are you up?"

"Up and dressed, Joe," she said, grinning as she considered the task ahead. "I'll scout around in here and see what I can find to cook."

"Cam said to tell you there's a slab of bacon hanging outside the wagon. You'll have to wipe it off, get the dust washed away, and I've brought you three eggs from Jennie. She has a little coop of chickens on her wagon and was agreeable to selling some for Cam's breakfast."

Excitement rose in Elizabeth, and in moments she had pulled her shoes on and made her way to the back of the wagon. A box in the corner opened readily and tin plates and mugs rested within, along with a small assortment of forks and spoons. On the frame overhead she found a skillet hanging, and made ready to climb from the wagon. The towels she had used and rinsed out during the past days were dry and folded and she dampened one in a small pan of water, drained from Cameron's barrel.

Before she wiped down the skillet and plates, and cleaned the bacon of dust, she would wash her own face, she decided. Taking up the bone comb Cameron had given her to use, she lifted her right leg over the tailgate and began the descent to the ground.

A strong hand grasped her arm and steadied her, keeping her from falling, and she managed to land upright, wobbly and feeling a bit shaky as she brushed down her skirts and peered up into Cameron's rugged features.

He was grinning at her. "You pret' near fell on your face. Good thing I was here."

Fumbling for balance, she grasped his forearms. "I didn't expect you so soon. Joe hasn't got the fire built yet."

"It's built, just not burned down to coals yet," Cameron said, looking her up and down as if he doubted she was able to do the chore he'd assigned her. "I'll help you," he offered, "just as soon as I take care of my horse and get washed up."

"I need to comb my hair, first," she told him. "As long as the fire isn't ready yet, I'll spend some time making myself decent."

His grin displayed even white teeth, and a lurking dimple in his cheek was exposed by the movement of his mouth. "You're decent, ma'am. What you're going to do is make yourself prettier."

She blushed at his words. "You're a scamp, Cameron," she told him with a wave of his comb.

"Can I do something to help over here?" Dora Perry asked,

drying her hands on her apron. "I've fed my bunch, and I can give you a hand, if you like."

Her eyes scanned Elizabeth cooly, and whether she sought some signs of wanton behavior or truly wanted to help was not at first apparent. And her next words solidified that thought, her reproof offered in phrases that made Elizabeth cringe.

"You shouldn't be out here in front of all these men combing your hair, Elizabeth. Didn't your mother ever teach you about propriety, about modesty?"

"I suppose she did," Elizabeth answered, aware that Cam had opened his mouth to defend her, and then fallen silent as she spoke. "The problem is that I don't remember my mother, or father either, for that matter. If my social skills are not appropriate, I beg your pardon. My dress is covering me adequately, I think, but my hair is too long and messy to comb in the wagon. I'll go behind the wagon to braid it if you think it would be more modest of me."

Cameron made a noise that sounded strangely as though he were choking and turned aside, coughing into his kerchief.

"Are you all right?" Elizabeth asked, turning to him, putting the woman in front of her out of her mind.

"Yes, ma'am," he managed to whisper hoarsely. "Just got a gnat in my throat."

"Humph." Dora expressed her displeasure with a snort and turned away. A few feet from Cameron, she turned back. "You'd do well to make an honest woman of Elizabeth, you know. Folks will talk. In fact, they're already talking."

"I'm sure you're helping them find something to talk about," Cameron said sharply. "Miss Elizabeth and I are two adults, thrown together by circumstance, and trying the best we can to muddle through."

Elizabeth looked over his shoulder to where Joe squatted by the fire, his own shoulders shaking with laughter. "I'll just wipe out the skillet, Cameron," she said, hoping her change of subject would result in Dora's retreat. "Would you hand me the slab of bacon, so I can wipe it down?"

"Yes, ma'am. I'd be most happy to," he said, turning his attention from the woman who was stalking stiffly back to her own wagon.

"I suppose it was rude of me not to accept her help," Elizabeth said. "But she seemed possessed of the idea that we were over here living in…" Her eyes widened and her mouth pinched shut as she halted her words.

"Sin?" Cameron asked. And then he offered an opinion that was designed to placate her worry. "It's my opinion that sin is making accusations with no foundation of truth to back them up, sweetheart. The lady is looking for trouble where there is none."

He lifted the half slab of bacon and held it before him as Elizabeth wiped it with her towel. "If you'll cut some slices with that knife of yours, I'll comb my hair on the other side of the wagon so I don't tempt any of these fine, upstanding gentlemen," she said, her voice sharp and sassy.

"Fire's about ready, Cam." Joe stood and sought out Cam's cooking stone from the back of the wagon, placing it on the coals to heat.

His knife was as sharp as his honing stone could make it, and Cameron had no problem with slicing off a dozen thick pieces of bacon for their meal. He placed them in the skillet Elizabeth had cleaned and placed it on the stone.

"Won't take long before it's sizzlin' up a storm," Joe said. "You got any bread?"

"Yeah, part of a loaf. One of the ladies baked bread the other night in her campfire and brought me some." Cameron dug into the barrel that held foodstuffs and brought forth a half loaf of sourdough. "Here we go," he said. "No butter, but I still have a bit of jam."

"Jam?" Elizabeth laughed aloud. "You brought jam along?"

He glanced at her, his look one of chagrin. "I've got a sweet tooth. Packed three jars of jam when we left St. Louis."

The skillet was sizzling, the bacon beginning to curl on the edges, and Elizabeth grabbed for a fork from the barrel. "Here, you get to watch the bacon while I tie my hair back. After all this fuss, I'll wait and braid it later."

Cam took the utensil and grinned at her. "Leave it hang loose, will you?"

"Too messy," she said, pulling the length behind her head and fishing in her pocket for a bit of ribbon she'd found there the first day. With swift movements of her slender hands, she tied a credible knot and bow, and then tossed the comb inside the wagon.

"That does it," she announced, taking the fork back and settling near the fire. Joe had brought a block of wood for her to sit on and she smiled her thanks at him as she lowered herself to its surface. The bacon cooked nicely, and she kept it turned and evenly browned, inhaling the welcome scent as she tended it.

"Here's some newspaper to drain it on," Cam said, sorting through a stack of things in the wagon. He turned the sheets to the center, where they were at least fresher and cleaner than the outer pages, and placed them on a tray he'd dug from his barrel.

In ten minutes' time, the three of them sat near the fire and ate from tin plates. The jam was still good, and Cam was pleased that it hadn't begun to mold in the heat. They each ate an egg, Joe demanding that Elizabeth have her share of their bounty.

"How I could possibly settle in so quickly, I don't know, but this feels like home," she said, wiping up the last of her egg yolk with the crust of bread she held. She popped it into her mouth, relishing the flavor, and then picked up a second piece of bacon.

"For now, this is your home," Cameron said. "You've got Joe and me to take care of you, and a wagon to ride in and food to eat."

"I can't thank you enough for rescuing me the other day," Elizabeth said, looking down at her lap. "I'd be dead by now if you hadn't found me."

"Just doin' our job, ma'am," Joe said, grinning at Cameron over her head.

"Best morning's work we've done since we left St. Louis," Cameron agreed. "Didn't know we'd find a prize like you when we rode out that morning."

"Not a prize," she countered. "A woman with no memory and nothing of her own to bring along on this journey. I'm a liability to both of you."

"Not me, ma'am," Joe said quickly. "I kinda like havin' you around. I've enjoyed watchin' you cooking our breakfast this morning. Maybe you'll feel like puttin' together some supper tonight. I heard that one of the men got a deer early on, before dawn. Bet he'd share a bit with the scouts. What do you think, Cam?"

"Almost guaranteed," Cameron agreed. "We'll see if he's got it all cut up yet."

"Will he mind sharing?" Elizabeth asked.

"Naw," Joe drawled. "He'll dole it out to anyone who wants fresh meat for supper. It won't keep long in this heat anyway. Probably be all used up by tomorrow. Lots of folks here to eat it."

"What will he do with the skin?" Elizabeth asked.

"If you want it, I'll ask him," Cameron said. "If you're planning on making something from it, it'll have to be readied first. You know, the Indian women chew the hide to make it soft. Think you're up to it?"

She almost gagged at his words. "Hardly. But I'll bet I could make something out of it, if he wouldn't mind selling it to you for my use. And then I'll pay you back, Cameron."

"And how will you do that, young lady?" he asked with a wide grin.

"I'll make you a shirt out of it, if you like."

* * *

The bachelor who'd shot the deer brought them a piece of roast for their supper, and Joe showed Elizabeth how to prepare it for cooking. A large kettle hung beneath the wagon and she washed it, then filled it halfway with water, hanging it over the fire after breakfast. "I'll give it a head start," she explained to Cameron. "It'll take a while to cook, but at noon, I'll give it another dose of heat and by suppertime, it should be about halfway done."

"I've got a couple of onions hanging inside," Cameron said. "They're still good, and one would taste mighty fine in the pot with the meat."

"I'll pour the bacon grease in it, too," Elizabeth said. "Seems like I heard somewhere that bacon cuts the wild flavor of the meat." She frowned and shook her head. "Wish I could remember where that came from."

The call to clear the camp came sooner than she'd hoped, but Elizabeth did her share to ready the wagon for the day's travel. A pot of hot water on the side of the fire warmed nicely by the time she had the plates and forks ready to wash, and the final chore was to wipe out the skillet. No soap was allowed to touch the iron surface, and she couldn't remember why, only knew it to be true.

The mountains seemed to creep closer by the day, and midmorning they presented a sight for sore eyes, Elizabeth thought, looking up from her stitching to gaze upon the sight of towering peaks in the west.

The deer skin would not be hers until tomorrow, Cameron said, the young man still working on it, making it pliable and ready to cut and form it into whatever she pleased. That was easy enough to decide upon, because what she'd already decided would give her the most satisfaction was to turn it into a shirt for Cameron. He'd seemed pleased at her plan, and she had found one of his shirts in the trunk where he kept his clothing, using it as a pattern.

So it was that the next day found her awake early, awaiting the arrival of the prized deer hide. She held it before her, profusely thanking the hunter for allowing Cameron to purchase it for her, then folded it and placed it in the wagon.

She spent an hour inside the wagon, working the leather, rubbing the surface with a stone and cleaning off the bits and pieces he had missed, as if it were a skill she'd once learned, a talent not forgotten. Holding it up before her Elizabeth examined it carefully. When she considered it ready, she spread the hide on the floor, then cut it into the required pieces for Cameron's shirt.

"When we stop for noon, I'll measure this against you and see how it will fit," Elizabeth told him, leaning on the seat at the front of the wagon, catching a breath of fresh air.

He walked beside her, his occasional comments and words making the time go swiftly. He spoke of his plans for a ranch in Colorado, of the piece of land where a river ran through the back of the property he'd claimed as his own.

Now he looked up at her, his smile pleased as he watched her stitching the deer hide. She was in her glory, Cameron thought. Give a woman something to do, some project to work on, and she was happy. The end result being a shirt for him was enough to give him a big head, he thought. He'd figured she would make herself something from the leather, but unless he missed his guess, there wouldn't be enough left to make more than a small pair of moccasins. Maybe that was her plan. With a glance down to where her dress pooled at her ankles, he decided it wouldn't take an awful lot of leather to cover the feet that were now shod in shabby shoes.

She'd been barefoot when he brought her to his wagon, and one of the older girls had contributed an old pair of nondescript shoes for Elizabeth's benefit. She'd accepted them gratefully, but he suspected the worn leather pinched her toes. Frequently, she slipped them from her feet and, without a word of complaint, rubbed those pink toes absently as she sat atop the wagon seat.

If the deer hide provided enough leftover leather to make her a pair of moccasins, he'd be more than delighted. But it seemed her own comfort rated second to his, for the project she'd begun with was a shirt she'd mentioned, one she sewed with precise stitches, and obviously designed as a token of her appreciation to him. She'd made the offer and he'd decided, no matter how it turned out, he would look forward to wearing it.

As promised, the unfinished work was measured against his back and shoulders, after their simple noontime meal was prepared and consumed. She hung the cooking pot with the venison in it over the last of the glowing coals, and then she readied the unfinished shirt for fitting.

The front pieces lay against his chest as she stood back and surveyed her work. "I think just a narrow seam will work," she said musingly, adjusting the soft leather to his body. "You're a little broader in the chest than I'd thought."

Cameron suppressed a shiver. If the girl had any idea what her gentle touch was doing to his state of mind, let alone the condition of his body, she'd no doubt climb into the wagon and hide for the rest of the day. Innocence was enticing, he decided, holding his arms out as she held the front and back of his new garment together, her head tilted to one side as she gauged the fit.

He looked down to where her bare toes almost touched his own boots and could not refrain from the words that jumped from his tongue. "You should be making yourself some moccasins before you worry about my shirt," he said gruffly, only to cringe as she shot him a look of confusion.

"I wanted to do something for you," she said softly, her hands falling to her sides as though she had only just now realized that she'd been using them to measure the breadth of his chest. "I'm used to going barefoot," she continued, "and I'm riding most of the time, anyway. My feet hardly get dirty, let alone bruised up from walking."

Cameron found himself wishing for different circumstances. If only he'd met her at a dance or party back East, or maybe noticed her first as a member of this wagon train. As it was now, he was responsible for her safety, and that obligation weighed heavily on him, well aware that most of the possibility of danger she was in at the present could be laid at his own feet.

He'd thought himself immune to women for years, only allowing his body's needs to be satisfied on rare occasions, when it seemed that he'd been alone for too long a time to be borne. Now he found himself watching this female almost constantly, the days being measured by the hours and minutes he spent in her company.

When the sun set and the pot of venison roast was but a tasty memory, Cameron crawled beneath the wagon, punched his flat pillow into a reasonable lump and thought longingly of the feather tick and down pillow he'd donated for Elizabeth's use in the wagon overhead. Not that he would take them back, for he cherished his honor, and once a gift was given, it was out of his hands forever, so far as he was concerned.

He'd only like to share the bedding with her. And at that thought he grinned widely, his attention arrested by the sound of Elizabeth turning over, then sitting up and muttering unintelligible words just out of his hearing. She wasn't sleeping soundly tonight, he realized, and not for the first time, she'd been dreaming.

He settled down again, thinking of the woman he desired with every fiber of his being, wondering if he dared rush her into a commitment that would include marriage when they reached Denver. Granted, as Dallas said, he'd only known her a short while, but some things happen rapidly in this world, especially in situations such as this. Life was fraught with danger, always had been, always would be. But if he could gain the role of protector of the woman he'd rescued, on a permanent basis, it would make his life complete.

Marriage had not been nearly so much a priority in several years. He'd been bitten by the bug once, and had thought himself immune to the females who flitted in and out of his life. Elizabeth was not flitting, he thought with a grin. She was in his wagon, sleeping on his bedding and using the only decent pillow he owned. That should give him a head start when it came to expecting her response to his proposal.

He considered that theory for a few minutes, the edge of his concentration nudged by the feminine sounds of distress from over his head. Quiet sobs reached to where he lay, and without a second thought, he rolled from beneath the wagon and stood at the tailgate, peering within to where Elizabeth was rolled up at the far end of his feather tick.

"Elizabeth. Honey, are you all right?" His whisper was low, but he knew it carried the few feet to where she curled beneath the sheet. Not awaiting an answer, he climbed lithely over the tailgate and crouched just inside the wagon. "Elizabeth?" His calling of her name seemed to gain her attention, and she sat bolt upright, her eyes wide and staring, tears streaming down her cheeks.

"Don't let them kill me," she whispered, her face twisting in an agony of despair.

With less grace than haste, Cameron made his way to her side, untangling her from the sheet and lowering himself to sit beside her. His strong arms swept beneath her and he lifted her to his lap.

"I could get used to this in a hurry, sweetheart," he murmured as he rocked her in his embrace and buried his face in her hair. Fragrant with the flowers she'd soaked in the rinse water before she washed it earlier, the silken strands flowed beneath his hands and tempted his nose with the aroma of fresh meadow daisies and tiny purple flowers that seemed to thrive on the prairie.

"Cameron?" She roused from whatever dream she'd been immersed in, her arms reaching for his neck, her face buried in the hollow above his collarbone. "Hold me tight, please," she begged. "I need to feel safe."

"You were dreaming, sweetheart," he murmured against her ear. "I heard you from down below."

"Thank you for coming to me," she said, her voice faint as if she hesitated to speak the words. "I needed to know I was safe, needed to know you were here to take care of me."

"I'm planning on doing a lot of that in the future. Taking care of you will be my number one priority from now on. Once I get you to Denver and find us a preacher, I'll have the right to be with you all the time, and I'll be able to give up that bedroll under the wagon."

She wiggled a bit, sitting upright, as if leaning against his strength was somehow forbidden. "I must have been dreaming, or maybe remembering. At any rate, I saw Ben running from the wagon and my father went after him. They went to the river and then disappeared beneath the water. I fear that my father drowned there."

"Ben?" The single word was harsh, Cameron's voice almost choking on the single syllable. "Who is Ben?"

"He was with us. A friend of my father's, a man who wanted to marry me, I think. He went along on the trip to help Daddy with the animals and keep an eye on me." Her face assumed a look of distaste. "I didn't like him much, Cameron. He was always touching me, not in a nasty way, but as if he had the right to be familiar with me."

"He and your father left the wagon train when it was attacked?"

"Ben left. My father chased after him, called him a coward and knocked him into the water. I was still on the wagon, and when the attackers saw me, they pulled me down to the ground." She shuddered, closing her eyes against the memory.

"Did you ever see your father again? Or Ben?" Cameron felt futile rage clamp its talons within his chest as he visualized the woman who had been abandoned and left to the savages.

"No, I was knocked down by a man's fist, I think. I saw it coming and then I remember I hit the ground. Someone tore at my throat, probably after my necklace, and then he slapped me and punched me." Her eyes seemed to see a vision he could only imagine. "I thought they would kill me or take me along with them. I don't know why they didn't, only that one man was left with me and he carried me farther from the flames, and then seemed to change his mind."

Hot tears streamed anew down her cheeks, and Cameron held her close, his voice a soft murmur against her face. "Don't think about it anymore, sweetheart. It's over, and done with. You're here now, and you're safe with me."

He closed his eyes against the rage that still engulfed him. How could a man who'd been interested in this woman run off and leave her to die? Her father had at least tried…for surely his attempt at catching the elusive Ben was his way of ensuring his daughter's safety. Being protected by two men would have made her less vulnerable to the men who had attacked them.

At least she was remembering bits and pieces of the past, not that they were guaranteed to give her peace of mind.

"What was your father's name?" Cameron asked quietly.

"George Travis," she said without hesitation. "I'm Elizabeth Travis." A slight smile curved her lips as she considered that fact. "I have a name, Cameron. I was afraid I'd never know even that much about myself."

"Do you think your father got away?" he asked. "Could he swim?"

"A little. But if he had found safety, I think he'd have come back for me. Don't you?" It was a pathetic query, and Cameron reserved judgment. It seemed that Elizabeth had been the responsibility of two men, and neither of them had done their job.

"We'll ask around in Denver about him. He may have gone there."

She shuddered again and subsided against him. "Just hold me for a minute or two, will you? I don't want to be all alone right now."

"You'll never be all alone again," Cameron vowed harshly. "If I have to fight all the ladies on the train, I'll still take care of you by whatever means I must. So long as you trust me and know I won't humiliate you in any way, I'll stick to your side like glue. And once we find a preacher, I'll marry you and make a lifelong commitment to you."

"I'll have to decide about that. I need to know more about myself before I talk to you about marriage."

"Are you fearful of me, Elizabeth? Afraid I'll take advantage of you?"

She shook her head with a quick movement. "No, I know you wouldn't hurt me, Cameron. I just don't want you to be misjudged in any way. It's my fault you're in here with me right now. But folks will blame you if they know you ended up inside the wagon in the middle of the night. I'm afraid I'll ruin your good name."

He edged her onto the feather tick and maneuvered his long body to lie beside her. His arm slid beneath her head and his other hand sought the middle of her back, turning her to face him. There was no force in his touch, only the warmth of a man who is deeply aroused and has sworn not to take advantage of the woman in his arms.

"It's your name I'm concerned with. A woman is always looked down on in a situation like this. I don't want that to happen to you."

She relaxed gradually, her legs twining with his, her arm circling his waist, and her head cushioned on the pillow they shared. With a sigh of what might have been relief, or perhaps contentment, she burrowed against him and relaxed. "I'll be fine," she said with a yawn, and then she breathed deeply, as if her trust in him was not an issue. And for that reason, sleep came easily to her, he decided, as she became limp in his embrace. All but for the slender arm that stretched to the middle of his chest, the fingers that gripped his shirt and clung with a strength that pleased him.

Chapter Five

The morning sun filtered through the white canvas of the wagon, stirring Cameron from his sleep. It was past dawn, he realized, and he should have already been on the trail, scouting out the land ahead. With that, a grizzled face appeared at the rear of the wagon, a face he knew well.

"Joe. What time is it?" Cameron asked softly.

"Well, I'm back from scouting out five miles of the trail," Joe said, his grin speaking his thoughts silently. "I thought you looked pretty comfortable in here a couple of hours ago, so I didn't wake you. Is our girl all right?" His smile disappeared and a look of genuine concern took its place.

"She was dreaming, enough so she remembered a few things, and she needed to talk."

"Talk?" Joe asked. "Did that involve you sleepin' with her?"

"What you see right now is what went on all night," Cameron told him, his words loaded with honesty and, yet, a good measure of menace, his hands in full view.

"No one's gonna doubt your concern for the girl," Joe said. "But you know as well as I do that at least one old biddie will be comin' around before you know it, and raisin' Cain."

"No doubt," Cameron admitted. "But I'm about to announce my engagement to Elizabeth, and I defy anyone to cast any slurs against her or cause her pain."

He rolled from the sleeping woman he held and sat up carefully, trying not to disturb her rest. "I'm getting up. If you'll start a fire I'll get breakfast going."

"I'll help." In a husky voice, Elizabeth revealed her awareness of the situation.

"You don't need to," Cameron said quickly. "Rest for a while."

He rose and crouched low as he went to the tailgate and climbed over to the ground. His boots sat side by side near the wagon and he slid his feet into them and pulled them up, then stomped his feet to settle them inside the carved leather footwear.

Joe had already started piling wood and kindling for the fire and Cameron leaned back into the wagon, searching out the skillet and the cooking stone.

"I'll bring the bacon," Elizabeth offered, folding the sheet she'd used during the night. "I need to find a little privacy before I cook, though." Her cheeks were rosy as she bent over the box where foodstuffs were stored. The slab of bacon appeared in her hands, along with the turning fork, and she looked to where Cameron stood, watching her.

"Will you slice this with your knife? I won't be long in the bushes."

He grinned. "Want an escort, ma'am?"

Her blush deepened as she shook her head. "You're bound to cause trouble as it is, Cameron. Don't make it any worse. I'll just scout out where the other women have gone. I'll bet there are still a few around, and I'll join them."

"You're no fun," he said mournfully. "Leaving me to cook while you take a walk, and turning down my offer."

Her eyes sparkled as she sought out his comb and began making inroads on the long length of her hair. Within moments, she had pulled it back and braided the length of it, tying a bit of string around the end of the tail. Then with a quick, saucy grin, she tossed his comb back into the box and set off on her walk.

"Don't look so downhearted," Joe said. "She'll be back in a minute."

"I know. I'm just hoping no one has anything to say to her about my sleeping in the wagon."

Elizabeth was relieved to find Jennie leaving the safety of the circle at the same time she sought a private spot for herself. With a quick wave, she hurried to catch up to the other woman. "There's not a lot of cover, is there?"

"Not much, but I'll stand in front of you, and then you can return the favor," Jennie offered. "The men know not to be nosy, but it still grinds my gizzard to do my duty just a few feet from a slew of menfolk."

"Have you begun breakfast, yet?" Elizabeth asked as they walked toward a lush grove of bushes. "We're getting ready to fry bacon if you'd like to join us."

"That sounds good. I'll bring over some eggs to fry."

Elizabeth delighted in the friendship that was forming between Jennie and herself. So much so, that she was willing to share the news that was causing her to walk on air.

"Cameron has asked me to marry him," she said softly.

"I'm not surprised to hear that, Elizabeth. He spent the night in your wagon," Jennie said, her face showing the concern she felt. "He'll have gossip running wild today. It's a good thing he's made the offer, or a couple of the women would be hounding him already."

"Does everyone know he stayed with me?" Elizabeth asked, stunned that the knowledge had spread so quickly.

"Most everyone. But then, I think Cameron wanted them to

know that he was laying claim to you, and that was probably the easiest way to go about it."

"He crawled into the wagon when I was having a nasty dream, a nightmare, you could say. The only good thing about it was that I remembered some things that were missing from my mind. I saw my father's face, and I know that another man was traveling with us."

"Not your husband? I've noticed the ring you wear around your neck on a chain."

"I'm not married," Elizabeth said forcefully. "At least not to Ben. I didn't really like him, and I sure wouldn't have wanted him for a husband. He was a friend of my father's back East, but neither of us thought much of him by the time we'd been a couple of weeks on the trail."

"Where is he now? And where is your father?"

Elizabeth shook her head sadly. "I wish I knew. I saw Ben run off when the Indians appeared, and my father went after him. I suspect he had plans of bringing him back to help defend our wagon and keep me safe, but then Daddy fell in the stream and I didn't see him again."

"I wish you could have remembered something that would have given you more pleasure than that," Jennie said sadly. "Surely you have a mother. Wasn't she with you?"

"No. I can't even recall a face right now. I wonder if she's even alive." Her hand went to the ring that lay in the hollow of her throat. "Maybe this is her wedding band. I know it isn't mine."

"That makes sense. Especially if she's not been a part of your life for a long time," Jennie said. "My mother died when I was a child, and I came on this wagon train with my father and two brothers." She cast down her eyes, and her smile was faint. "I'm hoping to find a man I can love before we get to Oregon. I'm going to need a husband, and thus far, there aren't many prospects around. You've caught the best of the bunch."

"I wasn't trying," Elizabeth said firmly. "I'm hoping that Cameron doesn't feel obligated to marry me just because he found me all alone and injured."

Jennie laughed aloud. "Never fear, my dear. Cameron Montgomery doesn't do anything just to please propriety. If he wants to marry you, it's because he's attracted to you and wants to spend his life with you."

"Does 'attracted' bear any relation to 'love'?" Elizabeth breathed softly. "I'm attracted to him, I know, but I've never known what loving a man is all about."

"With men it's different," Jennie said quickly. "They don't need to feel love in order to act on an attraction. I think there are lots of men who don't know what the word love even means." She grinned suddenly. "But I suspect that Cameron might be one of the ones who do. For your sake, I hope so."

They'd meandered across a hundred feet of prairie and found themselves in the depth of the grove of greenery. Tall bushes and willow trees fought to form a verdant spot in the midst of the flatland that was mostly grasses and flowers waving in the breeze.

"This is a likely spot," Jennie said. "I'll bet this is where most of the women headed earlier. I wouldn't be surprised if there's an underground stream hereabouts that's causing all this green stuff to flourish."

"You're probably right," Elizabeth agreed. "Wish that stream would come to the surface and give us a chance for a bath and doing laundry."

Jennie laughed. "Can't have everything. Just finding this shelter for doing our business is gift enough for today. I think we'll run across a river up ahead, according to the map my father has."

"I surely hope so." Elizabeth shaded her eyes with one hand and looked to the West. "There are trees ahead, but they're probably miles away. Maybe your river will show up by tonight."

Jennie turned back to the current business and sought a place where the bushes had thinned to a sparse cover, then stamped down the grass in a circle. "You watch for me," she said, adjusting her clothing.

Elizabeth turned back to where the wagon train seemed to be bustling with early morning activity. "There's no one around," she said quietly. "Just a couple of the women heading over toward our left. I think they're looking for a spot, too."

Within minutes, the two of them were heading back to the circle that offered safety for those gathered in the midst of wagons and animals. Several campfires glowed, the scent of coffee and frying bacon reaching them before they climbed between two wagons to join the group.

"Hungry, ladies?" Joe wielded the turning fork over the skillet and tended the bacon with a practiced touch.

"You bet," Jennie said. "I'll go get some eggs and be right back. My father will no doubt be joining us, too."

"What about your brothers?" Elizabeth wanted to know.

"They've already sorted out a couple of girls who are busily trying out their cooking skills. We don't see a lot of them."

"Come sit down," Cameron told Elizabeth as Jennie walked across the circle to where her father waited. The chunk of wood awaited her, and Elizabeth sank onto it gratefully. "How about some coffee?" he offered, and then without waiting for a reply, he handed her the tin cup. "Careful, sweetheart," he admonished. "It's mighty hot."

"Thank you." She had difficulty meeting his gaze this morning, and sensed the eyes of others from the various campfires upon them as they sat together and drank coffee. "Jennie said we're a topic of conversation," Elizabeth murmured.

"I expected that," he said agreeably. "I've already put the word out that we'll be getting married when we reach Denver, or a preacher, whichever comes first."

"Do I get to have an opinion?" Elizabeth asked sharply.

"I don't like to sound heavy-handed, but in this case I'm afraid I'll have to. You're in a fix, and so am I. Folks will expect us to set things to rights as soon as we can. And that involves a preacher and a ceremony."

"You're planning on staying near Denver, aren't you?"

"That's where my land is. Won't that suit you?"

"I had a hankering to see Oregon. That's where my father wanted to settle."

"At the risk of sounding cruel and unfeeling, I have to tell you that what your father wanted is no longer valid, Elizabeth. You can't go alone to Oregon, you know that. Not unless you marry one of the other men in the party, and I don't see that happening."

"I'll make up my mind later on, when things add up to me."

"And what is that supposed to mean?" Cam asked bluntly.

"When I see Denver, I think I'll know if I'll be satisfied there. If I'm not, I'll ask to stay on the wagon train all the way to Oregon."

Cameron's nostrils flared and his mouth tightened in a gesture that spelled trouble. "You'll choose where you want to live over the person you live with?" he asked.

"What makes you think I want to live with you?"

"I'll take you inside the wagon and demonstrate what I'm talking about if you like," he said forcefully. "But I think you're a smart lady, and you're well aware that I'm mighty attracted to you, Elizabeth. I've laid claim to you, beginning back at the fire when I picked you up out of the ruins of your wagon and brought you back here. Since then I've done nothing to indicate that I've changed my mind. If you don't understand my claim on you yet, I'll demonstrate it to you more fully."

She flushed, her face crimson, her throat above the collar of her dress sharing the vivid color. "I'll let you know my choice, Mr. Montgomery, when we reach Denver. And I'm assuming it won't be long before we get there, will it?"

"A week, maybe," he said, wondering if he'd botched the whole deal. Making her angry had not been his purpose, but sure enough, she was madder than a wet hen right now. "I won't rush you, Elizabeth," he promised. "Just think about it, consider your choices, and make up your mind."

"I won't welcome you into my bed again," she said with a glare in his direction.

"Don't make threats you have no way of fulfilling," he told her. "This is my wagon and my feather tick, and above all, you're sleeping on my pillow."

Joe stifled a hoot of laughter, his ears obviously overhearing the heated discussion. Apparently, the mention of Cameron's pillow had tickled his funny bone. He turned to cast a furtive grin in Cam's direction and shook his head with a puzzled gesture. "You sure ain't goin' about this the right way," he muttered. "Women like to be fussed over and wooed, you know. You can't just tell a gal what's what and expect her to like it."

"When did you get so all-fired smart about the ladies?" Cameron asked, aware that the object of their conversation was hiding her face in her hands.

"Been livin' a few years longer than you, boy. Had my share of ladies makin' eyes at me. Even…" He broke off suddenly, as if thinking better of his next statement, and then jutted his jaw forward as he glanced again at Elizabeth. "This here female is a lady, Montgomery, and she ain't about to give in to high-handed shenanigans."

"I'll handle Miss Elizabeth," Cameron said quietly. "Now just turn that bacon and get ready for the eggs. Miss Jennie is heading this way with her hands full."

The day got off to a late start, with everyone working at a slower pace than usual, but Dallas Smith bode his time, recognizing that his people were weary and needed the comfort of the river they would find just a few miles ahead.

Sunset found the group circled next to the stream, for it was less than a river, more than a small brook. The water flowed clean and clear, probably from a mountain runoff, Dallas said. Fit to drink and plentiful enough for bathing and laundry, it was a welcome sight to the group, especially the women, who bore the responsibility of keeping their families' clothing as clean as possible.

Campfires were built quickly and food prepared for cooking before the flowing water was visited by the men who rolled empty barrels onto a wagon, then drove it upstream where they had decided the water would be the cleanest and fittest to drink. The wagon was pulled to the location chosen and the barrels filled with buckets. A slower trip back to the camp saw the barrels unloaded onto their owners' wagons, assisted by much muscle and the loud groaning of those involved. Supper was made ready, with Elizabeth preparing a hearty soup from venison, shot by another of the men early on in the day. She found wrinkled potatoes in the wagon to add to it, and plants on the prairie that resembled onions, adding even more flavor.

Gathering dirty clothing was simple, for the task included almost all of the wardrobe she and Cameron owned. A gallon jug she'd once thought held a supply of rotgut turned out to be a supply of glutinous soap. Certainly easier to use for laundry than the coarse yellow bar she'd been using. Two clean towels had been set aside for just this circumstance, and a bath was in order once the clothes washing had been accomplished.

The bank of the stream was alive with an assortment of women and a few men who were forced to do their own clothing. Two of the ladies ran a thriving business doing the washing for several bachelors. One of their erstwhile customers, a grinning Cameron, was even now smugly kneeling beside Elizabeth as she scrubbed his clothing along with her own. A long line was strung between trees for the use of the ladies, and Dallas had said they would not break the circle tomorrow, until everyone was rested and the ladies had all of their chores completed. Comparatively speaking, it would be a day of rest for all. Although the women-folk disagreed, since it was up to them to sort out the clothing and restore it to its rightful owners once it was dried and folded.

The children planned for a picnic on the banks of the stream on the morrow, then a swimming party farther west, closer to the water supply, where the bottom of the shallow runoff could be readily seen. Some of the men took horses and sought live game for their meals during the next day or so, and found that rabbits were in good supply.

Excitement ruled the encampment as the clothing fluttered in the breeze and the sun set in a blaze of glory. Coffee was set to brew over campfires as the children were tucked into bed and the adults enjoyed the time of visiting and relaxing before they faced the mountains ahead.

"Dallas said we'd pack up after noon sometime tomorrow," Joe told them as he filled his tin cup to the brim with the strong coffee Elizabeth had brewed. "He wants the ladies to have time enough for their wash to dry, and for you and me to go scouting a little, Cam. He says we'll be in the foothills by tomorrow night if we move right along."

"And then we'll be in Denver, right?" Elizabeth asked buoyantly, feeling the effects of being clean and well fed. Washing in the cold stream had not been anywhere near having a warm bath drawn back East, but considering the bits and pieces she'd been able to wash in a basin over the past weeks, she felt greatly refreshed.

The men had waited their turn in the stream, watching for stray riders as the ladies frolicked in the water. The women had dried themselves quickly, dressing before they went back to the wagons, gathering up shotguns and rifles and then returning to keep watch while the menfolk splashed and carried on.

It was fully dark by the time Elizabeth made her way to the back of the wagon, and Cameron followed her apace, lifting her from the ground and into the wagon bed where she scurried to the feather tick. He leaned over the tailgate and called her name.

"Elizabeth, come here, please. I need to talk to you for a minute."

She turned from fluffing the feather tick and frowned. "Don't you dare climb inside, Cameron. We're in enough of a fix already. Several of the women wanted to know your intentions, and I was hard put to make any explanations."

"All you had to tell them was the truth," he said quietly.

"I don't know yet what the truth will be," Elizabeth said, with a catch in her voice. "What if I find my father in Denver? And what if he wants me to go on with him to Oregon? I can't just turn my back on him."

"In the first place, you haven't found him yet, sweetheart, and in the second place, you owe me some bit of loyalty, I think."

"More than a bit, Cameron," she told him quickly, making her way to where he stood. "But I need to try seeking him out. You must understand that."

"I do. But the first thing I'm going to say when we find him, is that he's going to be privileged to walk you down the aisle of the nearest church. Your reputation is in my hands, Elizabeth. And I'll take good care of it…and you. If you'll let me."

He reached for her, catching her wrist and drawing her closer. Both hands clasped her shoulders now, and he brought her up against the tailgate, bringing her within reach of his kiss. It was different this time, more demanding of her, seeking out the pulse spots in her throat, the softness of her cheeks and the sweet taste of her lips.

"Cameron, I've never…I mean to say, no one has ever…"

His groan was heartfelt as he released her, and then with a quick move climbed inside the wagon. His words were hoarse, deep and guttural.

"I know that, sweetheart. You're a woman of virtue, and until our wedding night I mean to keep you that way. Kissing me won't damage your status anymore than it has already."

His arms circled her, his hands warm against her ribs and back, and then he eased her from him the slightest bit, looking down to where her breasts formed beneath the dress she wore. "I want to touch you, Elizabeth," he breathed softly. "Will you let me put my hands on you?"

Even as he spoke, she felt the puckering of the flesh beneath her clothing, felt the thrill his words sent skimming down her spine, and the anticipation of his fingers actually forming to her curves. "I don't know why that part of me is so appealing to you, Cameron, but if touching me will please you, I won't stop it from taking place."

He smiled, his eyes narrowing, his jawbones firming and his nostrils flaring, as if they caught a scent about her that was pleasing to him. His fingers undid the buttons she'd so recently put in place, first one, then the second and finally the third, allowing him access to the shift beneath her dress. Tiny pearl buttons fastened it over her bosom and with gentle care, he freed the fabric and exposed her warm flesh to his sight.

The moon rising cast its glow through the rear opening of the wagon, bringing to life the pearly glow of her skin, turning the gentle curves and hard, beaded crests into a sight he welcomed. His hand slid beneath the fabric of her shift and he lifted one breast from its covering, holding it, as he might contain a priceless treasure in his palm. For indeed, the fact that Elizabeth was allowing this intimate venture was akin to him opening a chest of the most precious jewels in the world.

She caught her breath as his fingers tightened on her, whispered his name as he brushed the puckered peak with his fingertips, and then looked up into his eyes with a latent hint of passion that brought him to a full, stunning erection. She was ripe, ready for his loving, and yet not so, for her natural resistance to this seduction would call a halt should he attempt to gain any more ground tonight.

"Cameron." It was a whispering sound that told him of her desire for him, that promised a full surrender to him, once the promise of their wedding night was fulfilled.

He bent to her lips again and took what she offered, blending his tongue with hers in a foretelling of the joining of their bodies that would come. He was careful, cautious, well aware of her unfamiliarity with such intimacy, and strove for patience lest he frighten her with the fire of his hunger.

But to his surprise, there was no withdrawal, no retreat of her lips from his, only a warmth that lured him further, an invitation of such innocence he felt awed that she would allow his touch upon her. With care, he opened her shift wider, his gaze unhindered as he bent to touch his lips against the flesh thereby exposed. His mouth moved closer to the center of her breast and she inhaled quickly, as if she feared the touch of his lips and teeth against her.

"I won't hurt you, sweetheart. Just let me kiss you here," he begged, touching the dark crest with his tongue and then drawing it into his mouth. She shivered in his grasp, a low moan sounding from her throat, an unspoken phrase that resounded in his mind. She wanted him. This beautiful, untouched girl desired his touch, would marry him and be his wife.

Triumph rose in his chest, spilling out in words of love he could not contain. "Sweetheart." The single word was heartfelt, a groan from his depths, and he inhaled, as if he sought breath for his declaration. "Elizabeth, I love you. I've never said that to another woman in my life, I swear it. I want to live my life with you and keep you by my side so long as we live."

His hands rose to her shift, there to button and hide her beauty from himself. The fastenings on her dress were dealt with next and he was gentle as he moved her apart from himself, looking with longing on the gown that hid her from his sight.

"Please, Cameron," she whispered, her voice a sigh. "Let me think. You have my mind in a boggle, and I'm not sure just what you've done to me. I only know that I'm hot and cold at once and my skin is burning, even while I feel chilled. You make me into someone I can't recognize, and that frightens me. I'm not fearful of you or what you do to me, only of myself and the choices I must make for my future."

"Whatever your future holds, I'll be a part of it," he swore firmly. "I'll help you try to find your father, and I'll make it right with him, so that he knows I love you and am prepared to look after you. That's all I can promise for now, Elizabeth. But I want your acceptance of my offer."

He waited, his hands once more on her shoulders, watching carefully lest his ultimatum should place her beyond his reach. "Can you care enough for me?" he asked softly. "Enough to marry me?" He watched closely as her eyes closed for a moment and then smiled as her eyelids fluttered a bit. Blue eyes looked into his, and tears filled them to overflowing as she attempted to speak.

"I care for you, Cameron. You know that. But I can't make any promises until I at least look for my father."

He nodded. "I can live with that answer. Once we get to Denver, we'll set out on a search."

Chapter Six

The morning sun was hot and the clothing strung on rope lines dried quickly. Before noon, the ladies had finished their chores and Cameron had gone out to roll up the rope he'd volunteered for their use. His gaze swept westward as he worked, idly estimating the time it would take to reach their goal. Three or four days would do it, he expected.

Three days or so in which to lure Elizabeth further into his web, for that was surely what he was doing. Weaving his way into her heart was a pleasant prospect, he decided, and capturing the girl as his own would complete the plans he had for his life.

The wagons lined up right after the noon meal and started out, the oxen and horses fresh from the extra time they'd spent watering at the stream and finding fresh food to crop beneath the trees and bushes. Elizabeth spent the next hours inside the wagon, straightening and folding, moving Cameron's supplies to and fro, until she was satisfied with the arrangement she'd brought into being. Unfolding the clean sheets she'd washed and hung to dry, she caught the fresh scent of clean air and prairie flowers in the fabric, and hugged the sheet to her, inhaling the welcome smell. The white material floated like a falling leaf to the feather tick and she folded it in around the edges, fluffing the pillow, now covered with a clean case, and putting it in place.

A quick trace of guilt touched her as she thought of Cameron sleeping beneath the wagon on the hard ground, with only a flat, useless pillow beneath his head. Tonight she'd swap pillows with him. And with that thought, she climbed back on the wagon seat, catching Cameron's eye as he walked beside his team of oxen.

"Tonight, you get the good pillow," she announced with a grin. "I'm not going to be selfish anymore. From now on, we'll take turns."

His look was accented by a raised eyebrow as he dropped back a few paces to walk directly beside the seat where she perched. "In a couple of days, I'll be entitled to share that nice fat pillow with you every night, sweetheart. And the feather tick, too."

She blushed, not an uncommon thing for her these days, she thought. It seemed that Cameron had the ability to bring a hot flush to her cheeks with only a few words or gestures. She thought of his kisses and the warmth of his hands on her body. It was almost too much to be considered, that his whole body would one day touch hers, his potent masculinity would lay claim to the feminine parts of her that even now yearned for him.

"What are you thinking, sweet?" he asked in a low, coaxing voice she had heard before. "Thoughts of me?"

"You make me all flustered. But my thoughts are my own, I'll have you know. One of these days…" She broke off as Joe rode toward them, his smile wide and triumphant if she was any judge.

"We're in the foothills, Miss Elizabeth. Not too steep a grade this side of Denver, not like going over the mountaintops, but dangerous enough to be ready for any event."

The oxen did not seem to strain unduly as the trail developed an upward slant throughout the afternoon, but they tired earlier in the day than was usual, and Dallas called a halt to the wagons well before sunset.

Campfires blazed and food was consumed by the hungry travelers as the talk between the men centered on the coming climb to the city that was rumored to be surrounded by clouds. Plans for using ropes to help the teams haul the wagons uphill were made, and the women and children were warned that they would have to walk most of the day tomorrow and probably the next. The weight in the wagons must be lightened as much as possible, and only one very pregnant young woman would be allowed to ride during the struggle to climb upward to the city that awaited them.

Euphoria gripped Elizabeth as she planned ahead to the search for her father. The memories of her past were coming together as might a patchwork quilt, the days of her childhood yet a blur, but the memory of her mother coming clearer to her as she searched the corners of her mind for that lady's face and form.

A tall Christmas tree seemed to be important, gifts beneath it piled and waiting for eager hands to tear aside the colorful wrappings. Her mind dwelt there for long moments, aware of the happiness she'd owned, the love that had surrounded her.

A house with many rooms; a cat with a litter of kittens, and the green grass of a city called Philadelphia came to mind. It was where she had lived, she knew it as a fact, and the anticipation of sharing her new memories with Cameron filled her to overflowing.

She walked now beside Cameron, having fulfilled her duties after the early morning meal and packing bread and meat for their dinner at nooning. They would not stop for that meal, just eat it as they walked, halting long enough to feed and water the animals should the occasion arise.

As it happened, by the time they were thinking once more about a meal, a river appeared at their left, flowing down the mountains in a rush of white, tumbling water that the children were warned to steer clear of, lest they be sucked away by strong currents. And this river would be crossed, up ahead at the tree line that loomed at the far reaches of her clear vision.

They found that, by placing their wagons next to trees, they were assured of not tumbling down the mountain that night. It was a touchy procedure, but Dallas refused to go any farther once the sun had gone over the mountain peaks. Night fell swiftly, and the usual campfires were lit for only a short time, with travelers finding their beds early. Dallas had said that tomorrow would bring a rigorous few hours when the river was crossed, and the menfolk were adamant that they should all rest as much as possible in preparation for the tasks ahead.

Cameron found Elizabeth still sleeping when he crawled into the wagon early in the morning. His touch roused her immediately, and she turned to her back, smiling up at him joyously. "Good morning," she whispered. "Is everyone up and about?"

"No, just a few of the men. We'll be leaving as soon as we find food enough to eat while we walk. Should reach the river crossing by noon."

"No cooking this morning?" she asked, surprised at the unusual change of schedule.

"One campfire with several coffeepots over it. We'll take canteens full once we've drunk our morning coffee here, and other than what we have ready for our breakfast, we'll do without until after we cross the water."

"I've got bread sliced, along with cold sausage left from supper, and I found some cans of tinned peaches last night," Elizabeth offered. "We can eat the bread and meat, and then open the fruit later. The juice will taste good."

"You're a good sport, Miss Elizabeth," he said, bending to kiss her quickly. "I'll take my clothes and change behind the wagon while you get ready for the day."

Her heart lifted as Elizabeth thought of the crossing today and the lure of Denver just ahead. To see real stores and wooden houses on actual streets was a thought that kept her going for the whole of the morning as they walked and struggled up the mountain. She clung to trees as she went, at times almost on her hands and knees.

"I'm not as strong as you are," she complained to Cameron as he strode upward, seemingly without effort.

"I'm a man, and my muscles are probably better equipped for this than are yours, or those of any woman for that matter," he explained. "Men are stronger than women, but women are softer and cuddly, just the way men like them to be. That's why it's so easy to care for womenfolk. A man knows that his woman will respond to his concern for her and give him the warmth he needs to keep him happy."

"Will I be able to keep you happy?" she asked wistfully. "I sometimes think you don't need me along. I'm only a burden to you."

"Ah, yes. But one smile, or one kiss gives me all the strength I need to tote you along with me, sweetheart. I love taking care of you, and making certain you're safe and sound."

She walked on beside him, inwardly proud of the man who slowed his pace to match hers, a man who gave without stinting of all he had for her comfort. How could a woman not love a man such as Cameron Montgomery? For if this feeling of joy and gladness while she dwelt in his shadow and in his presence was not love, she had no notion of what that emotion might entail. She wanted to find ways of pleasing him, recalling his pleasure in the shirt he wore, even now. She'd cut buttons from the antler of a deer, the same one who had given his hide for Cameron's benefit, and pounded holes carefully in their centers so that she could sew them in place. The shirt was soft and supple, the sleeves turned up now, due to the heat of his exertion, and she beamed as she watched him, knowing that he wore the garment with pride.

And then they were at the chosen place for a crossing, the river before them, the rocks and swift current looking more dangerous by the minute. The men seemed assured of success, and Cameron himself told her he had already conquered this crossing three times before, and therefore knew the best place to enter and leave the water.

"Promise me you'll hang on tight while the wagon goes across," Cameron said sternly, readying his team, tying down anything that might wash away in the current. "I want you on the seat where I can watch you, and I'm going to tie you down. I'll fasten a rope to your waist and then to the seat, but I'll leave it so that you can undo it should the water tip the wagon and douse you in the current. Don't worry, sweetheart, I'll be watching you every minute, and I'll take care of you."

"I know that," she said confidently, sure of his word.

The reality of the crossing was more traumatic than she had planned for. The water washed up over the sides of the wagon, sloshing about and soaking into the contents inside. She had put everything up as high as possible before they'd gone forward early in the morning, but some of their belongings were still liberally doused with the cold mountain water. She clung to the seat, feeling anchored by the rope holding her in place, even more secure in the knowledge that Cameron knew what he was doing and that she had only to follow his lead. There was much to be said for belonging to a strong man, she decided, and then felt her heart flutter within her bosom as she considered that thought.

She belonged to Cameron, as much as did his oxen and wagon and the very basics of his life, his clothing and food, and the rest of his paraphernalia. And yet she knew that of all he owned, all he claimed as possessions, she was the most valued item of which he boasted.

The climb up the riverbank was treacherous, and two of the wagons tipped, their contents being washed away, except for the few items the men were able to salvage. The wagons were set upright and the men formed crews, repairing and hammering fresh boards in place so that they might be fit for the trail. Women brought items to the two families and provided for their needs, clothing and food being supplied readily by those who were willing to share of their own bounty for the less fortunate travelers.

The trail leveled out by late afternoon and a fairly flat piece of land, perhaps two or three acres of grassy surface, was welcomed as a spot to halt for the night. Trees surrounded their oasis in the midst of the wilderness, and the wagons seemed to huddle even closer than was usual in the chosen place. One of the menfolk produced his Bible and read to the assembled group from the Scriptures, that which described the trials and tribulations of those who had lived centuries before, but who had shared in the perils of overland travel in their quest of a homeland.

Elizabeth listened to the words of comfort and promise and sat close to Cameron as they shared a quilt on the grass. The eyes of many of their fellow travelers dwelt upon them, perhaps gauging their relationship, or wondering about the days ahead and what they had planned once the outskirts of Denver were reached.

"I'm sleepy," Elizabeth said softly. "Would it be rude to gather up our quilt and go to bed?"

"No." Cameron looked around the circle. "Several folks have already headed for their wagons, but I don't want you going anywhere by yourself, sweetheart. I'll come with you."

Together they approached his wagon and sought out the darkness behind the overland vehicle, there where the light of campfires did not reach. Cameron leaned over to place the quilt he'd carried inside the wagon and then reached for Elizabeth. His arms held her against his body, his lips found the skin of her forehead and temples and then he held her apart from his body, and peered down at her in the darkness, smiling as his words spoke of their future.

"I'll build you a house as soon as I can," he told her. "We'll need at least three bedrooms eventually, to hold our family, but I think just one will do for a while. I have money in the bank in Denver, enough to buy furniture and whatever else we need to set up housekeeping. I'm glad you're familiar with a needle and thread, sweetheart. We'll need curtains and all sorts of things to make a home. Some we can buy, but—"

She shushed him effectively with fingertips touching his mouth. "Yard goods are a lot less expensive than ready-made stuff from the catalogue. All we need is a store with dry goods in supply and I'll be happy. We'll need a good length of oilcloth for the kitchen table though. My mama couldn't abide bare wood to eat on. We always had fresh oilcloth for the kitchen table every spring."

She inhaled sharply. "I'm remembering more and more all the time, Cameron. That little item came out of nowhere into my mind, and I could see the yellow daisies on the printed oilcloth we had last, before she died. Mama made curtains that had the same daisies all over them, and I helped her with the sewing. I think I can manage to recall the specifics of keeping house and sewing and all the rest. I can remember her teaching me how to cook and even the foods my father enjoyed the most. Mama always catered to him, spoiled him rotten, he used to say."

"Will you spoil me the same way?" he asked, hugging her as if he could not help but show his affection.

"Probably," she said agreeably. "I have a notion you'll pretty much have your own way."

"I'll try to make you happy, Elizabeth," he vowed, "and since pleasing you makes me happy, we should get along just fine."

She tilted her head back and sought his lips, whispering against the firm line of his mouth. "Kissing you pleases me, Cameron. I know there's a lot more to this business of being married, but when the time comes, I'll enjoy whatever you give me."

His legs weakened beneath him as he considered her words. "I think I'd better lift you inside the wagon, love," he said, his voice sounding rough and yet soft against her ear. "I don't think my self-control is going to last for much longer. I'm too ready to make you mine right now, and I can't do that. I've already been tempted almost beyond my ability to resist you."

She sought his gaze in the darkness, the moon lending a bit of light to the endeavor. "You mean when you touched me and kissed me in the wagon?"

"Exactly," he agreed. "I had the devil's own time not getting rid of your clothing and holding your warmth in my arms. I'm not trying to scare you off, Elizabeth, but you spoke the truth when you said there's a lot more to being married than just kissing."

"If you want to…" she began hesitatingly.

"No." His voice regained strength as he denied her offer. "When we find your father, I want to be able to look him in the eye and tell him that I've taken care of you, not taken advantage of your innocence."

"*When* we find my father?" she asked. "Are you so sure?"

"I'm sure," he replied. "My daddy always told me that a man should ask for the hand of his bride from her father. I did it once, and I'll admit that I wasn't sure what I was getting into, but this time I'm certain of my ground. We'll have a good marriage, Elizabeth, and it's gonna start off right."

With strong hands and arms that were muscled from hard work, he lifted her into the wagon and, to his credit, only snatched one quick kiss before she found her way to the bed he'd given her, disappearing from his sight in the darkness. Without hesitation, he crawled beneath the wagon, having scooped up his quilt first and the flat pillow that offered little comfort. Only his boots were removed as he settled down for sleep, and he yawned widely, pleased with the few minutes he'd spent with his future bride.

He reached for the bottom of the wagon bed and rapped twice with his knuckles. An answering sound from above made him grin and he heard, faintly, but clearly the simple words she spoke for his hearing alone.

"I love you, Cameron Montgomery, but I forgot to give you your pillow."

* * *

The trail into Denver was not without hardship, but the members of the train bore it with no complaint, happily anticipating the sight of an actual town and the chance to see a general store wherein they could buy supplies, and even clothing if they so chose. The children were regaled with tales of long candy sticks that would probably be available for sale, stored in tall, glass containers. Although some of them might have to share such a treat with a brother or sister, they didn't seem to mind the scarcity of such luxury in their lives.

Elizabeth heated water over the campfire the morning before Denver city-proper would be reached. It would be a rushed job, she knew, but clean hair was a necessity, and behind the wagon was as good a spot as any to do the deed. Jennie approached her as she gathered her towel and soap, smiling as she approached, bearing her own bucket of warm water and the necessities for such a task.

"You're about to wash your hair, aren't you?" Jennie asked in an undertone. "I thought I'd join you when I saw you heating water. I knew it was either for a bath in a basin or a hair-washing and I was hoping for the latter."

"I can't bear not having it clean any longer," Elizabeth told her. "Scrubbing my head in a cold stream was a necessity but not a pleasure. I can hardly wait to feel the warm water on my head and the soap being scrubbed into my hair."

"I'll do yours if you'll do mine," Jennie offered. "It always felt so good when I was a little girl and my mama washed my hair over the kitchen sink for me. She got right down to the bottom of things and it made me have chills down my spine when she poured the warm water over my head."

"Well, I may not be able to do as well as she, but I'll do my best," Elizabeth told her. "And having you back here behind the wagon with me makes me feel better. I'll appreciate your company."

They poured the liquid soap over each other's hair and took turns with the warm water and the washing and rinsing of long lengths of shimmering locks. It was not an easy task, but much more fun with two of them sitting together in the sun, using their towels on the wet strands before they combed out the snarls.

Elizabeth's golden blond tresses and Jennie's dark locks were a contrast to Cameron's gaze as he watched them silently. Both of them pretty women...and then he revised that thought. They were beyond pretty. Lovely or beautiful were words that would better describe them.

He smiled as he watched Elizabeth's hair dry, the sun turning it into the color of clover honey from the comb, shades of brown with sunshine mixed in, making it a sight for a man to dwell on with only one thing occupying his mind. Cameron's would not be deterred from the wedding to come and his smile of pleasure as he gazed on the woman he'd chosen was but an outward sign of the deep hunger for her that filled his being. A need he must set aside now in order to concentrate on the day before them when his duties as a scout would be needed on the trail ahead.

Cameron and Joe rode in the next morning from scouting the trail that led from the mountains onto the flatter lands that were the outskirts of Denver. Their presence brought welcoming smiles from the womenfolk, who sensed that civilization was not far off. But no smile was wider than that of Elizabeth, busily finishing up the bacon and making toasted bread over the fire on which to serve the meat for their breakfast.

Her happiness was tinged by her awareness of Jennie's leaving. The two women would soon part company, probably forever, once Denver was reached. For Jennie's father was determined to go on to Oregon, was planning on settling there, leaving his daughter no choice but to go with him. Jennie had not complained, but Elizabeth knew that the parting would be painful for both of them. Finding another woman who was compatible was not easy, indeed the other ladies on the wagon train were married, with families for the most part, and Elizabeth had not found close friendship with any of them.

Now, she watched as Jennie approached, comb in one hand, a length of ribbon in the other. Without being asked, Elizabeth reached for the comb, and stepping to the back of the wagon, began braiding Jennie's hair for what might be the final day of travel. Without speaking, she turned her back for her friend to return the favor. It was a task she could have accomplished alone, but one that she would be able to remember with pleasure in the future as she thought of these final days together.

Cameron called her name from the other side of the wagon and she watched as he rounded the corner afoot, pausing as if he would not infringe on her grooming.

And then he grinned as he saw that the two women were finished with the dressing of their hair. "Want me to tend to your fire, ladies?" he asked. "We're about ready to break up camp, and we need to grab a quick bite of breakfast and then y'all need to be getting ready to move out."

"I still have things to pick up and sort out," Jennie said, rising and scurrying toward her father's wagon. "I'll see you later," she called back to Elizabeth. "Save me some bacon."

"I'll go inside the wagon and straighten things up," Elizabeth said, hanging her towel over the tailgate. "You and Joe can feed yourselves, I suspect."

"We don't have far to go this morning, sweetheart. Another couple of hours and you'll see civilization, at least the Denver variety of it."

"Will there be a hotel there, with an honest-to-goodness bathtub for me to use?" she asked anxiously.

"We'll get a room and stay in town for a few days," he assured her.

"One room?" she asked, lifting her eyebrows at him.

"Yeah, one room. We're going to look for your father later today and see if he's been seen or heard of here. If we can't get married right off, we'll put you in the room and I'll sleep in the wagon until things work out."

The hotel was impressive, Elizabeth thought. A large two-storied structure, painted white with dark green shutters on the first floor, and a fancy front door that was obviously imported from the East. Etched glass adorned it, the sunlight shining through it onto the hotel lobby's floor casting lovely patterns of flowers and leaves entwined together. She paused to admire the effect and then turned as she heard Cameron speaking to the clerk at the desk.

"We'll need a large room to share," he said. "We'll be married later on today."

"I'll see what I can find for you, sir," the young man asked, shooting an admiring look at Elizabeth as she waited beside Cameron.

"We also need some information," he said, watching as the desk clerk handed him the pen and turned the registration book to face him. "We're looking for the young lady's father," Cameron told him. "He survived a wagon train attack some ways east of here, and we're hoping he might have ended up in Denver."

"Maybe the sheriff would know something," the young man said. "He's pretty well kept up on things going on in town."

"Well, first we'd like to see a room, and I want to order a bath for Miss Travis."

"I'll show you the room, and notify the kitchen that you'll need hot water and a tub, sir," the clerk told them. "I'll take your bag, Miss Travis," he said, reaching for the small leather valise Cameron had given her from his wagon.

"I'll take care of Miss Travis," Cameron said shortly, narrowing his gaze at the clerk and then grasping Elizabeth's bag in one hand, his own in the other. "If you'd give Miss Travis the key, we'll find the room."

Without hesitation, Elizabeth was handed the key to a room on the second floor, and together they climbed the curving staircase. "You were a bit rude to that nice fellow," she said reprovingly.

"That *nice fellow* was giving you the eye," Cameron told her harshly. "You might as well know right now that no other man looks at you thataway. You're mine, Elizabeth, or at least you will be by tonight."

He was jealous, Elizabeth thought, happily aware for the first time of a man who would not allow any untoward attention to be fixed on her. Cameron had truly staked his claim, as he'd told her weeks ago, and had no intention of releasing her from his care.

The room was large, with a bed big enough for two, a dresser, complete with mirror, and two chairs. A wardrobe stood against one wall and Cameron put their valises inside.

"I'll empty those out," Elizabeth told him. "I see there are hooks to hang my dresses on, and my other things can go into one of the drawers. Shall I take care of your clothing, too?"

"Might as well," he said, turning from the wardrobe to offer her a smile that encompassed her as a whole. "You'll be sorting my things out for a lot of years to come, I'll guarantee."

A knock at the door announced the presence of two young men carrying buckets of water. "We'll be right back with the tub," one of them said, furiously blushing as he cast his eyes on Elizabeth. They backed out of the room, returning in minutes with the large, metal tub Cameron had ordered.

"I'll leave you to your bath, ma'am," he said with a bow. "I'm off to see the sheriff and look around a little. I'll give you an hour of privacy before supper. Will that do?"

"Yes, of course," Elizabeth said distractedly, hardly able to keep her eyes from the steaming water that filled the tub. "I won't be long."

"Go ahead and enjoy it," Cameron said. "I'll order you a tub from the catalogue once we get to the general store, but it'll probably be a couple of weeks at least before we get it. More like a month, I imagine." He shut the door firmly behind himself and then opened it again, poking his head inside the room.

"I'm going to lock this thing from the outside, Elizabeth. I'll use the key when I come back and I'll knock first." The door closed again and she was left alone with the promise of a clean body and a good meal to follow, one she did not have to cook, one that would not come from over a campfire. Life was almost perfect.

The sheriff was a fount of information, Cameron found. "I know who you're looking for," the tall, husky man said. "George Travis came into town with a couple of fellas from a ranch east of here. He'd walked as far as he could, and as luck would have it, those two cowhands found him under a tree, all tuckered out."

"Is he all right?" Cameron asked anxiously. "Where can I find him?"

"He's fine, far as I know," the sheriff said. "And he's staying at Ma Brown's boardinghouse, down the street." He opened the door of his office and motioned Cameron to step out onto the sidewalk with him. Lifting one hand, he pointed his index finger to the north a ways. "See that sign, past the hotel and post office? It says Boardinghouse on it, and that's where he's living. Might not be there now, but it's likely he'll show up there by suppertime."

Cameron thanked the lawman and set off on foot to where he'd been directed. The house was large, set back from the road with a large porch across the front. The door was open and Cameron leaned inside, seeking the proprietor of the business. A large lady bustled down the hall from the back, where he assumed the kitchen was, her hands buried in her apron, wiping them dry.

"Yes, sir, can I help you?" she asked. "If you're looking for a room, I'm full up, but I can offer a meal in about an hour."

"I have a room already," Cameron said, removing his hat and holding it at his side, "but I'm looking for a gentleman named George Travis. Have you heard of him?"

The lady grinned widely. "I sure have. He came in here a couple of days ago and took a room and he's been all over town ever since, trying to find trace of his girl. They were on a wagon train that was attacked and burned. He got away, but when he managed to get back there the next day, there wasn't no trace of his daughter, not hide nor hair."

The fact that George Travis had sought his Elizabeth's presence gave a boost of pleasure to Cameron. The man obviously was concerned for the girl, and would be happy to see her. "I know where Elizabeth Travis is," he told the landlady. "Where can I find her father?"

"He's out scouting around, like I said. But he'll be back about any time now. He don't miss a meal, George don't. Will you join us?"

"We had planned on eating in the hotel restaurant, but this sounds like a good idea to me. I know Elizabeth will be happy when I tell her we've had success in finding her father. Just don't spill the beans, all right?"

As the woman nodded in understanding, he slapped his hat in place and left the house, his good humor abundant as he imagined Elizabeth's reaction when he gave her the news. The hotel was only ten minutes away, and Cameron's long legs carried him there quickly. He gave a quick salute to the desk clerk as he headed for the stairs, and got his key out of his pocket, anxious to open the door where Elizabeth was waiting for him.

His quick rap announced his arrival and Elizabeth turned from the dresser with a smile. "I feel like a new woman," she said. "I'm clean as a whistle, and hungry as a bear."

"I've found your father." All his plans for a gradual explanation of George's arrival in town and the finding of his lodging place flew to the four winds, and Cam was delighted to clearly read the stunned expression of pure joy on Elizabeth's face. She seemed paralyzed for a moment, and then flew across the room, her feet barely touching the floor, so quickly did she arrive in his arms. Her head tilted back and her eyes shimmered with tears as she gripped his neck, her hands sliding into his hair, her fingers tugging on his head, lowering it to hers, their lips meeting with an enthusiasm he cherished.

"I can't thank you enough," she whispered between sobs of joy.

"You just did, sweetheart," he told her, his voice husky with an emotion he could not name, only knew that the woman in his arms was the source of his happiness at this moment.

"Oh, Cameron, I can't believe it. You've found him." she cried, her tears falling even though her smile was wide and her expression joyous. "Where is he?"

"In a boardinghouse at the north end of town. At least he's going to be there for supper in a few minutes. I told the landlady we'd join them for the meal if it was all right with you."

She laughed aloud then. "What do you think? Did she say he was all right? You didn't see him, did you?"

"No, I didn't see him, but he'll be there when we get there. You get ready and I'll take you to him."

Her hair was damp, her face shiny, and yet he thought she was the prettiest thing he'd ever laid eyes on. And she would be his. One way or another, he'd lay claim to this woman and make her his own.

Chapter Seven

Elizabeth had never dressed so quickly, never worked so rapidly at drying her hair, and then forming it into a knot at the back of her neck. It made her feel older, more like a full-grown woman, and it seemed that the days of girlhood were long behind her. Those long-ago memories she could now recall, when her hair flowed free, waving and curling halfway down her back.

Yet the look on Cameron's face when he took her measure was one she cherished. He smiled, and the movement of his mouth promised pleasure to come. He reached for her, his hands careful as he held her waist and inspected her with interest.

"You've never looked so much like a woman as you do right now. Your eyes are glowing and your skin is flushed. And your mouth is tempting me, sweetheart. I want to claim your lips, and then take off your pretty dress to see what lies beneath it."

She felt heat rush over her body, a satisfying flush of triumph. This man wanted her, needed her, if she was any judge of matters. His hands trembled as they rounded her waist, his big body offered safety and comfort and above all, promised pleasures she had only dreamed of. Even if he didn't marry her, she would surrender to him, and that knowledge made the heat rise within her once more.

"We're going to have to find us a preacher before nightfall," he said quietly, his hands tightening their grip on her. "I don't think I can last another night without you in my bed, Elizabeth."

"I'll do whatever you ask of me," she said, the words offering him her very soul, should he demand it. "I'll do whatever will please you, Cameron. I only ask that I be allowed to see my father first. I need to know why he and Ben left me behind during the attack."

"That bothers you more than you want to admit, doesn't it?"

"I think I suspected Ben was a coward." She shuddered at an errant thought. "I couldn't have let him touch me, Cameron. Marriage to him would have been a living nightmare. But I need to understand why my father left me there unprotected."

"Get your shoes on, sweetheart, and we'll take a walk. You may have all your answers within the hour." He settled her on the chair and sought out her low shoes from beneath the edge of the bed. "Here. Lift your foot and slide this on," he told her, holding the shoe as she put it on. The second one slipped easily against her white silk stockings and the leather wrapped around her narrow foot.

"I think I'm ready," she said breathlessly.

"A kiss for courage," he told her, kneeling before her and wrapping his arms around her once more. His strong hand cupped the back of her head and he brought her closer, his mouth offering the gentle touch of warm lips against her own.

"Thank you, Cameron," she said, rising as he tugged at her hands. "I'll never be able to thank you enough for my life. For taking care of me and bringing me here."

"I had selfish motives, sweetheart," he confessed. "I wanted you in my life, not just for days or weeks, but for all the years to come. And now I have you. You're mine, Elizabeth."

He escorted her to the door, locked it behind them, and then held her close as they descended the stairway to the lobby. "Are you up to taking a long walk?" he asked, bending to speak next to her ear.

"Of course," she told him with a wry glance. "I'm young and strong and anxious to find my father."

It seemed a shorter walk to Cameron, with Elizabeth by his side. She matched her steps to his, and he slowed his own to accommodate her shorter stride. They passed the shops that were closed now for the day, waved at the barber who swept his floor, the newspaper man who carried a stack of fresh newsprint, and slowed their pace as they looked into the windows of the Emporium.

"We'll need to come back here tomorrow," he said. "We'll get supplies before we look for a rig to buy, to take us to my land."

"Tomorrow?" she asked, her voice shaking. "We'll leave town tomorrow?"

"Unless we have to wait to find a minister to marry us. I'd like to honeymoon with you tonight," he told her, and felt the trembling that signified her fears. "Don't worry about it, Elizabeth. I'll be happy to hold you in my arms. I won't make any demands of you."

"I'm not afraid," she said, and rued the trembling of her voice. "I'm really not."

"Look. Just up ahead." He pointed his index finger to a small house, nestled next to a simple, white chapel. "I'll bet you that's the parsonage. Let's stop for a minute."

Before she could offer an objection, he turned her through the open gate and up onto the porch. A quick rap of his knuckles on the door brought a young woman into view, a dish towel in her hands, a smile of welcome on her lips.

"Hello, there," she said brightly. "I'm Pastor Timothy's wife. Won't you come in?"

"Just for a moment," Cameron said, ushering Elizabeth before him into the small foyer. "We want to be married later on this evening. Does that seem like a possibility?"

Eagerness brightened the features of the small woman before

them. "Timothy will be back in an hour, and we have no plans for the evening. When will you return?"

"Let's say two hours' time," Cameron told her. "We're going to have supper with Elizabeth's father, and all three of us will be back."

So easily it was plotted, and the wheels set in motion, Elizabeth thought. She held Cameron's arm, her grip tight as they walked down the steps and back to the street.

"You said you wanted to talk to my father first," she reminded him.

"I will. Just as soon as we see him," Cam said firmly. "You haven't changed your mind, have you? You told me in the hotel that you're still willing to marry me and live here, even when your father goes on to Oregon."

She only nodded, but her warm gaze told him what he wanted to know. She would not be an unwilling bride, of that there was no doubt. He stepped up the pace a bit, anxious to reach their destination, and discovered in the next few moments that he was not the only man who awaited this meeting anxiously. For coming toward them was a tall, broad-shouldered gentleman of perhaps middle age, his dark hair touched by gray at the temples, his eyes so like Elizabeth's that there could be no doubt of her heritage at this moment.

His gaze fastened on the woman by Cameron's side. His hands clenched as he walked, his mouth worked as he met Elizabeth's gaze and his eyes filled with a glaze that could only be tears as he reached for his daughter, and held her closely to his chest.

"Elizabeth." George Travis spoke her name as if he'd never thought to address his daughter again in this life. "Ah, Bethy, I've been so worried about you. I've tried to find you and had almost given up hope. Now this gentleman has brought you to me. I can't thank you enough," he finished, looking up at Cameron.

"I've brought her to you for two reasons, sir. First, because she was so worried about you, and needed to find you. Second, in order to ask your blessing on our marriage," he finished.

"You're married?" George seemed stunned, but rallied quickly. He set Elizabeth away from him, the better to look down into her eyes.

"Not yet," Cam said, "but before nightfall. That's if we eat quickly and get back to the parsonage in a couple of hours. The preacher is expecting us. All three of us."

His words were careful, letting George Travis know his presence was needed for the ceremony to come. He heard Elizabeth's soft sigh. Surely her father would…

"I'll be honored to give my daughter to you in marriage," George said quietly, looking into Elizabeth's face. "If marrying you is her desire, I'll gladly give you my blessing. But first I think you'd better introduce yourself, and tell me how you came to be my daughter's future husband."

Elizabeth spoke quickly, her words breathless. "He rescued me, Father. Brought me to his wagon train, kept me with him and took care of my wounds. Actually, the doctor who was traveling with the train sewed up my face, but Cameron was there through it all. He kept me safe, gave me his feather tick and his pillow and his wagon to sleep in."

"Do you want to marry him, Bethy?" her father asked, his smile sad yet filled with a tenderness he made no attempt to hide. "Does he make you happy?"

"I could live without him, Daddy, but I'd mourn forever if I lost him. Finding a life with Cameron seems to be a fine goal for my future. Here, where he has property and wants to build me a house."

"Where is your property?" George asked his future son-in-law.

"Just north and a bit west of here," Cameron said. "I have over a hundred acres, enough land to run a herd of horses, enough money to build a house and barn, and muscle enough to make a good home for your daughter. If you'll give us your blessing."

"You have it, son," George said, a hitch in his voice that signified deep emotion.

"I hate to lose you again so soon, Daddy," Elizabeth said softly. "I know you're determined to go on to Oregon, but you can always come back here if you want to. To visit or even make your home with us."

George looked down at her. "Somehow, Oregon doesn't seem so inviting anymore," he said with a smile. "I wanted us to find our future there, but it looks to me like you've found your own way without my help. Perhaps I'll consider staying near Denver."

Elizabeth wrapped her arms around the man who had fathered her, hugged him close and wept against his chest, her hands gripping tightly to the flannel shirt he wore.

"Don't cry, Bethy," he said, lifting her face with long fingers beneath her chin. "I want to know that you're happy. And if marrying this man will make it so, I'm in favor of a wedding tonight."

"Sir." Cameron's eyes darkened as he gained George's attention. "I need to know about the man who traveled with you. I believe Elizabeth said his name was Ben."

"It was," George said harshly. "Now it's the name on a bit of wood stuck in the ground at the head of his grave."

"What happened?" Cameron's eyes were dark with a fury he did not attempt to conceal.

"I shot him," George said. "He ran off when the raiders began burning the wagons. I almost drowned before I caught up to him. All I could think of was my girl, left alone, and that rotten excuse for a man left Bethy behind without a second glance. I was almost out of my head, torn between taking my girl with me or chasing Ben down, hoping to bring him back to help me keep her safe. But he said he wasn't going to lose his scalp for any woman, and I lost it. I killed him, and then buried him, and made up a board with his name carved on it. Even that seemed to be stretching my Christian duty, I fear. After that, my memory has an empty space, until the next day."

"Your daughter almost died there," Cameron told the man. "It was only through the mercy of an Indian brave that she survived. He could have taken her scalp or even carried her back with him to his camp. He did neither, just left her there to be found."

"How was she injured?" George asked, his hand lifting to touch the scars on her chin and forehead. Rough, reddened flesh that had not yet faded. He winced as he waited for a reply.

"The men who grabbed her from the wagon threw her to the ground, and at least one of them hit her. I could still see the marks of his fists when I found her the next morning." Cameron closed his eyes as though he were recalling the event, those moments when he'd feared for her survival.

And then he took Elizabeth's arm and motioned for George to join them, walking toward the boardinghouse where their supper awaited.

It was good, solid, nourishing food. Mrs. Brown was a talented lady, Cameron decided, able to feed over a dozen men and one very beautiful lady, with little trouble, it seemed. Elizabeth was scrutinized by the men who lived in the house, her natural loveliness a source of pleasure to the hardened men who seldom saw a real lady.

Cameron felt his protective instincts rise, and then realized that no harm would come to her here. His impatience for the meal to be over weighed heavily on him though, and when the last plate was cleared, the apple pie dished up and pronounced nectar from the gods, he was ready to leave. He drank his coffee hurriedly, his gaze fixed on the woman he wanted, and would soon claim as his own.

As if she didn't notice his fretting, she spoke quietly with her father, told him of the past weeks, inquired about his own health and safety, and then when he whispered something that pleased her, she laughed, a silvery sound of joyful delight, wholesome and happy. Her head turned to Cameron as he inhaled sharply and rose to escort her from the table.

"You're happy to see your father, aren't you?" he asked quietly, so low that only she heard his words.

"Oh, yes," she said, sighing a bit. "The best part is knowing he'll be close by."

"He can come with us, if he wants to, Elizabeth. We'll build a house large enough for all of us to live together. Even extra rooms for the children we have."

"Can we afford all of that?" she asked, looking up at him in awe.

"I'll have to impress you with my bank account," he teased. "We can afford whatever you please. I've worked for years, dug gold from the earth and led four wagon trains across the country, and every penny is in the bank, here in Denver."

She followed him from the dining room, remembering to thank their hostess for her hospitality. She'd watched her father pay the amount required for their meal, but knew that her own thanks would be welcome to the lady who had fed them so sumptuously.

They left the house and walked in the twilight back to the small church. A young man awaited them on the porch of the parsonage and led them into the white church building next to his home. A familiar sense of awe enveloped Elizabeth. She walked down the aisle beside her father, noting with pride the tall, handsome man who would soon be her husband standing at the altar. Who now awaited her with a semblance of patience, an emotion she was willing to guarantee he was not in possession of tonight. He was ready for a wedding night, needy of his wife by his side in that room at the hotel.

Elizabeth could only hope she was able to please him, willing though she was, she laid no claim to knowledge of the marriage bed. She only knew that she loved this man, was willing and eager to spend her life with him.

The words of the ceremony were brief, the reading from the Bible admonishing them to be loyal and honest and faithful. And she had no doubt that Cameron Montgomery was all of those, that he would be a good husband to her.

George Travis walked away, back to the boardinghouse where his belongings would be packed by morning, his future assured by the man known as Cam Montgomery.

"We'll pick you up after we get some supplies together," Cameron said, and George waved in acknowledgment as his daughter left his side to become Cameron's wife.

The hotel was silent as they crossed the threshold, the desk clerk sleeping at his post, his head cushioned on the leather-covered book Cameron had signed earlier. Quietly, the newlyweds made their way up the stairs and down the hallway to their room. The key slid into the lock and the tumblers clicked as Cameron turned his hand, then twisted the doorknob and opened the portal into the room where his marriage would begin.

"Are you all right, sweetheart?" he asked quietly. "Do you want me to go downstairs and leave you alone till you get ready for bed?"

"No." Elizabeth shook her head quickly. "Don't leave me, Cameron. I'm just a little worried about all this, but I know I need you here to help me."

"Can I undress you?" he asked hopefully. His hands went to the buttons on her bodice, and not waiting for permission, he undid them carefully, slid the simple gingham dress down her arms and onto the floor. She stood before him in her white petticoat, her vest and drawers as pristine as the woman whose body was covered by their fabric.

With care, he knelt, taking her shoes and stockings from her legs and feet, then stood before her again, his hands grasping the white muslin undergarments she wore and carefully removing them, to reveal the shimmering beauty of her body. She was rounded, yet slender, her curving breasts looking all the more abundant because of the narrowness of her waist. Her hips filled his hands and he brought her against himself, gritting his teeth, lest he frighten her with his aroused body.

It was not to be, for she lifted her hands to his shirt and undid the row of buttons, giving her a view of his chest, of the mat of dark hair that curled there, inviting her fingers to touch as she was being touched, of finding the muscular frame beneath the satin skin, of pressing her palms flat against him, her eyes closing as she explored the skin she'd exposed to her sight.

"There's more," he reminded her, undoing the waistband of his trousers, allowing them to fall to his feet. And then she was before him, pushing him to sit on the bed, kneeling at his feet to remove his shoes and stockings, sliding his trousers down, even as she eyed his drawers with barely concealed apprehension.

He would not allow her to become frightened. Her gaze had attached itself to the bulge of his manhood, and even as he drew in his next breath, he realized the arousal had grown beyond that which he normally attained.

Lifting her to her feet, he stood before her again, turned her in his arms to face away from him, and removed the drawers that hid his manhood from her. She shivered as his warmth pressed against her, inhaled sharply as his hands lifted to possess her breasts and then sighed with pleasure as he owned the softness of the woman he held.

His hands were slow in movement, sure in their aim, and she knew but a slight moment of apprehension as he placed her on the bed and joined her there, the candle burning beside them burning low.

"Blow out the candle," she whispered, and her eyes pled for his understanding. Without words, he leaned toward the table, his big body covering hers, and with the sound of his breath toward the flame, the room was dark. His hands found her again, and he lay beside her, his breathing harsh, his body trembling. He bent to her, his mouth touching her breasts with care, lest she be frightened, and he felt a surge of delight as she clung to him.

"I want to be your wife, Cameron," she whispered. "I don't know much about all of this, but I'll do whatever you ask me."

She should have known better than to give him free rein, for his flesh surged at her words, his passion almost out of control. His bride was truly innocent, unaware of a man's needs, and so had offered to accommodate him in any way he chose. A choice that might make any man forget himself. But Cameron had vowed to himself that he would be patient.

And so his choice was simple. He chose to pleasure her. With strokes designed to arouse her desire, kisses that were intended to entice her passion, and with hands that strove only to give her a woman's delight, he led her down the path of seduction. Yet it was not truly a seduction, for she was willing, her hands exploring him with tentative movements, stroking fingers finding new places to visit. And when her palm reached his arousal, and did not hesitate, but circled that throbbing organ, he heard the sigh of surrender she offered.

"You're hard, yet soft and silky at the same time," she whispered and he smiled at the awe she made no attempt to conceal.

He relished the slender touch of her fingers, the reaching of her hand for the source of his masculinity, and knew afresh that he'd been blessed beyond measure.

Rising over her, moving her legs apart and exploring the treasures exposed, he sought the center of her being, caressed the warmth of her womanhood, and bent low over her, whispering words of love as he made her his wife.

Cameron's head bowed as he found his place in her depths, his heartbeat rapid, his breathing harsh and yet he would not be satisfied until she had received pleasure to match his own. He rose to his knees and touched her more intimately, his hand roaming over her breasts and stomach, finally claiming the center of her pleasure and leading her to a knowledge of the joy her body was capable of.

* * *

It was not really a painful ordeal, such as she'd expected, but a blending of bodies, of minds and of the souls of two people who had found love in an unlikely time and place. Elizabeth felt the small stab of pain at his entry, lifting to contain him and gifting him with the prize of her virginity. For she was truly virgin, truly untouched, a woman of purity and virtue.

"I love you," she whispered, after her heart had finally stilled a bit. "I want to spend my whole life with you, Cameron."

"I know." He kissed her then, and repeated the vow of love she offered, his words firm and filled with promise. "I love you, too, Elizabeth. I love you now, I'll love you as long as we live, and I'll always be there to take care of you and our children."

"I'd like to have a baby," she whispered, her hand rising to touch his face, her fingers tracing the long line of his jaw, the firm texture of his skin, the warmth of his mouth.

"As soon as we can," he promised.

Epilogue

Six years later. Spring, 1854

The house was large, growing yearly as Cameron added rooms, the one-room cabin he'd started with now spreading to offer four bedrooms, a big kitchen and parlor. They shared the space happily with George Travis, who delighted in being a grandfather to the children of his daughter's marriage. He thrived there, aware that Elizabeth and Cameron were happy, fulfilled and enjoying their life together.

That they had chosen to include him in their plans was a bonus he'd not expected, but he'd been given free rein with a herd of horses, training, breeding and, with Cam's help, developing a profitable line of buying and selling the horses that were necessary to life in the West.

Now his third grandchild was about to be born. In fact, if the sounds he heard from the big bedroom down the hall were to be believed, his newest delight was even now being delivered. He heard the sharp cry of a baby, the sound of Cameron's deep voice, and finally the words he'd waited to hear.

"Daddy? Cam, where's my daddy? Is he here?" Bethy asked,

her voice carrying through the bedroom door Cameron had just opened. He walked through the portal, down the hallway to the parlor where the rest of his family awaited.

"I have something to show you," he said, his arms holding a tiny bundle, his smile looking like that of a smug warrior who has won a hard battle and glories in it.

"A girl?" George asked hopefully, rising from the sofa, and Cameron's answering nod gave him the answer he delighted in. "Can I hold her?"

"Here's your grandpa, little one," Cameron said softly and de-livered the child into the waiting arms of her grandfather. From the sofa beside their grandfather, two small boys ran full-tilt, toward their parents' bedroom.

"They'll be fine," Cam said as George watched them racing toward their mother.

"Can I see Elizabeth now?" he asked and at Cameron's nod, he walked down the short hallway to the big bedroom at the back of the house.

Elizabeth was propped up in the bed, three pillows beneath her head, a joyous smile on her lips, her arms filled with two small boys who could not be refrained longer from seeing their mother.

"Isn't she beautiful?" she asked her father, her eyes on the bundle he bore, and was not surprised by his choked reply.

"More beautiful that anything I've seen," he said. "What will you call her?"

"Faith." Without explanation, with a smile of beauty, Elizabeth named her daughter. And George understood. For faith had brought them thus far in their journey. It had sustained them through danger, uplifted them in the hard times life brought into being and given them courage to walk unfalteringly into the future.

"Faith." It was Cameron's deep voice that spoke the name now. "Faith Elizabeth," he said. "The first girl to be born into this family, but hopefully not the last."

Elizabeth raised weary eyes to him, yet found a smile for the man she loved. "No, not the last," she vowed.

George placed the babe in her mother's arms and lifted the two little boys from the bed. "Come on, fellas," he said, eyeing the small replicas of their father who looked up at him with adoration. "Time to feed the horses. Your mama needs to rest now."

In moments, the doctor had finished his work, and with a promise to return in a few days, left the house, leaving Cameron alone with his wife.

"You're beautiful," he told her and she smiled.

"You always say that, Cam. I don't feel very beautiful right now. Just lonely in this bed. Do you suppose you can come lie with us for a minute or two?"

So it was that they slept, mother and father with a tiny bundle between them, the man's strong arm circling his woman's waist, his watchfulness fading into slumber as he knew once more the peace and happiness of being with the woman he loved.

It was almost dark when George closed the bedroom door, leaving the three of them alone to rest. Caring for the two little boys was a pleasure, and George Travis happily fed them both and then undressed them for bed, keeping them quiet to ensure their parents a restful night.

And then he sat on the porch, watching the stars, admiring the moonbeams that silvered the land. Land that was surely more to his liking than would have been Oregon. For here was the family he'd longed for, the children of his old age, the daughter and son who would look after him. And three little ones to fill his days with happiness.

In the house, Elizabeth roused and was hushed by a kiss from the man she slept with. "It's all right, sweet," he whispered. "Your father has put the boys to bed and he's out back. This little one between us is waking up a bit, wanting her mama to feed her."

"Umm." Elizabeth opened her gown and settled the newborn at her breast, her nose buried in the fragrance of the child, that definitive scent that would disappear all too soon, but now filled her with love for the helpless infant.

Her murmur was soft, a whisper of happiness she could not contain. And the man who held her smiled as he recognized the delight that filled her voice as she spoke, was filled with joy as he watched the serene features of the woman he loved.

"Faith." It was a single syllable, a word of promise and a pledge for the future.

* * * * *

Dear Reader,

I hear from many readers who ask about characters from past books, so it was a pleasure to give Luke and Annie from *Sweet Annie* and Noah and Kate from *His Secondhand Wife* roles in this story.

After her cousin Annie married, Charmaine was promised the next too-good-to-be-true man who came along. Charmaine is more than ready. She has dowry trunks stacked against the wall in her bedroom. Idealistic to a fault, Charmaine tries to be the perfect lady to entice a perfect young man. When challenged with writing her story, I asked myself, "Who would be the perfect man for Charmaine?" And then I brought in the most unlikely fellow I could imagine. Once married to a half-Cherokee woman, Jack Easton is a man solidly grounded in reality. Nothing frivolous for Jack. He has time for nothing but work and his son.

I love taking story people of differing backgrounds and with opposing goals and watching them fall in love. Charmaine and Jack are just this couple. I hope you enjoy their spring love story! It was a pleasure to write.

Cheryl St.John

ALMOST A BRIDE

Cheryl St.John

It's my pleasure to dedicate *Almost a Bride* to my readers.
Thanks to each one of you who has ever taken time to
write. Your letters and e-mails are an encouragement
I deeply appreciate. I have kept every last one of them.
To those who have sent pictures of yourselves, I want
you to know those photos are thumbtacked to the bulletin
board that surrounds my desk. Your faces remind me that
each story I write is for you. Thanks for your support.
You are special to me.

Chapter One

❦

Copper Creek, Colorado, 1892

"Spent three winters in the stable, you say?" Jack Easton studied the appaloosa with dark spots on white hips, brown-and-white leopard pattern in the middle and white speckling on dark head and forelegs. The haltered filly trotted around the perimeter of the corral with the other horses Jack had come to look over. He appreciated the animal's erect ears and ease with their presence. The signs promised acceptance of a rider's demands.

Noah Cutter, owner of the Rockin' C, nodded. "She's halter and saddle broke."

"Used to havin' her foot lifted?"

"She's been shod for a year," the rancher replied. "But she doesn't have long lines or a deep chest. You buyin' for yourself?"

Jack shook his head. "For my son. I want him to train his own horse. She's not broke to gaits?"

"Nope. But she can be ridden. My wife has exercised her several times."

Since Noah raised the finest horses this side of the Rockies and Jack was a saddle maker, Jack had done trade with Noah on many occasions. Because of the man's past evasiveness, dealings had been strained, but since his marriage, Noah had been conspicuously more approachable.

"Want to see her ridden?" Noah asked. He flicked away a fly, drawing Jack's attention to the back of his hand.

The scars that marred his hands and face had never bothered Jack much, now he hardly noticed. "I trust you, but I would like to see how she moves. Would your wife oblige us?"

Noah actually grinned. "She has her gaggle of women friends comin' over this afternoon, but maybe she'll spare us a few minutes before they descend." He glanced over his shoulder. "Newt!" he called to one of the hands. "Run up to the house and ask Kate if she'll ride the appaloosa for Mr. Easton."

The ranch hand waved his compliance and loped toward the house.

As they waited, the men discussed the animal's size and how much growth was still to come.

"How old is your boy now?" Noah asked, catching Jack by surprise. He'd brought Daniel along a few times, but this was the first Noah had shown interest.

"Just turned eight."

"Our Rose will be three soon. And little Levi is just one."

Jack wasn't sure how to respond. They'd never discussed anything more personal than the types of leads and snaffles they preferred. "I bought a place outside town," he said finally.

"Heard you'd moved closer to town. Wife knows all the latest news. Don't even need to read the paper."

"What are you saying about me?" a teasing female voice asked.

Jack noticed the expression on Noah's face soften even more and turned. Katherine Cutter was a fine-featured woman with a bright smile. She wore a practical split riding skirt and a pair of kid gloves. She raised her hand to shield her eyes from the sun.

"Kate, this is Jack Easton."

She gave him a friendly smile. "We spoke at the mercantile last week. Good to see you again, Mr. Easton."

He quickly doffed his hat. "Mrs. Cutter."

"Kate," she corrected. "Mrs. Cutter is my mother-in-law."

She and her husband shared an amused glance. "Where's this filly you want me to parade? I have tea cakes waiting to be frosted."

Jack and Noah entered the corral and herded the horses until they could approach the appaloosa. Noah grabbed the lead, opened another gate and led the animal into the connecting corral. Wooden steps sat in the dust, and Kate climbed to the top, then waited for her husband to walk the horse alongside.

She mounted and walked the filly inside the boundary of the enclosure. Jack liked the way the horse responded, appreciated its form from all angles. "This will be a fine horse for Daniel."

A commotion caught their attention, and all three turned to observe the carriage that had drawn into the dooryard. One by one, colorfully dressed women stepped down, holding their skirts aside with gloved hands.

"Oh drat! They're here and I haven't dressed." From atop the horse, Kate waved to her friends. "Ladies! I'll be there in a moment."

The women wore billowing dresses of varying hues, styles and patterns, plumed hats of all shapes and sizes, pristine white or delicate pastel gloves and dainty satin shoes. One by one, they spotted their friend and carefully made their way toward the corral, gingerly holding their skirts aside to avoid weeds and holes.

"Look at Katy!"

"Kate, you're a natural."

"Noah, have you put her to work, breaking the horses?"

The women laughed among themselves and continued onward.

Jack recognized only Diana Sweetwater, whom he'd met at the elementary school both of their sons attended. None of the other faces were familiar.

Noah helped his wife dismount, then tethered the horse to the fence, and the three of them exited the corral.

"Come meet my friends," Kate said, gesturing for Jack to follow.

He did so reluctantly, immediately encompassed by a fragrant cloud of exotic floral scents, strikingly contrary to the barn and corral smells to which he was accustomed.

"Ladies, meet Jack Easton. This is Annie Carpenter. Her husband, Luke, runs the livery."

"Ma'am." Jack knew the livery owner.

"And Diana Sweetwater. They're sister-in-laws."

"We've met," Diana said with a friendly smile.

Kate continued. "This is Pamela Stevenson and Lizzie Halverson. Janie Barnett. And this is Charmaine Renlow. Charmaine and Annie are cousins."

"Are you confused yet?" Charmaine asked with a twinkle in her blue eyes. Jack thought he detected a slight Southern accent. Charming dimples winked from her cheeks when she smiled. She wore a light green dress with a ruffled collar and hem and had artfully arranged a matching ribbon through her blond curls. When she moved, her sparkling emerald earbobs swung. She carried a napkin-draped basket over her forearm.

"Not at all," he replied. "Pleased to meet you—er—all of you."

"You'll join us for refreshments, of course," Kate said.

Jack opened his mouth to decline. He'd be more comfortable thrown into a pit of rattlesnakes, but the ladies smiled encouragement and nodded vigorously, sending long colorful feathers swaying.

Kate placed a hand on her husband's arm. "Give me half an hour to finish the tea and frost the cakes and then bring Jack to the house."

Jack watched them go, bemused at their chatter and dumbfounded at their fragrances and fresh appearances.

"They're something, aren't they?" Noah adjusted his hat.

The sight of that many fancified women was an oddity for certain, but Jack drew his attention back to their business. He had a horse to buy.

* * *

"What have you brought?" Annie asked Charmaine. The two of them had hurried into the kitchen to help Kate finish the refreshments while the rest of the ladies seated themselves in the dining room and chattered.

"My sponge lilies," Charmaine replied.

"You've outdone me at my own tea party," Kate said with a grin.

"I hadn't thought of that." Charmaine whisked the basket from the counter to stow it away.

Kate grasped it by the handle and got it away from her. "I was only teasing. Goodness knows I can use all the help I can get with this fancy stuff."

"Where are Rose and little Levi?" Annie asked.

"Marjorie took them for the morning." Marjorie was the wife of the ranch foreman, and she helped with the house and garden. "Levi and her boy Fuller nap together, and Rose helps her garden. I appreciate my morning alone, and I keep Fuller for her whenever need be."

Annie nodded. "My mornings when my mother has the children are a godsend. Not that I don't adore the little darlings."

Charmaine heard the pleasure in their voices. Their families were everything she'd ever wanted. At twenty-two, Charmaine was the last unmarried woman over the age of seventeen in Copper Creek.

"Sometimes I despair that I'll never have what you two possess," she confided to her cousin and her friend.

For the past four years, she'd been seeing Wayne Brookover. Wayne had apprenticed for the druggist and now ran the apothecary, but so far no marriage proposal had been forthcoming. "Every time I think Wayne is ready to take the step, the moment passes in burning disappointment."

Kate turned to her with an expression Charmaine couldn't decipher, but Annie wrapped an arm around her shoulder. She and Annie had been closer than most sisters their whole lives. Annie had always come to stay at the Renlows' whenever her parents traveled. Back then, her parents had considered Annie an invalid, but because of her husband, Luke, Annie had gained self-confidence and strengthened her leg so that she could walk and live a normal life.

"Wayne is sure to come around soon," Annie told her. "He's crazy to keep you waiting for so long. I truly don't understand the man."

"It's not that difficult to understand a man," Kate said with a smile. "Food and a willing—er—spirit. That draws them every time."

Warmth climbed Charmaine's cheeks. Wayne had kissed her on occasion, and she hadn't discouraged him. She was definitely a good cook. So there had to be something wrong with her. Something missing. She just wasn't as extraordinary as her cousin or as brave and adventurous as Kate.

She'd figured out the problem. As hard as she tried to do everything just right, there wasn't anything special about her.

Kate uncovered Charmaine's baked goods and arranged them on a glass tray.

The back door opened. Noah and Jack Easton entered the kitchen and hung their hats on pegs. Their sleeves were damp from an apparent wash at the pump.

"You're just in time," Kate said with a bright smile. "Lead the way, Charmaine."

Charmaine picked up a tray of cups and led them into the dining room, where the women were seated on straight-back chairs around the perimeter. The lace-draped table had been pushed up against one wall to hold china and napkins.

The ladies stopped their prattle to greet the men again, and Kate set the food on the table. "Charmaine, will you serve the tea, please?"

From the sideboard, she poured tea and in turn asked each person their preference and carried their cup to them.

"Sugar, please, miss," Jack said. He appeared decidedly uncomfortable with the situation, but was following Noah's cues. Charmaine added sugar to his tea and stirred. As his hand dwarfed the dainty china cup, she had a moment to notice his long tanned fingers and blunt nails.

He raised his gaze and their eyes met. His were rich brown, his eyebrows lighter than his dark hair, and he wore a neat mustache that left his lips visible. He had a pronounced bow to the upper one, a sharp chin and good cheekbones. A very interesting face, now that she studied it. A twinge of embarrassment—or discomfort—rose in her chest, and she realized her inspection was too forward. Not to mention *disturbing*.

She yanked her gaze to the teapot in her hand. "I'd better go for the other pot of tea."

Kate helped her pour the steaming liquid into the china pot. When they returned, Kate served the pastries.

Jack would've rather wrestled a grizzly than sit here with these women and their dainty little tea cakes. His fingers didn't fit in the cup's handle, and he glanced to see how Noah was managing his. The rancher held the delicate china without using the handle, so Jack did the same.

The two men's gazes met, and Noah's held a decidedly amused glimmer. He gave Jack a nearly imperceptible nod, as if to say, "You're doing all right. This isn't my favorite pastime either."

Jack's skin prickled beneath his shirt, and the temperature in the house seemed to have risen at least twenty degrees. The last ten minutes had stretched like an entire day. Didn't these people have something more useful to do? He had an afternoon's work ahead of him.

He'd felt obligated to accept their invitation, and Noah was taking it in stride, but he wished he were anywhere else.

Noah's wife had changed into a dress as frilly as the other women's, and now she was standing in front of Jack with a tray laden with pastel frosted squares and some sort of sugary cookies that were shaped like flowers! He tried not to stare like an idiot. How much effort had gone into those?

Noah had taken a napkin first, so he did the same.

"Charmaine made the sponge lilies," Kate said. "I can't manage anything near as exquisite."

Jack took two square cakes and two of the flowers just to make sure he didn't offend anyone. The center of each delicate cookie held a yellow candy bean. He'd never put anything so pretty in his mouth before, and the confection melted on his tongue.

He watched how the ladies held their napkins on their laps and the cups in their hands and managed to copy them without spilling on himself. His food was gone in a few bites, and he was glad he hadn't actually been hungry.

"Kate tells us you make saddles, Mr. Easton," one of the ladies said.

His head buzzed. Now they expected him to *talk?*

Chapter Two

He thought the woman's name was Lizzie, but the introductions had gone by in a blur.

"Yes'm," he replied. "Saddles, harnesses, collars and the like."

"Fine workmanship," Noah added. "I own several myself."

"How did you learn your trade?" Diana Sweetwater asked.

"My father caught and trained wild horses. I grew up helping him and apprenticed with a saddle maker when I was fourteen."

"Is your father still alive?" Charmaine asked. She toyed with a gold locket on a delicate chain around her neck. Her hands were small and dainty, soft-looking.

"No, ma'am."

"I'm sorry. Has your mother passed on, too?"

"Indeed. I was a boy when a fever took her."

"How unfortunate for you." Her expression seemed one of genuine sympathy.

"Noah lost his mother at a young age, too," Kate told him.

With discomfort, Jack glanced at the man beside him. Had the two of them been alone, they'd never have learned of each other's pasts.

"Where did you live before you came here?" Diana asked.

"On land my father left me. In the mountains," he explained. "Moved my business here so my boy could go to school."

"Daniel's a delightful young man," Diana told him with a smile.

"Thank you, ma'am."

"Your son lost his mother at a young age, too, then," the young woman named Pamela said, her tone sympathetic.

"She died when he was just a baby." Growing more and more uncomfortable with their avid curiosity, and not wanting their sympathy or their attention, he tried not to squirm on the chair. He didn't want to discuss his wife and her Cheyenne heritage—nor did he want to deal with their disapproval. He wasn't ashamed and he didn't want his son to be either. Neither did he want it to be an issue. The less said about her, the better.

"Kate says there's a shoemaker settin' up shop in town." Noah's comment was completely off the subject.

"He's from Denver," Lizzie offered. "Can't imagine why he's come to Copper Creek when there's so much business in the bigger city."

Speculation arose from two or three woman at once.

As the women's conversation swelled around them, Noah looked to Jack with a raised brow.

Jack held back a chuckle. How easily the man had diverted their attention.

"Been a pleasure, ladies," Noah said. He rose to set his cup and saucer on the table. "Jack and I have business to finish, so excuse us."

"Thank you, Mrs. Cutter—"

She held up a hand.

"Kate," Jack corrected. "The tea was fine. The cakes, too." He set his cup beside Noah's, itching to escape the room and the curious eyes. "The lily cookies were a real treat, Miss Renlow."

Her fair cheeks turned pink at his words, and she stood. "I'll send some for your son. Let me wrap a few."

He waited in the kitchen, impatience clawing a ragged hole in his self-possession, while she wrapped several cookies in paper and tied the package with string.

He accepted the gift. "Daniel's never seen anything like these. I never had."

"Really? Well, they're just…cookies."

He glanced over his shoulder to see Noah waiting by the door. Jack glanced from the package in his hand to the young woman's hands clasped in front of her, once again noticing her delicate white skin and slender fingers.

He pictured her shaping all those cookies and wished he'd taken a little longer to eat his.

"Thanks, miss."

"Mr. Easton."

He turned and grabbed his hat from beside the door and fled on Noah's heels.

"Damnedest thing I ever saw, that tea party." He adjusted his hat.

"Yeah."

"You do that often?"

"Only if Kate can find me. I have trouble sayin' no to the woman."

They entered the corral, and Jack inhaled scents of hay and manure that were as familiar as his own skin. "Let's get on with this deal."

The following morning Charmaine entered Annie's dress shop.

Her cousin looked up from the comfortable chair where she sat basting a sleeve. The other sleeve, held together with straight pins, was draped across her lap. "You're early."

"I woke at dawn when Daddy went out, and I had all my chores finished by breakfast."

"Charmaine!" Rebecca squealed. Annie's four-year-old daughter had been stacking blocks on the hardwood floor around the rug that set apart their play area, but she stood, scattering the pile, to wrap her arms around Charmaine's skirts.

"Goodness, dearling. You'd think you hadn't just seen me day before yesterday."

"I missed you."

Charmaine knelt for a warm sweet-smelling hug. "Mother was coming into town to see Mrs. Davidson, so we rode together," she said over the child's shoulder.

Two-and-a-half-year-old Ruth toddled over to join them. "Say me good morning."

Charmaine laughed. "Good morning, Ruthie." She gave the child an equally affectionate hug and a kiss on the cheek. "I'll read you both a story at teatime, would you like that?"

The girls clapped with delight and went back to playing with their toys. Both of them had accompanied Annie to the shop several mornings a week since they'd been born, and Charmaine came most of those mornings.

Charmaine opened the box beside the other chair and took out a voluminous gauzy veil she'd been working on for the past month. Settling in the other chair, she opened a drawstring bag, poured seed pearls into her palm, and used straight pins to stick them at the ready in the padded arm of the chair.

"I have something to tell you," her cousin said.

Charmaine discovered Annie's eyes sparkling with pleasure. "What is it?"

"Luke and I are going to have another baby."

With the surge of joy she felt for her cousin came a wave of disappointment she had to forcefully hold back. "Oh, Annie, that's wonderful!"

She slipped from her seat to kneel in front of Annie and take her hand. "I'm so happy for you, really I am."

"I know you are. I wanted to tell you first. No one except Luke and myself know yet."

"Not even the girls?"

She shook her head. "We thought we'd wait a few months to tell them, so the wait won't seem so long."

"Luke must be very happy. And no doubt he's hoping for a boy this time."

Annie smiled and leaned forward. "He hasn't said as much, but I'm certain."

The two women hugged. Charmaine sat back on her heels for a moment, studied Annie's face, then moved back to her chair. Picking up a needle and thread, she reflected over the past several years. There had been a time when she'd believed—and hoped—that Luke had been interested in her.

Because of the Sweetwaters' resistance to having him court their daughter, Luke had invited both Charmaine and Annie out for ice cream and buggy rides. But it had soon become clear that his interest and devotion was all for Annie.

She'd been delighted for her cousin. Thrilled, because during the time when Annie had been treated like an invalid, she had despaired ever having a husband.

Little had they known back then that it would be Charmaine, the outgoing one, the healthy one, who would languish into spinsterhood.

After several minutes of companionable silence, she asked, "How many wedding veils have I made now?"

Annie glanced up. "A few, I guess."

"More than a few. I make them to add to the trousseau that has grown to such immeasurable proportions that I've begun stacking trunks in my room."

Annie gave her an understanding nod.

"But then I give them away. I gave one to Kate, one to Darlene and one to Janie. I've helped all of our friends plan their weddings. I've probably made a million boutonnieres. Remember how young and excited we were when Lizzie got married, and we all dreamed we'd be next?"

"I remember."

"I'm at my wit's end as for knowing what to do." Her emotional venting had brought tears to her eyes, and when the pearl she held blurred, she quickly wiped them away. "I'm sorry. I didn't mean to spoil your moment of joy."

"You haven't." Annie set down her work. "I have to ask you something. Are you sure you want a man who has dragged his feet for so long?"

Charmaine blinked. "Of course I want Wayne."

Her cousin gave her a penetrating look. "Do you truly love him?"

Charmaine's defenses were riled. "Or is he just the only man left? Is that what you mean?"

"Of course not."

"It's certainly not flattering, I can assure you, to have been picked over like the bruised apple in the bin. Why, Mary Lou Hollister even got a husband, and she's mean and spoiled and—"

"I wanna apple!" Ruth called.

"I'll slice you one at teatime," her mother replied, then said in a low voice to Charmaine, "Now don't be unkind—"

"I'm not being unkind, I'm being realistic. I'm being honest. And while I'm being honest, is there any reason why Wayne wouldn't want to marry me? My features aren't perfect, but I've never curdled the cream."

"Dear one, you are lovely. Lovely, do you hear? Why, I always wanted to look like you, to have your poise and your gift of conversing. I envied you my whole childhood."

Charmaine stared at her. "You did not."

"Did so."

"Why?"

"Well, for one thing your parents were always loving and accepting and treated you with respect. For another you were healthy and able to attend school and play croquet—even though you sat out many an activity to keep me company, and I loved you all the more for it. You treated me with dignity, and you were my best friend. You still are."

Charmaine wiped another tear from her cheek. "And you're my best friend. No one except a friend would tell me when I'm behaving like a fool. Remember when I used to affect that breathless Southern accent?"

"You did it yesterday."

"I didn't!"

"You did. When you spoke to Jack Easton. Ever so slightly, but it was there."

"I shall continue to work on that. But the whole point is, Annie, that either I accept that there's something wrong with me—that I'm incapable of endearing a man—or I believe that Wayne simply needs another nudge to be convinced."

"What are you planning?" Annie asked, her tone skeptical.

"Nothing specific yet. I'll figure it out."

"Just think about my questions, okay?"

"I think about my plight day and night."

Annie moved back to her seat and picked up the other sleeve. Her fingers moved deftly, threading the needle in and out of the fabric. "It's nearly teatime."

The cousins were sipping tea midmorning when Diana entered the shop. "Good morning, ladies."

They greeted her, and the girls ran to hug their aunt.

"I'm in need of a favor," Diana said.

"What can I do?" Annie asked.

"As you know, the Founder's Day celebration is coming up in just a few weeks."

The other two women nodded.

"I serve on the city council planning board, and we have weekly meetings for the next month."

Diana was a forward-thinking female, and her husband, Annie's brother, had always encouraged her. She was always involved in civic matters and was active in supporting political candidates.

"What do you need, a costume?" Annie asked. "I ordered a pattern for a dress with a jacket that will suit you perfectly."

"That sounds lovely, but I'm afraid it's another matter. The school needs assistance with their activities for Founder's Day, especially with their float for the parade and the booths at the picnic. Burdell and I simply don't have time, and each student is expected to have adult assistance."

"That sounds too physically challenging for Annie," Charmaine said, not really thinking of her cousin's leg, but of the new life she carried.

"Of course it is." Diana's gaze was directed at Charmaine. "I was hoping I could count on *you* to fill in for me again. I know I've asked you several times and you've never declined, but this is especially important to Will."

Charmaine often stood in for her cousin Burdy and his wife, and she didn't mind doing so now. She didn't have brothers and sisters of her own, so her Sweetwater cousins were her family. "I'll be glad to do it."

"Wonderful!" Diana swept forward and bent over Charmaine to give her a hug. "Thank you! There's a meeting at seven tomorrow night. Will you be able to attend and learn your assignment?"

Charmaine nodded. "I will."

Diana turned to Annie. "May I bring Elizabeth over to play with the girls tomorrow morning?"

"Rebecca and Ruth are always delighted to have their cousins over," Annie said with a smile.

"It's only Elizabeth, now that Will's in school," Diana clarified. "Thanks, I'll see you in the morning. And thank *you* again, Charmaine."

The door closed behind her and Annie and Charmaine released their breath, then grinned. "She'll be running for office one of these days, wait and see," Annie said.

Charmaine agreed. Some women seemed to have it all.

Chapter Three

Mort Renlow readied a team of horses and a rig for his daughter to take into town the following evening. It was still light, but the western sky was streaked with purple clouds. "You can leave them hitched in the schoolyard for a couple of hours," he told Charmaine. "If you'll be any longer than that, you take them to the stable."

"I shouldn't be longer than that," she assured him. She'd been taking herself places since she was thirteen. Her father had taught her how to handle a team as well as a rifle, which was now lying loaded under the seat.

She stretched on tiptoe to kiss his cheek, and he stepped back as she made her own way up.

"You and Mother enjoy your evening alone."

"We'll just be waiting for you, daughter," he laughed.

Charmaine drove the team toward town, and her mind wandered to all the times Annie had stayed with them. Smiling, she reminisced about the adventures they'd had. That part of her life had been missing ever since Annie had married Luke. They'd grown up. Annie had her own family now.

And Charmaine was still living with her parents. Her smile faded.

Several rigs and horses were already parked in the school-yard when she arrived. She set the brake, tethered the animals and brushed dust from her gloves and hem before entering the schoolhouse.

Nothing ever changed. The inside of the schoolhouse looked as it had when she'd attended. She knew everyone, and spent a few minutes greeting the parents. Several children occupied benches at the back of the room. She took a seat at one of the smaller desks in the front, because she could fit and many of the adults couldn't.

Walter Hutton was the teacher, and he and his wife were seated on a pair of chairs.

"Good evening, Miss Renlow," Walter said. "Pleasure to see you. Are you representing your cousin?"

"I'm here with William Sweetwater," she explained.

"We're pleased to have you join us."

She was sure they were pleased to have Will in their school. Burdy and her uncle Eldon owned the bank and probably made hefty contributions to school fund-raisers, even if Will's parents didn't always show up in person.

Additional parents arrived and the meeting was soon under-way. One by one tasks were assigned, and though Charmaine offered to assist with the booths, her request was overlooked. The subject of the float was presented last.

Mary Chancelor spoke up then. "Charmaine has worked on floats for school and church in the past. She'd do a good job or-ganizing that."

Several others seconded and Charmaine agreed. "As long as I have a committee to help and a good dry place to build the float."

Several parents offered to help. Charmaine jotted down their names. "We still need a barn or a stable," she said. "I'd offer ours, but it's quite a ride from town. We need a convenient place so that the float remains nice on parade day."

"I have space in my barn."

All eyes turned to see who'd spoken. Jack Easton sat on a bench along one wall, his hat hooked on his knee. "My place is only a couple of miles to the east."

"That will be perfect," Walter Hutton said. "Put Mr. Easton's barn down. Charmaine, you speak with your committee afterward and schedule work times."

She nodded.

The committees divided off to discuss their plans, and Charmaine found herself leading a group of nine. "I've made enough crepe paper flowers to fill an ocean," she told the assembly. "The Ladies Aid always does crepe paper roses, so let's think of something else. Something more suited to school."

"What do you suggest?" Darlene Redman asked.

Glenda Harper tossed out a few ideas, and her husband, Tom, countered with how impractical they were. "We can't make a wagon look like a book. Or a lunch pail."

"Maybe we could make it look like a schoolhouse," Charmaine suggested.

"How?" Darlene asked.

"Build a miniature schoolhouse right on the back of a wagon," Jack said, speaking up for the first time. "Paint on windows, but cut a real door."

"And have a bell to ring!" Glenda added.

"Construction would be up to you men," Charmaine told them.

The fathers voiced their amiability with the plan.

Glenda grinned and nudged her husband. "Let's keep our float a secret."

The committee members looked at each other and concurred.

Charmaine checked her list. "We need a wagon. My father has one to spare."

"We're all set then. When do you wanna start?" Tim asked.

"This Saturday?" Charmaine suggested.

Everyone agreed and a time was set.

A boy with black hair joined Jack at the back of the room, and Jack touched his shoulder, indicating the child should wait until Charmaine had gone through the doorway ahead of them.

It was full dark outside, and she tugged on her gloves and pulled her shawl around her shoulders.

"Do you have a ride home, Miss Renlow?"

She gestured to where all the horses and buggies were nestled in the darkness. "Over there. Is this your son?"

"This is Daniel. Daniel, say how do to Miss Renlow. She's the one who sent the cookies home for you."

"How do, ma'am. The cookies were almost too pretty to eat, but I ate 'em all."

"Pleased to meet you, Daniel. Are you enjoying school?"

"Yes'm."

"My nephew Will attends class with you."

"Will's my friend."

She smiled, wishing she could see him in a better light. He stood close to his father. "I'm pleased to know that. Do you think I can be your friend, too?"

"You're pretty big."

She couldn't resist a laugh. "Big people make good friends."

In the darkness, the boy looked to his father. "I'll have to ask my dad."

"Of course," she agreed. "Well, good night. I'll see you Saturday."

"Are you alone?" Jack asked as she turned.

"Pardon?"

"Is someone seeing you home?"

"I got myself here. I'll get myself home."

"We could ride alongside until you're close to your place. My mount is right over here."

"Thank you, but that's not necessary. I'll see you in a few days."

He remained where he was, but watched as she untethered the horses and climbed up onto the seat of the wagon. It wasn't a fancy enclosed rig like her aunt and uncle and cousins drove, but that had never bothered her.

What bothered her was that she *was* alone. And that this man was feeling protective of her. The attention was flattering, she couldn't deny that. No one besides her father had ever expressed concern over the fact that she elected to take a team to town on her own. But he had taught her to handle the horses and protect herself and that was that.

After she'd been on the road a few minutes, the sound of hoof-beats reached her. Knowing instinctively who it was, she looked over her shoulder to see the horse and rider approaching in the darkness. Her heart leaped in anticipation.

The horse drew alongside her wagon, and in the moonlight Jack was clearly visible, his son seated behind him. He said nothing.

"I told you I didn't need an escort," she said as the horses lumbered onward.

"Daniel wanted to take a ride."

"This is out of your way, isn't it?" She knew it was. He lived southeast of Copper Creek and she to the west.

"Not much."

Charmaine couldn't remember ever being at a loss for something to say before, but this situation felt awkward, and so far Jack Easton wasn't much of a conversationalist.

They rode along in silence, an occasional raccoon scurrying out of their path. The creak of Jack's saddle and the plodding of his horse's hooves accompanied the sound of the wagon wheels. When they reached the fields that her father had tilled and planted, she said, "This is our farm."

He rode another half mile, then reined in his horse. Over her shoulder, she observed them in the moonlight, his wide shoulders and the tilt of his hat, Daniel's head peeking around his arm.

She gave a little wave, then faced forward. When she looked

back minutes later, she could no longer see them, and the sense of loss was unexplainable.

Jack was an unusual man, indeed. A lot of men seemed uncomfortable around womenfolk, but with him it was something more. Almost as though he didn't trust her…didn't like her…. Now that thought was silly.

On Saturday, Charmaine helped her father hook up the team. She drove the spare wagon past Copper Creek to a fork in the road, and followed directions to the Easton house and stables.

A few of the parents were already there, and Glenda Harper greeted her. "Hello, Charmaine! I brought sandwiches and drinks for a lunch."

Glenda was Mildred Sweetwater's housekeeper, and Charmaine had eaten her delicious cooking more times than she could count while visiting Annie over the years. "How thoughtful of you. I should've thought of it."

"I'm guessing this will be our longest work day, what with the men having to figure out how the structure will be built and getting the frame together."

"I'm sure you're right."

Glenda's husband, Tom, joined them. "This is the wagon?"

"It is. Do you want me to take it into the barn?"

"Why don't we leave it out here for now," he replied. "We can move it inside when we're finished for the day."

She tied the reins and climbed down.

Jack had been standing to the side, but he walked forward now to unhitch the team. He spoke to the animals in a soothing low-pitched tone. The horse nearest him, nudged his chest in a friendly manner, and Jack scratched its forehead. He led both horses to one of his corrals and released them.

Isaac Redman, Darlene's husband, had brought boards and scrap lumber in the bed of his wagon, so the men inventoried their supplies and got to work. They built the frame on the ground, then lifted it to the flatbed wagon before adding the sides, which would make it heavy.

Harry Stevenson had brought a partial bucket of red paint, and he assigned the women the chore of stirring it and readying the brushes.

Daniel Easton hung back from the Parker boys who were playing marbles on a hard patch of dirt. He was a slender child, with midnight-black hair and a wary look in his deep brown eyes. His eyes were like his father's, Charmaine noted, shuttered eyes that made a person wonder what he was thinking.

She walked over to stand beside him. "Do you like to play marbles?"

He didn't look at her, but shook his head.

"How about jacks?"

He shook his head again.

"What *do* you like to do?"

He glanced to where his father was working, then up at her. "I have a bow. I like to shoot arrows."

Charmaine was fascinated. "I've never seen a real bow and arrow. Only pictures."

He looked toward his father again, indecision on his young face. "I can show you."

She checked and saw that Jack and the others were occupied. She could spare a moment or two. "Okay," she said with a nod.

He grinned and gestured for her to follow.

Delighted, she ran after him. She'd made a new friend.

Chapter Four

Charmaine had worn her oldest dress and shoes, so she didn't mind picking her way across the dusty ground to the rear of the barn. Nearly a dozen animals had been created out of burlap bags and set in various hiding positions beside clumps of buffalo grass and patches of weeds. Charmaine recognized a coyote, a raccoon, birds, rabbits, a squirrel and a fox. Each of them bore holes exposing their straw stuffing.

"Did your father make these for you?"

Daniel said he had. He walked to a chest set against the rear of the barn and took out a bow and a quiver of arrows.

She admired the quiver made of soft leather with intricate beadwork. "That's beautiful."

He slung it over his shoulder and proceeded to take a stand in the grass. Reaching back for an arrow, he placed the nock into the waxed string, drew the bow tight and squinted along its length.

With surprising agility, he released it, and the arrow soundly pierced the chest of the coyote target.

"That was amazing!" Charmaine had never seen anyone shoot an arrow before. "Can you do that every time?"

"It's easy to hit a standing target," he told her. "Harder to hit the real thing. Coyotes don't stand there, still-like."

"Have you ever actually hit a real animal?"

"Yes'm. Me 'n' my pa hunt turkeys and rabbits. Arrows don't scare off the rest of the game like a rifle."

"I wouldn't have thought of that. But then I've never hunted. Do you cook the game you catch?"

"Had possum stew last night," he replied. "I caught the possum."

"I like turkey, but I don't believe I've ever eaten a possum. Is it good?"

"One of our favorites." He withdrew another arrow and swiftly anchored it in the shoulder of the burlap rabbit. "That wasn't a good shot. Just wounded the critter and that's not kind."

"I see. Has it taken you an awfully long time to learn to do that?"

"Yes'm. Got a little bow when I was four."

"Do you think you could show me how?"

Daniel glanced around, as though wondering if his father would object, then locked his dark gaze on her. "Why do you want me to show you?"

"I don't know. I'd just like to see if I can do it."

"You might be too big for this bow, but I'll show you." He instructed her how to stand, showed her how to hold the bow with her hand on the section of polished horn, then how to lock the arrow into place and stretch the bow taut. He stepped back and encouraged her to do it just the way he had.

She did her best imitation, but the string slapped her arm and the arrow fell at her feet.

Daniel laughed, and though she was sorry she hadn't been more accomplished, she was pleased her clumsiness had amused him.

She picked it up and tried again. After five minutes, she actually got it to land a few feet in front of the stuffed squirrel.

"I didn't know where you'd gone off to."

Charmaine turned toward Jack's voice. He strode from the corner of the barn to join them in the practice area.

"Daniel was showing me his skills with his bow and arrow.

I'm afraid I would need a lot more practice to actually hit one of the targets." She handed Daniel his bow and curled and uncurled her sore fingers, then rubbed the inside of her stinging forearm. "His bow is strong and flexible. It's an ingenious creation."

"The deer tendons make it like that," Jack replied.

"Oh." She didn't want to think about where deer tendons came from or how they'd acquired them. "His quiver is beautiful. Wherever did you buy it?"

"Daniel's aunt made it for him."

"It's amazing work. She's talented." She thought a minute. "You made the bow yourself?"

"I did."

He *had* done things with deer tendons. Unconsciously, she brushed her palms together. "Thank you for the lesson, Daniel."

"Yes'm."

"I didn't mean to shun the work effort, Mr. Easton. I'll paint now. How is our little school coming along?"

"We'll put a roof on sometime during the week."

She headed around the side of the barn and he followed. "Do we have roofing?"

"I have a stack of wooden shingles in my lean-to."

"How generous of you."

"They're pieces mostly, nothing fancy, but we can make do."

Glenda had the paint stirred and Charmaine hurried to climb onto the wagon and help her brush the first coat onto their now-sided structure. Someone had drawn on the windows with charcoal, and those would be painted black with white trim for the sills and sashes.

"Isn't this just the cutest thing you ever saw?" Charmaine asked, as they stroked red paint on the wood.

"We're sure to win," Glenda replied. "No one has ever done anything this clever."

The men took a break in the shade of two interlocking oak trees, where Jack had fashioned benches and a table from thickly sliced tree trunks. Tim sprawled on the ground, his face covered by his hat.

From beside her, Glenda commented, "Jack has a nice place here, doesn't he?"

Charmaine glanced around. The house was small and had seen a good many seasons, but the exterior was well cared for with fresh whitewash and clean windows. The barns and stables were more numerous than her father's, but equally as neat and sturdy-looking.

"His workshop is in that barn down there," Glenda said. "The boys and I rode out with Tom once when he was buying harnesses."

"There's no garden," Charmaine noted.

"Probably wasn't here in time for spring planting, and it looks like he has a lot to do, what with the house and the shop and no mother for Daniel."

"He's a charming boy."

"Talk is he's part Indian," Glenda told her.

Charmaine glanced at Daniel, once again standing off to the side watching the other children. Of course. Straight black hair and an aunt who did bead work. Jack's wife had been an Indian. How much of his standoffishness was self-imposed and how much was a result of being ostracized? "He doesn't join the others. Do the other children treat him any differently?"

"Not that I've seen. Children learn from their parents, though. I've asked the boys to include him. He seems untrusting, doesn't he?"

Like his father.

Charmaine's gaze drifted back to the men. Jack was sitting with his back against the trunk of a tree, his hat on the grass beside him, looking directly at her. His intense study made her skin warm.

"Handsome father and son," Glenda said.

Charmaine turned to find the woman watching her. She busied herself with her paintbrush. "I suppose so."

"Wayne might be jealous if he saw the way that man was looking at you just now."

Charmaine's cheeks warmed at Glenda's teasing. "He was watching us paint."

"I don't think so. His attention was on you. Has been most of the morning—except when you disappeared, and then he kept glancing around for you."

"Nonsense, I'm sure he was looking for his son."

"Uh-huh."

Charmaine reached over and dabbed a red dot on the back of Glenda's hand, then went back to her work.

A moment later, the other woman's brush entered her vision and the bristles touched the tip of her nose.

Surprised, Charmaine jerked her gaze up.

Glenda chortled with laughter, and Charmaine found a rag to wipe away the paint.

"You'd skin our boys for doing that," Tom said, jumping up on the wagon, a grin on his lips.

"That's why they're not helping with this part," his wife replied.

He leaned over her, and their noses almost touched. Charmaine looked away in embarrassment. Unfortunately, she looked right at Jack, who was once again watching her, and she felt warmth climb her neck and cheeks.

She resumed her task, and the men went back to work, eventually gathering the scraps and cleaning their work area. Their little schoolhouse still needed the windows painted, a roof and a bell. They'd discussed setting a few small bushes and flowers in buckets around the outside to give the completed project an outdoor look.

One by one the committee members headed for home and chores, until only Charmaine was left.

"We'll see you home," Jack told her.

She'd neglected to ask one of the other families to tie her horses to their wagon and give her a ride, like she'd intended.

Jack offered her a rag dampened with turpentine to remove paint from her hands. She worked at it the best she could while he brought his wagon around and tied her father's horses to the rear.

She handed him the rag.

"You still have some on your nose."

She chuckled. "That's Glenda's doing."

"Stand still."

She obeyed while he held her chin with one hand and dabbed at her nose with the other. The smell made her light-headed, and she blinked up into his mysterious dark eyes.

"There," he said, releasing her. "There's soap and clean water on the back porch."

Her chin tingled from his touch. She rolled back her sleeves as she approached the house. The back door stood open, with no screen door, and she glanced into the simply furnished kitchen. Feeling nosy, she looked away and washed her hands and face, then made her way out to the yard while Jack washed.

Daniel joined them, taking a seat in the back of the wagon.

"You may sit with us, if you like," she offered, climbing unassisted up to the bench seat and thinking to place the boy between herself and his father, but Daniel silently declined.

Jack climbed up and took the reins.

"I'm pleased with our progress today," she said. "Glenda and I think we're sure to win the contest. Our float is entirely original."

He glanced at her, then watched the road.

"What was your wife's name?" She wanted to bite her tongue for asking that, but she'd been curious ever since Glenda had mentioned her.

He didn't look at her for long uncomfortable moments, and she was just forming an apology when he replied, "Silver Moon."

"That's beautiful. She was an Indian?"

He looked straight at her then as though gauging the sincerity of her question and whether or not he wanted to answer. "My son's mother was half Cheyenne."

"I've never lost anyone except my grandparents. My grandma

lived with us when I was little." Charmaine gazed out across the expanse of a meadow dressed in spring wildflowers. "Annie lost a baby once. That was a sad time. She blamed herself and didn't think she was a good wife to Luke. But that man adores her, plain and simple. They met when we were just girls, Annie and I. Her parents and brother didn't approve of him, though, and years later, they had to see each other secretly. It was all incredibly romantic."

She was blathering now. The last time they'd been together she'd been at a loss for words and this time she was blurting anything that entered her head.

She wished she didn't feel obligated to him for a ride home. "Why don't the two of you stay for dinner?"

This time he didn't look at her. Daniel scrambled to stand behind them, holding the back of the seat for balance and seemed to be waiting for his father's reply.

"Please," Charmaine coaxed. "My mother would love the company, and we always have plenty. My father enjoys having another man at the table."

"I have chores to get back to."

She glanced over her shoulder at Daniel's hopeful expression. "I should have helped you," she told Jack. "I don't want this project to set you back. But you have to eat. This way you won't have to take time to cook."

They were driving alongside her father's fields, where corn and hay sprouted from acre-long rows in healthy green shoots.

He changed the subject. "Does your father have hired hands?"

"The farmers take turns helping each other with planting and harvesting, and he hires on older boys during busy seasons. Perhaps one day Daniel will hire himself out."

"We don't know much about farming."

"I noticed you didn't have a garden."

"Didn't have time."

"You could still have a late crop."

They reached the Renlow spread, and Jack pulled his wagon up before the barns.

Mort had heard their approach and sauntered out to greet them.

Jack jumped down and untied the pair of horses from the rear of his wagon.

"Daddy, this is Jack Easton."

Jack took a few steps forward to shake the older man's hand.

"I invited Jack and Daniel to stay for supper," she added.

Jack looked up at her, then glanced at Daniel, who scrambled down to the ground.

"The missus put on a roast earlier," Mort said, taking one horse's lead while Jack held the other. "I've been smelling it for hours."

Daniel sidled up beside his father and took his hand. Charmaine noticed the beseeching look he raised, and the way Jack's expression softened.

"Thank you kindly. We'd enjoy sharing your supper."

Charmaine hopped down and headed for the house. She had to change out of these old clothes and wash up. "I'm going to go help put the meal on."

"Mama?" she called, sailing in the door while removing her hat. "We're having company for supper. I'll be back down to help in a minute!"

"The Easton fellow?" her mother called on her return from the pantry.

"That's him. They're putting the horses away." Charmaine dipped warm water from the back well of the stove and carried the pitcher up the stairs to her room. She couldn't explain the tremor of excitement in her voice—nor did she want to.

Chapter Five

The walls were covered with rosebud paper, her furniture painted white and lacy curtains hung at two wide windows. It was a frilly feminine space. Charmaine and her mother had sewn the curtains, pillows and coverlet when she'd been quite young, then she'd inherited part of the furnishings from Annie when Annie'd moved away from her parents' home.

After pouring water into the basin on her washstand, she shrugged out of her dress and chemise and washed quickly.

Her face needed a good scrubbing and her nose was still red, whether from paint or irritation she didn't know. Opening a jar, she smoothed glycerin on her face and hands. She brushed out her hair, which had wilted, and settled for an upsweep with unsatisfactory curls before pulling on a fresh gown and powdering her nose.

Ten minutes later, she was wearing an apron over her dress and peeling extra potatoes.

Her mother inquired about the float, and she chattered until the hinges on the mudroom door squeaked.

The sound of the men washing and talking in low voices created a stab of nerves in her belly, though she couldn't imagine what she had to be nervous about. They'd had company to supper a hundred times.

"Mama, this is Mr. Easton and his son, Daniel. Mr. Easton, my mother."

He'd already removed his hat, so Jack nodded politely. "Ma'am."

Daniel copied his father.

"Welcome, gentlemen," Vera said with a broad smile. "Please take seats. We're not fancy on Saturday evenings. We eat in the kitchen."

"Supper smells first rate, ma'am."

"Just simple fare, roast and potatoes," she replied.

Once everyone was seated, the family lowered their heads and Mort, seated at the head of the table, asked a blessing for the food. Charmaine glanced across to see Daniel's inquisitive expression as he sat with his hands folded, his elbows planted on the table in imitation of Charmaine's father.

She couldn't resist a smile, and he ducked his chin in embarrassment.

The serving bowls and platters were passed, and Jack placed food from each on his plate, then a smaller portion on Daniel's before passing to Vera.

Seated directly across from Jack, Charmaine sensed his discomfort. Perhaps some relaxed conversation would put him at ease. "Mr. Easton has put a lot of work into his place already," she told her father. "His barn is as neat as a pin."

"Saddles and harnesses, I hear." Mort poured steaming gravy on his pile of mashed potatoes.

"I got my own horse," Daniel said. "My pa bought 'im for me."

"You do? That's a big responsibility, isn't it?"

"Yes, sir. I gots'ta give 'im feed and water every day." Daniel watched with wide eyes as Jack topped their potatoes, then the lad took up his fork and tasted. His look of delight had Charmaine and her mother exchanging a grin.

The men conversed on bits and bridles, and Vera questioned Daniel regarding his studies.

Charmaine passed a platter of sliced bread and buttered a piece for herself.

Both father and son cleaned their plates.

"Would you like another helping of potatoes and gravy, Daniel?" Vera asked.

He glanced at his father warily.

Jack nodded permission.

"Yes'm. And a slice of bread, please."

"Our bread doesn't hold a candle to this, Mrs. Renlow," Jack admitted.

"Charmaine makes the bread on Fridays," Vera told him proudly, buttering a slice for the young man beside her.

Jack's brows rose appreciatively, his dark gaze sliding to hers, and once again Charmaine experienced that surprising jangle of nerves in her belly.

They finished their meal, and Charmaine picked up the dishes, as she normally did, while her mother sliced a peach pie.

Charmaine turned from the cupboard to inquire, "Coffee, Mr. Easton?"

"Yes, miss."

She poured a cup for both of the men.

Jack noticed the change in Charmaine when she was around her parents. She appeared more relaxed, her posture and conversation at ease. This didn't seem like the same fancified woman who'd climbed down from that buggy at Noah Cutter's place, every perfect curl in place, her small hands encased in spotless white gloves.

When Charmaine set a cup of coffee before her father, she leaned over him, a hand on his shoulder. Without so much as a thought it seemed, the man raised his own hand to cover hers where it rested. The period of time their fingers touched was only a matter of seconds, the blink of an eye, but the wealth of uncomplicated love expressed by that simple gesture touched Jack in a place he figured had grown too callused to notice. With a swish of skirts, she moved away to pick up another mug.

When Charmaine walked toward him, his heart chugged to a rhythm he feared she would hear. Though he knew she wasn't going to touch him, the *possibility* turned his insides to jelly.

She leaned around his shoulder to place the cup at his right hand, and he caught a whiff of lilac water and soap, a smell so fresh, so feminine, and so out of his realm, he blinked in surprise.

Jack's head roared at her nearness. He couldn't look up. He stared at the mug—practical ironstone—heard her move away. The aroma of the brew replaced her scent, and he forced his hand to reach for it.

Raising his gaze, he met Mort Renlow's friendly blue eyes. Had her father noticed Jack's reaction? He didn't seem threatened or concerned. He was a man content in his home. Confident in the love of his wife and daughter. Secure in his ability to provide for them and protect them.

At that moment Jack envied the older man with all his being. Envied all of them their comfortable home and their uncomplicated family. This wasn't what he'd expected to see.

Charmaine had poured Daniel another glass of milk to go with his slice of pie, and the boy polished them off with obvious appreciation.

She seated herself across from Jack once again, this time with a dainty rose-patterned cup and saucer in front of her. To her tea, she added a spoonful of sugar from a matching sugar bowl, and blew across the surface of the steaming liquid.

Her rosebud lips formed a pretty *O* as he watched, mesmerized. She blew again, and his heart contracted. She glanced up, and an ache like a hunger he knew was impossible after the meal he'd just tucked away gnawed in his belly.

Her cheeks grew pink beneath his stare. She set the cup back in its saucer and squared her shoulders self-consciously. Her gaze slid to her mother, occupied with trying to draw Daniel into a conversation, then back to Jack.

He sipped from his mug, and the coffee was rich and strong. "I'm partial to chicory," he said, referring to the taste.

"The missus blends it," Mort told him. "Used to do it to make the grounds stretch, but now it's the way I like it."

"Old farmers get set in their ways." Vera's comment held a smile.

"As do old farmers' wives," he replied with a teasing twinkle in his eye.

Charmaine inclined her head toward Jack. "You haven't touched your pie."

He picked up his fork. "I'm savoring this meal. It's not often Daniel and I eat this well. You and your mama are fine cooks."

"Thank you, Mr. Easton." Vera folded her napkin and laid it beside her dessert plate. "We don't lead as fancy a life as some of our neighbors, but we have all we need and more."

"Vera's brother is the town banker." Mort washed down his last bite of pie with his coffee. "She could've had a fancy house and all the trimmin's like the Sweetwaters, but she chose to marry me and be a farmer's wife."

"My mama told me love doesn't shop according to price tags." The tone of her reply was more reproachful than teasing, leading Jack to think her husband's mention of her choice hadn't been the first time.

Mort chuckled, and Charmaine rolled her eyes at her parents' conversation as though she was used to it.

"Do you enjoy a good cigar, Jack?" Mort asked.

"On occasion, sir."

"Walk outdoors with me. I'll show you the old saddle and gear that belonged to my granddad."

Daniel's face lit up. "Kin I see it, too?"

"Sure, son. Come with us."

"Mind your manners and ask to be excused," Jack admonished his son. "And thank the ladies for the meal."

Daniel sank back onto his seat with a sheepish wrinkle across his forehead. "Can I be a-scused?"

"Yes," his father replied.

He glanced from Charmaine to her mother. "Thank you for supper."

"You're quite welcome, Daniel," Vera said. "We're pleased to have you as our guest."

Charmaine watched the three males exit through the mudroom, where she knew they'd stashed their hats.

"I'll finish the dishes, dear," her mother said. "You run along and get yourself ready."

Charmaine averted her attention. "Ready for what?"

"I thought there was an engagement at the Social Hall this evening. Someone's birthday?"

"Doneta's!" She had completely forgotten the birthday party. She glanced down at her dress. She had dressed a little fancier than usual for supper, but her hair was a fright. She'd been perfectly content to stay right here, but she'd already made the plans, so it would be rude not to go now. "Thank goodness I made her gift weeks ago." She raised a hand to her hair. "I have to curl my hair. Wayne will be coming for me."

Upstairs, she removed the glass lamp and lit the lantern on her dressing table. After brushing out her hair again, she held the curling iron over the flame. Tress by tress, she curled and arranged her hair, wound a ribbon through the mass and found a pair of black slippers to replace her scuffed shoes.

At the sound of men's voices below her window, she peered out. Wayne had parked one of Luke's rented buggies near the side porch, and was standing speaking with her father and Jack.

Extinguishing the flame, she checked her appearance and dabbed lilac water at her wrists and behind her ears. She grabbed her gloves, the birthday gift and a shawl before dashing down the stairs.

Charmaine called a goodbye to her mother and calmed herself as she stepped out the front door and navigated the wraparound porch to the side where the men stood.

Three sets of eyes turned. Her father had the same strained expression he wore whenever he was forced to make polite conversation with Wayne. She sensed Wayne's hurry to go when he offered a stiff smile. Jack's dark gaze traveled over her hair and dress, touching on her shoes, her gloves, the gift in her hand, missing nothing.

"I see you met Mr. Easton," she said.

"Yes, we've met." Wayne's tone was dismissive as he moved forward to take her arm.

"Did you meet Daniel?"

Wayne didn't have a chance to reply.

"He discovered the kittens in the corner stall and hasn't budged since," her father reported.

"Oh, aren't they darling?" She turned to their guest with a smile. "Mr. Easton, did you see the fuzzy gray one with the white paws?"

The corner of his mouth inched up in a grin. "I did."

She faced Wayne. "Would you like to see the kittens and meet Daniel?"

Wayne had the same coloring as his sister Glenda, reddish blond hair, fair skin and blue eyes. He had a classically handsome face, square-jawed and freshly shaven.

His complexion reddened slightly, clueing her that he would rather have hurried on, but didn't want to appear rude to her father. He gave a stilted nod and accompanied her to the barn, where she introduced him to Daniel and the litter of kittens.

"We'd better be going now," he told her after only a minute or two.

Jack and her father had moved to occupy chairs on the porch and were engaged in conversation. Her father raised a hand in farewell. She would have liked to join them and hear what they were talking about. She waved back, regret banking her enthusiasm. Charmaine felt Jack's notice as Wayne assisted her up on the buggy and she adjusted her skirts.

Wayne joined her on the seat and urged the horse into motion.

Jack's meal was weighing heavily in his belly as he watched Charmaine's beau help her up to the seat of the buggy. Earlier, she'd climbed up and down on her own with neither his nor her father's help, but he supposed etiquette dictated she allow her caller to lend a hand. Jack had kept his distance where Brookover had moved right into the task.

Gone was the informal young woman who had emerged for to-night's meal. Charmaine had changed back into the person he'd seen that first day—a gussied up female who put on airs. Seeing that proved his belief that people were two-faced. Insincere.

The horse pulled the buggy away from the house and yard.

Jack liked her father. Mort Renlow was a straightforward fellow. His wife seemed genuine. But their daughter was spoiled and pampered. She wore elaborate clothing and jewelry, drove her father's best rig and had time to bake fancy cookies, attend social events and go to tea parties.

She volunteered at the school, but that was probably just an amusement. Like a schoolgirl, she chattered about silly things, spoke of romance.

It didn't matter to Jack where she went or who she went with. Wayne Brookover worked for the druggist. Jack had met him previously when he'd stopped in to buy salve for an injured horse. Brookover probably suited Charmaine, he thought. A citified gentleman for a fancified woman.

As the buggy disappeared, Mrs. Renlow joined them, having removed her apron and fixed herself a cup of tea. She took the rocker and gazed out across the side yard. The sky was streaked with orange and lavender as the sun headed for the horizon.

"Charmaine tells me you're a widower," she said.

"My wife died when Daniel was a baby."

"Such a shame. He's a delightful child. She would have been proud of him."

"Thank you, ma'am."

Mort drew a hand down his face to his chin. "You teachin' him your trade?"

"I am. He's taking to it like a duck to water."

"He's a smart boy. One day he'll take over your shop and make you proud for sure."

Charmaine was an only child, Jack realized. She would probably inherit this farm. Was her father wondering what would become of it if she married the druggist?

Jack stood. "Reckon I'll round up my boy and head home to do chores. Thank you kindly for your hospitality."

"It was our pleasure," Vera said. "Thank you for seeing Charmaine home. Come back again soon."

Nearly half an hour later, Daniel slept on his shoulder as they passed the northwest corner of town. Lights blazed and piano music tinkled from the Social Hall. He spotted the rig Brookover had brought for Charmaine parked with others in the side lot.

He was night to day from those people. The place he had now was the closest he'd ever lived to town his entire life. He'd been raised in the mountains, his mother teaching him to read and figure. Occasionally, he'd attended school at one fort or another. His grandfather had caught and broken wild horses, and his father had trained horses for the Army. Jack had grown up around simple hardworking men who had no time for nonsense.

The women of his family had been wives, mothers and ranch helpmates. From a young age he'd learned to be practical, realistic and to live in the present. He'd moved Daniel here so his son would have a chance at a good education. Jack knew that alone he couldn't teach the boy all he needed to learn to succeed.

But Jack didn't fit in. He was going through the motions with this school project, and they would attend the parade, but that didn't make him or his son one of them. It had all seemed like a good plan until this unsettled feeling had lodged inside him and wouldn't be budged.

Charmaine was the reason, and he wasn't too blind to recognize it. He was wise, though, so after tucking Daniel into his bed and doing outside chores, he washed a few shirts and hung them on a line behind the stove. And all the while he gave himself a talking to. He had more sense than to let himself get addled over a woman—especially an unsuitable one like Charmaine. He didn't want impractical emotional clutter controlling him.

Looking at her might be disturbing, and smelling her might conjure up dozens of sensual images, but he wasn't going to let those useless things addlepate his brain. Not now, not ever.

Chapter Six

〜〜〜〜〜

All of her friends were there that evening, and Charmaine enjoyed their company as usual. And as usual, she was the only unmarried young woman in their gathering. Most of the guests had gone to school together; those who hadn't had married her schoolmates. Glancing around the Social Hall, she noted she'd been to every last person's wedding, in fact had helped plan most of them....

The fact that she was yet unmarried had begun to weigh upon her shoulders like one of her dowry chests. Watching Luke and Annie dance, her cousin's words echoed in her head.

Are you sure you want a man who has dragged his feet for so long?

Charmaine glanced over at Wayne. He stood talking to Benjamin Barnett, who worked on Noah Cutter's ranch.

Do you truly love him?

Of course she did. Why, she'd wanted to marry him for the past four years, hadn't she? If he'd asked on any given occasion, she'd have accepted and they would have been Mister and Missus by now. Perhaps they would even have had a child or two.

Her gaze went back to Annie, whom she now knew was expecting another child, and she observed the way she and Luke shared smiles and touches.

Where had she gone wrong? she wondered for the hundredth time. Why didn't Wayne long to hold her in his arms like that—why didn't he want to make her his wife and give her children?

Annie was special. She'd deserved Luke from the beginning.

Noah and Kate drifted past, diverting her attention. Originally, Kate had married Noah's philandering brother, Levi, and when he'd been killed, Noah had gone to find his brother's wife and bring her home. Noah hadn't deliberately shown his face in Copper Creek for most of twenty years until he'd fallen in love with Kate and she'd drawn him out of his shell.

Kate was special, too.

Charmaine had done her best to be charming. She'd shown Wayne she could cook and sew. She looked after her nieces and nephews, proving her ability with children. She went to great pains with her skin and hair and clothing….

Maybe she wasn't special, maybe she was just a farm girl who had improved herself, but she was smart and she deserved the same happiness everyone else here seemed to have.

Her cousin caught her eye, and Charmaine hoped her wistful thoughts hadn't been written on her face. A moment later, Luke escorted Annie to the side of the room and fetched her a cup of punch. Annie took a seat on one of the benches that lined the walls.

Charmaine distractedly watched the other dancers.

"Will you dance with me, Charmaine?"

Luke was standing before her, his hand extended, a smile in his blue eyes.

She glanced at Annie before taking his hand and letting Luke whisk her on to the dance floor. "Annie put you up to this."

"Her hip is tired."

"Don't forget, I've known her since I was born. She can pull that one off on someone else, but not on me."

He laughed and led her through the steps.

"What's wrong with me, Luke?"

He glanced from her hair to her dress. "Nothing I can see, why? Aren't you feeling well?"

"I'm fine. I mean why am I the only unmarried woman over the age of seventeen in this town? Is there something dreadfully wrong with me that I don't recognize in my mirror?"

"Of course not. You're beautiful."

"Do people tell things about me behind my back? Am I a pariah?"

"You've always had a flair for the dramatic," he replied, not unkindly. "But you haven't any flaws I've heard people whispering about."

"Why do you think Wayne holds back? Tell me truly."

Luke glanced over her shoulder, and she guessed he was looking for the man she was questioning him about.

His gaze came back to hers directly, honestly. "If I hadn't met Annie, I might have asked you to marry me myself," he said. "I've loved her since we were young, so there was never anyone else for me. But if I'd never known her…who knows?"

She studied his sincerity a moment, then glanced away.

"I don't have answers for you," he continued. "Personally, I think the man is daft to let you get away."

"What do you mean let me get away? It's not as though there are others asking for my hand—or showing interest for that matter."

"That's a shame. Sometimes a little competition is healthy. Makes a man work a little harder."

She tapped his arm in amused rebuke.

"I'm just stating a fact," he assured her. "Men are competitive."

"You're suggesting jealousy is a motivating factor?"

"I'm not suggesting anything. I was just thinking out loud."

The musicians wound the song to an end, and Charmaine took a step back. "Return to your wife, Luke Carpenter."

"Thanks for the dance."

He kissed her cheek and left her on the edge of the dance floor where Wayne was now waiting.

"That was forward behavior for a married man," he said, his mouth held in a disapproving line.

"What?"

"Kissing you like that."

"He kissed my cheek. He's my cousin's husband, for goodness sake. A friend. A good friend, you know that."

He handed her a cup of punch. Questions wound through her mind. *Was Wayne jealous of Luke? Was Luke right about competition inspiring men? Had Luke done that on purpose?*

She glanced to where Luke sat beside his wife, their entwined hands resting on his knee. Annie was saying something, completely absorbing his attention.

"You know," Charmaine said in a conversational tone. "There was a time when Luke escorted both me and Annie to events. Took us for ice cream at Miss Marples' and for rides to see the house he was building."

Wayne studied the man across the room. "Is that so?"

A twinge of guilt ate at Charmaine. She was entirely too pleased with the fact that Wayne was behaving in this petulant manner. She couldn't contain a smile.

Entirely too pleased.

"Tell Darlene I hope she's feeling better soon," Charmaine told Isaac Redman two nights later.

He closed his front door and Charmaine gathered the hem of her work skirt and walked back to her team and wagon. She and Darlene were supposed to paint the windows of the little schoolhouse this evening. Alone it would take twice as long. "Drat."

She glanced at the house to make sure Darlene's husband hadn't heard. Apparently, her poor friend had been feeling under the weather for two days.

Well, Charmaine had been to the Easton place once, she

could find it again. She glanced at the basket she'd secured beneath the seat.

She guided the team out of town and enjoyed the different perspective of the countryside. Thoughts of Wayne's reaction to Luke asking her to dance and giving her a sisterly kiss had plagued her since Doneta's birthday night before last. She was convinced that Luke had deliberately been affectionate to provoke a reaction from Wayne.

Pulling into the dooryard before Jack's one-story house, she led the horses toward the barn. Jack strode out of the interior. Once again that unexplainable shiver of anticipation shot up her spine.

What had come over her?

Did she really want to know?

Chapter Seven

Charmaine pulled the team to a halt and got down.

"Is Mrs. Redman driving out herself?" Jack asked.

"I'm afraid Darlene's feeling poorly."

Without showing a reaction, he quickly moved to tether the horses.

Charmaine climbed to the ground. "Where's Daniel?"

"He's around here somewhere." He turned to survey the grounds, and she followed his gaze. Daniel stood watching from the corner of the house.

Smiling, she beckoned him with a wave. "Come see what I've brought for you."

The boy shot forward, his dark hair whipping away from his face, then scudded to a halt in the dirt.

Reaching back for the basket, she pulled it toward her and lifted it out of the wagon.

"Is it bread?" Daniel asked, his voice excited.

"No, it's not bread." She glanced at him. "I'll bring you bread next time." Once the basket was on the ground, she gestured for him to check inside.

The boy looked to his father first.

Jack shrugged. "Go ahead."

Daniel opened the wooden lid, and she waited for his reaction.

His eyes lit up, and a smile creased his face. The small gray kitten poked its head up over the edge and meowed. Daniel knelt to scoop the noisy animal into his arms. "You brought me a kitten!"

"I hope he's the one you liked best. If not, you can trade him for a different one."

"I like this one! What's his name?"

"He doesn't have one yet. He's yours now, so that's your job."

"Really?" He petted the feline's head. "I'll think of a special name."

"Don't forget your manners, Daniel," his father said.

"Thank you, miss."

"You're welcome." She placed the basket in the back of the wagon and turned to Jack. "I'll paint the windows on our building now."

"I'll help."

She started for the barn. "That's not necessary. The use of your barn doesn't require you to do all the work or sacrifice your own duties."

"I was plannin' to help anyway. I have the black paint stirred."

"Oh." She always managed to say the most idiotic things around him. "I mean—thank you."

Jack had maneuvered the wagon into a block of sunlight inside the open doors, and Charmaine studied their project with fresh eyes. It was still a good idea, and the most difficult part of the work was finished.

After pulling a smock on over her work clothes, she tugged on an old pair of thin white gloves.

Jack stood a few feet to her side. "How did you know I wouldn't mind?" he asked.

"Mind...what? Me coming here without Darlene?"

"No, of course not. I meant my son having a cat."

The cat? Charmaine's cheeks flushed with warmth. "I—I never gave it a thought. I just knew how much he enjoyed playing with the kittens, and I thought he'd like one of his own. I'm sorry if it's a problem. I guess I didn't think."

He picked up a few rags from a pile on a barrel. "It's not a problem."

He had stirred the paint and softened the brushes, so she busied herself dipping a brush and outlining one window. There were four altogether, two on each side, so Jack followed her example on the one beside her. He had rolled his sleeves to his elbows, and she found the play of muscle and sinew in his forearms a powerful distraction. Occasionally, her gaze wandered to his profile, and her strokes would slow until she caught herself and forced her attention back to her task.

By the time they'd moved to the other side, the square of sunlight was gone. He lit lanterns and they continued their work. A chill breeze snaked into the barn, and Charmaine shivered.

"Daniel?" Jack called.

"Back here, Pa."

"Just checkin'. I'm shutting the doors." He pulled the double doors closed and resumed painting.

Sometime later Charmaine stood back to admire their handiwork. "That's all we can do until this dries. Tomorrow we can paint on the white sashes and panes. Darlene and I, I mean."

"I'll clean up." He opened the can of turpentine.

Smiling, she held up her gloved hands, stained with only a few splotches of black.

"None on your nose this time," he said.

She grinned. "No."

"Come wash up at the house now. We can have a cup of coffee."

"Well." She tugged off her gloves and removed her apron. "All right."

"Daniel?" Jack called.

"Yes, Pa."

"We're going to the house now, you comin'?"

"Kin Bitsy come in with me?"

Charmaine met Jack's dark eyes. Was the kitten going to be a problem?

"He can come."

Daniel met them at the side door, the kitten in the crook of his arm.

"Bitsy," Jack commented. "Is that a boy's name?"

Daniel's look said an adult should be smarter than that. "No. It's a *cat's* name."

His matter-of-fact statement tickled Charmaine, and she struggled to keep a straight face.

Jack secured the door behind them. "So it is."

Daniel ran on ahead, but he paused inside and held the door open so Charmaine could enter. "Why, thank you, kind sir."

The boy giggled.

Jack hung his hat on a peg and lit the wall lanterns, as well as another lamp on a long table against the wall. While he fed kindling into the potbellied stove, she glanced around the room, finding it spare, but orderly. Once he had a flame going, he added split wood and pumped water into a pail and a kettle.

After the water had heated, he set out a bowl, a bar of soap and a towel. "You first, miss."

Giving him a sidelong glance, Charmaine rolled back her sleeves and washed her hands. She dried them and stepped back so he and Daniel could have a turn.

Meanwhile Jack had set a pot of coffee on to perk. "We have some biscuits," he told her, peeling a towel from a small bundle.

"Oh, I…" She'd been about to decline when his gaze raised to hers. Daniel stood beside the small table, three plates in his hands. They were treating her like an honored guest in their home. She certainly couldn't insult them by declining. "Why, thank you. I believe I worked up an appetite."

Daniel set out mismatched plates while Jack opened a jar of apple butter and brought tin cups holding sugar and milk.

Jack held her chair, and Daniel waited until she was seated to pull out his own and sit across from her. "You're our first visitor," the boy told her.

"I'm honored."

Having placed the biscuits in a bowl, Jack offered them to her. "Nothin' as fancy as your cookies or as tasty as the bread you bake."

She took one and set it on her plate. "I hardly expect you to find time to bake when you have a business to run and a house to see to. Animals to care for, as well."

She broke open her biscuit and spooned apple butter on both surfaces. Her first bite proved it was quite tasty.

Jack poured her a mug of coffee and pushed the milk and sugar toward her.

Charmaine politely added some of each to her cup, then after a few more bites, dared a sip. She had never acquired a taste for the bitter stuff, and Jack's brew was strong and hot.

She did her best not to shudder, thinking that not even the tonics she'd taken for childhood illnesses had been this bad.

It was only one cup. She could get through this and be on her way. Attempting to hold her breath, she gulped down the coffee to get the torture over with.

A shudder crept up her spine, and it took all her fortitude to hold it back.

Pleased with herself, she smiled.

The biscuit was actually pretty good, so she worked on that.

Jack got up and returned from the stove with the coffeepot. Before she could chew and swallow, he'd refilled her mug.

Charmaine stared at the steaming black liquid with tears of dread smarting behind her lids.

Once again he passed the tin containers, and this time she added twice as much milk and sugar, so much that her cup brimmed.

"You have quite a sweet tooth," Jack observed with a grin.

"Yes, it would seem so." She blew on the liquid, not wanting to drink it quickly and risk the same mistake.

"My friend, Henry McPhillips, said you have a beau," Daniel said.

Jack swallowed the sip of coffee he'd taken, but stared straight ahead at the wall where the stove sat, his mug held in front of his lips.

"I do have a gentleman caller," she replied, and used the excuse of picking up her own mug to avoid further answer. She sipped, grimaced inwardly. Sipped again.

"Are you gonna get married to him?"

Her coffee was cooled off enough that it shouldn't have made her skin feel so hot.

"Daniel, it's rude to ask personal questions," Jack told the boy.

"Sorry, I just wondered."

"Wondering's fine, asking isn't."

"Sorry, I did a rude," Daniel said to her, his black eyes soft with regret and confusion.

"Don't give it another thought, dear," she told him.

"Are we gonna follow Miss Renlow home again?" he asked.

She set down her cup, grateful for the change of topic. "I can make my own way."

Jack lowered his mug. He wasn't three feet away from her, and in the glow of the lamps, eyes as dark as his coffee met hers. Her attention wavered to the pronounced bow of his upper lip beneath his mustache, the fullness of his lower lip, the crisp lines of his chin and cheeks

He was studying her, as well, and she wondered what he noticed, if he found her features half as fascinating.

"I appreciate your independence," he said. "I do. But it wouldn't sit easy with me if I didn't see you home safely. Your father might think less of me if I didn't."

So his attention was for her father's sake? "My father has allowed me to travel freely since I was…well, for a long time.

"I'm not questioning his judgment. I'm just telling you why I can't let you go alone. Perhaps if it was daylight."

Obviously there was no dissuading him.

"Kin me 'n' Bitsy ride on Miss Renlow's wagon with her, Pa?"

"That would be up to Miss Renlow." He stood and rewrapped the remaining two biscuits.

She nodded at Daniel.

He grinned and went to the box he'd placed in the corner and scooped up the kitten.

"You know you have to set him loose to do his business," Jack told him.

Daniel shot out the door quick as lightning.

Charmaine picked up their cups and Daniel's milk glass. "Thank you for the refreshments."

He nodded.

"I can wash those up while the water's hot."

"No need. I'll do them in the morning with our breakfast dishes."

She walked toward the door and he followed. The night was still and quiet. Daniel's voice came from the field nearby, where he was coaxing the kitten. "Do you have much stock?"

"A milk cow, a few hens and my horses. I think I'll get a couple of calves to fatten."

She picked up her gloves and apron where she'd left them on a crate and started toward her wagon. "Daddy might have a few to sell."

"You sound like a little girl when you call him that."

Charmaine clutched her apron to herself, unsure whether or not to be embarrassed. "I'm certainly not a little girl."

"No, you're not."

Now embarrassment tinged her neck and cheeks with warmth. "You say it like I'm long in the tooth."

His deep full laughter surprised her, but it started a glow in her chest, as well. "And you say that like you're a horse," he replied.

"It's true I'm perhaps a smidgeon past first bloom." The admission cost her.

"I hadn't noticed."

"Because you don't notice at all?"

"I notice."

She'd lost track of what they were talking about. They stood beside the wagon, now, but she forgot to turn and climb the wheel to the seat. Jack stood so close, she could see the reflection of the moonlight in his eyes.

She didn't know who moved first. Neither did she know if he'd been moving to assist her, but she stepped forward at the same time he did. His arms came around her to steady her, and she grabbed hold of his shirt where it tucked into his trousers at his side, as though she was falling.

Instead, she used it as leverage to pull herself up at the same instant he leaned forward, and their lips met in a warm, almost frantic crush. The brush of his mustache against her upper lip was a silky delight she hadn't expected, his mouth a warm inviting haven she was delighted to learn.

She barely knew him. She knew his kiss was a little bit wild, more than a little bit heart-stopping. She'd kissed Wayne on several occasions, but it had been nothing like this…nothing.

Charmaine untrapped the arm holding her folded apron, letting the bundle fall to the ground. Never had she experienced the desire to affix herself to a man and never let go. Never had she wished she was more educated on intimate matters between men and women so she'd know exactly what was happening and what could happen. Never had she been aware of this sharp rush of joy or felt a prickling of tears behind her eyes because of the confusing emotions.

Jack's arms were strong, his chest hard, but she fit against him as though she was made to be there.

Before she could change her mind, before the moment was lost, she reached up and cupped his cheek, felt the rasp of his beard against her palm, and threaded a hand into his silky hair.

Jack inhaled, drew away for a much-needed breath, and she prayed he wouldn't end the rapturous moment.

As though he heard her greedy prayer, he instead captured the back of her head, realigned their mouths, and ran his tongue over her lips until she understood and opened them. At the sensation of his tongue on hers, her heart tripped and her entire being recognized the rightness of it. Of course, she thought. Yes, of course!

She wanted this heat and excitement in her life. She hadn't realized until just that moment that she'd been craving *this*.

Chapter Eight

This was it, what Luke and Annie shared, what Noah and Kate knew…what she'd been ignorant of until this moment. Her head swam with enlightenment and the bliss of Jack's kiss.

Now that she knew, she didn't want to lose it. She wanted to grab on and keep this thrilling new feeling forever.

Jack lowered his flattened hand to her spine and pulled her flush against him. His body was hard and sinewy, radiating warmth, and it was the most incredible thing she'd ever felt.

He released her as quickly as he'd pulled her close, as though he'd dared only one forbidden moment and knew he had to let go.

Their lips parted last, as though breaking that contact was painful.

She stared up at him in the moonlight, not knowing him any better than she had before, but recognizing things about herself far more clearly. Her palm itched to return to his cheek, to stroke his raspy jaw. Her lips tingled and her heart hammered a rapturous beat.

Neither of them spoke. What was there to say?

"We're comin', Pa!" Daniel's voice broke the spell.

Jack knelt to pick up her apron and hand it to her.

She accepted it with trembling fingers.

He took a full step back and gestured for her to climb up on the wheel.

Gathering her hem, she did so.

Jack lifted his son up beside her. Daniel sat with the kitten tucked in the cradle of his arm.

"I have to saddle my horse yet," Jack said, backing away. His voice seemed a little lower and huskier than usual. "You go ahead, I'll catch up."

She unwound the reins from the brake handle and urged the team forward.

Beside her Daniel asked questions about cats.

"He'll catch mice for you when he's a little bigger," she told him.

He wrinkled his nose and looked up at her. "Will he *eat* 'em?"

"Probably not. Our barn cats leave them on the doorstep, like gifts."

She didn't want to think about cats right now. She wished she wasn't heading for home. Shamelessly, all she wanted was to wind back the clock, experience that earth-shaking kiss all over again. A warm glow burned in her chest, and the smile on her face felt positively silly. What was wrong with her?

Jack caught up within a few minutes and rode alongside the wagon. "Will you be back tomorrow night?"

"The float needs to be completed, and we did take on a sizable project."

"Maybe Mrs. Redman will be feeling better."

She'd never wished anyone sick in her life, and she wasn't about to start now. "Maybe."

"If not, I'll help you paint."

"Thank you."

"Does your father meet you to put up the horses?"

"Yes. He hears the rig and comes out."

"I can tend to it for him."

"He'd probably appreciate that."

They reached the Renlow place and Charmaine scrambled down. "I'll go tell him not to bother coming out."

Her father was just getting up from his rocker in the front room when she dashed in. "Daddy, you can rest. Jack is going to put up the team for you."

He eased back down. "Is he now? Well, thank him for me."

"I will." Quickly, she wrapped half a dozen sugar cookies and carried them out to Daniel where he waited in the dooryard.

He followed her into the barn, and they watched Jack remove the horses' harnesses and brush down the animals. "Do they have particular stalls?"

"The brown on the end and the dappled beside her."

He led them in and closed the gates. "Your father already had their hay and water at the ready."

Jack stopped beside the open doors and the lantern that hung there and glanced at her.

Charmaine felt her cheeks warm, and looking at his mustache made her stomach dip. His gaze was flickering over her face and hair as well, and then he reached up to turn the lantern down until the flame was extinguished.

All she wanted at that moment was for him to pull her close and make her feel the way he had just a little while ago. But Daniel was waiting for them, and even if he hadn't been, she didn't know if it would ever happen again.

They walked out into the dark and Jack closed the barn doors, dropping the board into its brackets.

"Night, miss," Daniel said. "Pa, Miss Renlow gave me cookies."

"Good night, Daniel," she returned. "You and Bitsy sleep well."

Jack lifted his son to the horse's back effortlessly, then touched the brim of his hat and pulled up behind him with a creak of leather.

Charmaine watched them ride away, and climbed the stairs into the kitchen. Dipping water in her usual routine, she passed her father and wished him good-night before going up to her room.

Removing her skirt and shirtwaist, she washed and changed into her cotton nightgown. After staring out her window for half an hour, she tiptoed down the hall to her parents' room. The door was open and her mother was seated in her rocker reading a book.

"Mama."

Vera rested the book on her knees. "I heard you come home earlier. Did you get much accomplished on your float?"

"We did. Darlene was sick, though, so I went alone."

Vera's expression changed to one of concern. "Was that wise?"

"I didn't think twice. The work needed to be done, and Jack did help a lot."

"He seems like a fine man," her mother replied. "I am concerned that someone would form the wrong impression, however."

Charmaine scooted a footstool close to her mother's knees and dropped to sit. "Mama, he kissed me."

Vera's brows drew together. "I thought he was a gentleman."

"He is. It wasn't so much that he kissed me, actually, as... well, that we kissed each other."

"And he remained a gentleman?"

Charmaine nodded. "But Mama..." She took a breath to collect her whirling thoughts. "I never knew. I just never! Wayne never kissed me like that."

Her mother reached to stroke Charmaine's hair in a tender caress. "Oh, my dear one. I like the man so much, but if he breaks your heart, I'll pray burning coals heaped upon his head."

Charmaine took her mother's hand and confessed, "I had a crazy thought. That perhaps if he showed interest, it would provoke Wayne to propose. But now I see the folly of that plan. I could never lead Jack to believe I'm interested in him only to use him that way."

"Thank goodness you used common sense on that one, darling. I understand your impatience. But you can't trick people into doing what you want them to do. It's for all the right reasons, perhaps, but not the right method."

"I know."

"These things have to come about naturally. If it's love, then it happens on its own."

"That's why you married Daddy, isn't it? You were too much in love with him to think it made a difference where you lived or what he did for a living."

"Unlike poor Mildred," Vera said, referring to her brother's wife. "She married Eldon because her family knew he was destined to be the richest man this side of the Rockies. I know he loves her, and he's given her a good life, but it took her years and years to come to terms with her situation. She was a miserable woman."

"But she does love Uncle Eldon now, right?"

"I think so. In her own way. At least she gives it her very best."

"Why do things have to be so complicated?" Charmaine asked. "Why can't I fall madly in love with a man and he with me, and we both know it and don't fight it?"

"I wouldn't cross that off your list of possibilities," her mother said with a smile. "You're not on the shelf yet, dear." She leaned forward to kiss Charmaine's forehead.

Charmaine hugged her mother, said good-night and returned to her room. Against the wall on the right were four trunks, stacked two by two. Her hope chests. Her trousseau. By sliding one forward, she was able to make enough room for the lid to open against the wall.

Inside, stacks of embroidered dish towels and linens were folded neatly beside lacy-edged pillowcases and crocheted doilies and antimacassars of every size and shape. Dozens of them were bordered with a purple-and-yellow pansy design she'd perfected. Charmaine ran her hand over them, recalling all the hopes and dreams stitched into each piece of fabric.

The trunk on the other side held personal items, satin night-gowns and dainty chemises and drawers, wrappers and aprons and—tucked away at the bottom—baby blankets.

Charmaine's memories took her back over years of stitching and dreaming, and she realized the man she'd planned to wear all these items for, the man she prayed would love her and give her children, didn't really have a face. At that moment she could not see herself slipping on this blue-ribboned satin gown and welcoming Wayne to her room—to her bed. In fact conjuring up Wayne's face somehow spoiled her wishful desires.

Her future husband had been a creation of her girlish fantasies, someone handsome and dashing and completely enamored with her. Someone who thought she was…special.

The more she thought about it, the more she realized Wayne did not think she was special. If he had, he wouldn't have wasted all this time dragging his feet.

Replacing the items, she carefully refolded the tissue around them and closed the trunks. A sense of melancholy swept over her, seeming to plunge her from her previous euphoria. She didn't even know how Jack felt about her—about what had happened. Perhaps she had characteristically blown the kiss out of proportion. Perhaps he hadn't even given it a single thought.

Jack gave up on sleep, pulled on his trousers and walked outdoors to chop wood. The pile was on the opposite side of the house from Daniel's room, so he was fairly certain he wouldn't disturb the boy. He had to do something. His head and his body had been a jangle of confusion and nerves ever since he'd been with Charmaine.

He wasn't an idiot. It was plain she was carrying out a shrewd ploy to make her hesitant beau move things forward. Jack was a convenient tool because he was new…obviously the most inappropriate person she could think of…and probably the only man around.

He swung the ax with enough vigor to split the limb and sink a good four inches into the stump. He had to jimmy the head out, working up a considerable steam as he did so. He wasn't good enough for her, anyone could see that. She was pampered and used to nice things. She'd been treated like a princess her whole life. Charmaine didn't have the first idea about working to put food on the table.

Jack set another chunk of wood on end and tempered his swing this time. The memory of Silver Moon came to him as sweat broke out on his forehead. His wife had grown up in a Cherokee village, knew nothing but hard work and survival.

They'd been happy when Daniel arrived, and she'd been a doting mother. But the following spring, sickness had taken her.

Jack hadn't been interested in another woman since. Another Cheyenne wife would have been practical, and his friend Gray Cloud had tried to give him a woman, but Jack had been content with his family the way it was.

Their arrangement here was working fine. Far enough from town for him, but close enough to bring out customers and for Daniel to attend school.

If he had feelings for a woman, everything would have to change. He wasn't going to give up who he was.

Tired and sweating, he carried the lantern and a bar of soap to the well. He dipped a pail, stripped and lathered himself with suds and cold water. Then he poured a second bucketful over his head and sputtered, dipping another and another.

Teeth chattering, he dried off with his shirt and ran to the house for clean drawers. He poured himself a cup of lukewarm coffee.

"Pa?" Daniel stood in the open doorway of his room off the kitchen, blinking at the light. "What are you doin'?"

"I was chopping wood and I got hot, so I washed."

"Ain't it the middle of the night?"

"It's late enough that you should be back in your bed. Scoot now."

He followed Daniel to his room, tucked him beneath the covers and brushed back the hair from his forehead. Thinking, he perched on the side of the narrow bed. "Do you ever miss having a mother?"

"I guess so. I really ain't used to it, but the other kids got mothers, and sometimes when I see theirs, I wish I had one."

"Your mother loved you very much," Jack told him. "She used to sing to you in the evening."

"What did she sing?"

"I only understood a few of the words, but they were about a boy shooting an arrow at a star."

"I bet Laughs At Bird knows the song," he said, referring to his mother's sister who lived with her people by the Little Snake River. "Will we ever see her again, Pa?"

"We'll go visit your aunt when you're older. Maybe a few more summers."

"She'll forget me by then."

"She won't forget you, Dan."

"Why don't Miss Renlow have no kids?"

"She doesn't have a husband."

"Is she gonna get one?"

"I expect so."

"Her kids will have lots of kittens to play with, won't they?"

He didn't want to explain that those particular kittens would be grown by then and that she wouldn't be living on her father's ranch when that scenario happened, so he held his silence.

"She said I can come see the rest of the kittens any time I want. She said she would show me how she makes those flower cookies, too."

The last thing he wanted was to drill into his son that people were untrustworthy, but neither could he stand to see him hurt and disappointed. "Sometimes people say things just to be nice, and then they forget later."

"She won't forget, Pa. She's a nice lady." The boy snuggled into his covers. "It would be good to have a ma sometimes. But we take care of each other fine. Don't worry."

Jack patted his shoulder through the covers. "Okay. Night, son."

"Night, Pa."

Jack closed the curtain that separated the small room from the kitchen and picked up the cup he'd left on the table. The coffee was cold now. He poured it back into the pot and kindled the fire. Once the tin pot was hot, he poured another cup and added sugar. Doing so reminded him of Charmaine, and he thought of how she'd sat here with them, daintily drinking coffee and eating biscuits as though she was at one of her fancy tea parties.

All the while he reminded himself of what a misfit he was in her world, he couldn't still the anticipation that swelled behind each thought. She'd be coming back tonight.

Chapter Nine

That night when Charmaine arrived, Darlene was on the wagon seat beside her. Jack's heart didn't know whether to be relieved or disappointed. "How do, Mizz Redman."

"Mr. Easton." The young woman allowed him to assist her to the ground.

Charmaine, on the other hand, climbed down the wheel on the driver's side and waved to Daniel, who came running forward. "I have something for you," she told him.

"What is it?"

Jack approached and kept his voice level. "Miss Renlow, I don't think it's a good idea to bring the boy gifts every time you see him. And we don't need any more pets."

"Oh, it's not a cat, I assure, you." Her blue eyes twinkled. "But there may be a cat's *eye* or two. Please, allow me to spoil him just this once?"

Daniel was looking up at him as though Jack held the fate of the world in his hands. "All right, but no more presents. I don't want him to expect things from people."

A little frown started to wrinkle the skin between her brows, but she smiled it away. "Don't be silly. Gifts are gestures from the heart, not obligations or expectations."

"And what did you bring my son from your heart today?"

"Don't mock me, Mr. Easton."

Darlene glanced from her friend to Jack with curiosity in her expression.

So it was Mr. Easton again, was it? he thought without much surprise. Maybe that was for the best.

She took a bag from the pocket of her skirt and held it out.

Daniel accepted it with an excited smile, and as he did, the contents clacked. His eyebrows rose and he stared up at Charmaine.

"Open the bag," she urged.

He did and a handful of colorful glass marbles spilled into his palm. "Marbles!"

"You shouldn't have spent your money so foolishly," Jack told her.

When she turned her gaze on him this time, their blue fire shot sparks. "As a matter of fact, I didn't spend a cent. I've had those in a bottom drawer for years and years. Levi Cutter gave them to me on my seventh birthday, and I played with them a few times. Never really got the hang of it. None of the other girls would play, because they didn't want to get their dresses dirty. Annie couldn't get out of her wheelchair back then, and the boys wouldn't let me join them."

"I never knew you had such a deprived childhood," he replied.

Charmaine's brows rose and her gaze burned into his.

"I'm going to the barn," Darlene said. She turned and headed the opposite direction.

"Thanks, Miss Renlow," Daniel said. "I saw how the other boys played. I'm gonna go practice. Wanna help me?"

"I'll join you after I paint," she promised.

He ran toward a shady flat spot on the ground a distance away.

"What is it that you don't like about me?" Charmaine asked as soon as Daniel was out of earshot. "Why are you so disapproving?"

"I don't want the boy spoiled."

"Like me?"

"I didn't say that."

"He's hardly spoiled. I brought him a barn cat that needed a home and a few marbles."

Jack took note of the pink tinge in her cheeks when she was angry. He looked away to gather his thoughts and compose his next words. "Okay," he said, looking straight into her eyes. "I don't want you to get him used to you being his friend and paying attention to him, and then have him hurt when you tire of your—your—amusement."

Her expression was wounded, almost convincing. Her eyes narrowed. "Is this about last night?"

"What? No. No, it's not about last night." He wasn't a good liar. He glanced at Daniel and back. "Maybe it's partly about last night."

"Because?"

"Because I saw how different we are. I came to Copper Creek so Daniel could go to school, not to be drawn into anything."

"And you think I'm dra-awing you into something?" She dragged out the word and waved her fingers at the same time, as though conjuring up a magic spell.

He ignored her sarcasm. "I think you're trying."

"What? What am I drawing you into?"

"Your little performance you have going on, for one thing." Her mouth opened to object, but he went on. "Tell me you haven't been thinking about making your reluctant beau jealous."

Her cheeks pinkened visibly.

"Daniel and I are not your playthings, Miss Renlow."

She clenched her jaw in indignation. Gathering her skirts, she spun to walk away, but paused, turned and marched right back to face him. "You're right. I did think about that. Forcing Wayne to move things along crossed my mind. But that was the last thing on my mind last night when you…when we…you know."

"Kissed?"

The blush crept all the way from her neck to her pretty ears. "Yes," she whispered.

"Do you really expect me to believe that?"

"What have I done to make you think I'm a devious person?"

"You change like a weathervane spins in a windstorm. One moment you're almost as regular as anyone, doing your share of work, climbing up and down from your wagon, wearing things like that." He gestured to her plain skirt and shirtwaist. "But the next minute you're prim and prissy with your fancy clothes and your—your *cookies* and that breathless accent."

"Dressing smartly and having nice things is *devious* now, is it?"

"Why is it you suddenly need help getting up to a buggy seat when your beau is around?"

"Well—it's rather unladylike to scramble up and down like a tomboy, so I...I don't want him to think I'm uncouth. It's just good manners. Is that so hypocritical?"

"If he doesn't want you for who you are, what's the point? Would you spend the rest of your life pretending to need his help?"

She didn't answer for a minute. Maybe she didn't have an answer. Maybe she hadn't been prepared for the question. "What does that have to do with you?" she answered finally. "And what threat is there to me bringing some old marbles for your son?"

"I explained myself already."

She placed a hand on her hip and studied Daniel playing with the marbles for a long minute. A number of emotions passed over her delicate features, and regret had a chance to worm its way into his conscience. He hadn't meant to hurt her. Hadn't meant to say some of those things. But then he hadn't meant to kiss her either. He chided himself. Confusion and self-doubt weren't excuses.

If she cried, he would crumble into a thousand pieces.

When her gaze returned there weren't tears in her eyes however, and he was relieved. She said in a thoughtful tone, "I've never had an argument with anyone except Annie in my entire life."

"So how was it?"

She shrugged. "I'm seeing myself in a new light. I never saw myself like that—like you do. I guess I do seem like two people.

The person I want to be…and the person I can't get away from. Just me. Just plain old me."

"I'm sorry if I was hurtful," he managed.

"Truly, I only *thought* of making Wayne jealous, I never acted on it. I'm sorry you can't accept that as true."

She paused and looked at her hands for a moment. "If I didn't believe Wayne just needed a nudge," she said, "then I was left to believe there was something wrong with me. As I've suspected for some time now. I guess I was trying to be perfect. Trying to be…special."

Jack was the one who got a lump in his throat at those words, which seemed to come straight from her heart. Her hurting heart.

"Forgive my foolishness," she said. "I can see that I'm probably not the best influence for your son. He's a delightful boy, really he is." Her voice quivered on that, and she pursed her lips before blinking and hurrying on. "You're a good father and you know what's best for him. Please assure him that he's done nothing wrong. He'll have plenty of friends at school."

Jack felt as though someone was twisting a spur inside his chest. He had hurt her. *Hurt* her. "I only wanted to get things clear between us," he explained. "I did it badly and I said things that were all wrong."

"No, I think you said them all right." She gave a little nod as though everything was decided and finished. "Don't be untrue to yourself by taking anything back now. It's okay."

"Charmaine…"

At her name on his lips, she raised her gaze to his, her attention diverting briefly to his mouth and twisting that spur in his gut again. "It's okay," she said again. "I'm a grown woman, not a child. You don't have to pacify me. This was good. I needed this."

What had he done? He'd been so narrowly focused on keeping his defenses in place, he'd erected a wall around himself. And around Daniel.

"I'd better go paint now, before Darlene thinks I've abandoned her."

Charmaine turned and hurried toward the barn, and Jack just watched her go, like a man watching his entire life go up in flames.

Darlene cast Charmaine a few inquisitive glances throughout the rest of the evening, but Charmaine kept her distress and wretched feelings to herself. While the women finished the windows on their schoolhouse and as night was descending, Jack found small trees and bushes to dig up, planted them in wooden buckets and galvanized tubs, watered them, and set them strategically around the little building.

"Frank Miller will be bringing out the cupola and the bell tomorrow night," Charmaine told him as they finished. "After that goes on, we're ready for Saturday."

"I think we should have all the young children sitting on the wagon and the older ones walking alongside," Darlene said.

"That won't leave any kids to watch the parade," Charmaine said in what she hoped was a cheerful tone.

Darlene chuckled. "You're right about that, but they'll have so much more fun being part of it."

"Indeed," Charmaine agreed. "I'll let all of them know, and I'll tell them it's our secret." She tucked her smock and gloves in a satchel. "I promised Daniel I'd play marbles with him before we leave. Give me a few minutes, please."

She didn't particularly care that she'd left Darlene and Jack to wait outside the barn. Apparently Jack had carried a lantern out to where the boy was practicing shooting marbles with his thumb, because he crouched in a circle of light.

He had obviously watched and knew how the game was played, and he was already better at hitting the target than she. But when she missed a dozen times they laughed together. When she finally got up, dust clung to the front of her skirt. She brushed it off best she could and shook the hem.

Daniel followed her to the wagon as she prepared to leave, and Darlene met her there. "Are we riding home with Miss Renlow, Pa?"

"We are, Dan," he answered while helping Darlene up to the wagon seat. His gaze locked unerringly on Charmaine's. "She'll be alone after she drops off Mrs. Redman."

"I'm perfectly all right," Charmaine assured him. "I've done this a hundred times, you know. Why should a trip home from town be any different?"

"I owe it to your father."

"No, you don't." She scrambled up to the seat unaided. "You don't owe him anything. Me either for that matter."

Darlene glanced between the two of them with a look of concern. "Charmaine, if the man wants to see you home safely, what's the harm?"

"Mr. Easton knows it's better not to do things one way one day and a different way the next, just because of what people will think. Like what my father would think. I've handled this team on my own for years. Why should I suddenly act as though I'm a wilting violet because a man wants to protect me?"

"Charmaine!" Darlene said aghast. "You're being rude."

"No," Jack said, raising a hand to the woman in defense of Charmaine. "She's being honest. I can appreciate that."

"Thank you," Charmaine said, taking up the reins.

"Thanks for the marbles, Miss Renlow!" Daniel called.

"You're welcome, dear."

"You said we kin come visit the other kittens, right?"

"You're welcome any time your father wants to bring you."

"'Kay!" He waved.

Without another look at the man or his son, she headed the team toward Copper Creek.

Saturday dawned sunny and warm, a perfect Colorado June morning, with fluffy clouds adorning the blue sky over the Rockies to the west.

Charmaine always wore one of her nicest dresses to Founders Day, and she saw no need to change that habit now. She dressed in her pale lime silk with ruffled hem and gathered bodice. The cream lace insert at the split in the skirt front had taken her hours and hours, and she'd done it all herself.

She wasn't attempting to fool anyone by wearing a nice dress and having her hair curled and ribboned. She adored pretty dresses with layers of crinolines, and her gold heart locket was her favorite—a gift from Annie many years ago.

"I am going to have a good time today," she told herself in the mirror, making sure she used no hint of that affected Southern accent. She pinched her cheeks for color. "I am going to see all my friends and enjoy the parade, and you know what? Maybe I'll just treat myself to ice cream at Miss Marples'. Yes, I do believe I will."

She laced and tied her favorite soft kid boots, then boxed up lily cookies, an iced white mountain cake and her special chocolate-filled walnut cake that had taken the entire previous afternoon to bake and layer.

Her mother had sliced ham and made sandwiches to share on the food tables. She took off her apron. "Do we have everything?"

"I believe so."

"I've never seen a color look so lovely on you," she told her daughter. "What an excellent choice. I do think you and your cousin have surpassed me with your skills."

"Thank you, Mama." Vera had taught Charmaine and Annie to sew when they were girls. "We've had a lot of practice."

Mort had the wagon hitched and ready and helped carry food to the back. "Can't wait to see the school's float," he said. "I'll bet it's something."

The church had kept their float a secret that year, too, as had the Ladies Aid Society. The mercantile had entered a float, as well as Luke's livery, the druggist, the hardware store and the newspaper. Last-minute entries were always welcomed, because there was an entry fee—so there was usually a farmer or two and a business that just pulled their buggy or rode their horses for the fun of it.

The contests were held while the morning was cool. Charmaine wandered among the crowd, observing games of chance, competitions of strength, footraces and even a frog-jumping contest.

In front of the bank, Eldon Sweetwater gave a speech on the history of Copper Creek, and Diana talked about the upcoming elections. Proud of her cousin's wife, Charmaine listened and clapped.

Occasionally she found a friend to walk with or with whom to visit, and when she ran into Luke and Annie and their children, Annie insisted she join them for lunch.

Charmaine prepared a plate for Rebecca and one for herself, finding the blanket Luke had pointed out. The Harpers were seated not far away, Glenda's mother and Wayne with them. Wayne waved a greeting and she nodded.

She had just seated herself beside Rebecca when Wayne joined her. "Charmaine, you look beautiful today."

"Why, thank you."

"Did you enter something in the cake contest?"

She glanced at him, but had difficulty meeting his eyes. "I did."

"I saw your lily cookies on the dessert table. They're always the fanciest thing there."

She studied the tables and milling townspeople below. "So they are." She hadn't made them to impress anyone this time. "I made them because I enjoy it."

"How fortunate for the rest of us."

Luke and Annie arrived, Luke carrying Ruthie on one arm.

"Your hands were full, so I brought you a drink," Annie told her. "Good afternoon, Wayne."

"Ma'am."

Noah and Kate joined them, Rose in tow, and the baby on Kate's hip. She sat him down and let Noah go get their food.

Charmaine noticed that the conversation was stilted while Wayne was sitting with them. As soon as he excused himself and moved on, Luke and Noah launched into a conversation, and Kate asked Annie if she'd seen her mother-in-law anywhere.

"There's Jack," Kate said, gesturing to the man and his son walking toward the hillside with plates and drinks. She nudged her husband. "Invite him to join us."

Chapter Ten

Noah got up and met Jack on the grassy slope. A moment later, father and son joined their gathering.

Jack noticed Charmaine and his step faltered for a moment. Kate unfolded another blanket and made more room.

"Hey, Miss Renlow," Daniel said with a smile.

"Hello, Daniel. Have you enjoyed the day so far?"

"Oh, yes! I watched the frogs jump and then I got to hold James Bixby's jumper. He said I kin come to the creek by his house and find a frog for my own self. Pa's gonna take me later. You could come!"

His excitement was a pleasure to see. She gave him a fond smile.

"Miss Renlow is wearing too fine a dress to go frog hunting, Daniel," his father said.

If they were friends, she would have told him she could go home and change first, but she held her tongue and glanced away.

The first person she saw was Wayne, seated with his family. He was studying the gathering in which Charmaine sat with a frown.

Diana and Burdy strolled by just then, and Will flopped down to sit beside Daniel.

Charmaine picked up her plate and the jar in which Annie had brought her lemonade. "I believe I'll see what the contest table looks like now that all the cakes have arrived," she said.

Annie looked at her oddly, but Charmaine gave her a smile and headed down the hill. After stowing her dishes, she found the cake table. She had a good chance, though Flora Sample had entered her Yankee ginger cake, so it would just depend on the personal likes and dislikes of the judges.

Charmaine studied her chocolate-filled walnut cake in the center of the table. Number twelve. It had always been so important to her to win a ribbon. So important that she be the best, that she do something perfectly.

At home, a drawer held a dozen blue ribbons she'd won over the years. Everyone knew she was one of the best bakers in the county.

But what had those ribbons earned her? she wondered. Admiration? Appreciation? Friends? Her friends would love her if her baked goods tasted like dirt. A husband? Obviously not.

Reaching across the cake-laden table, she plucked up the number twelve card and stashed it under the table. She then lifted the plate holding her cake and carried it quickly to the dessert table.

Charmaine located a knife and sliced her masterpiece into wedges. She tasted the frosting on one finger, inordinately pleased with herself, and placed the cake inconspicuously among the baked goods brought for lunch.

She picked up a tin plate and tried a sliver of an apple crumb cake. She took pride in her baking. She didn't have to be the best, but after tasting a peach pie that puckered her cheeks, she suspected she was. She left the remainder on her plate.

Under the leafy canopy of a spreading maple tree behind the picnic area, Glenda and the mercantile owner's wife were washing plates and jars in wooden tubs. Charmaine found an apron and joined them for half an hour, pleased to be useful.

She had just dried her hands and was removing her apron when she saw Kate and Darlene standing at the dessert table with their heads together. Kate tasted a slice of something on her plate and her eyebrows rose. They had discovered her walnut cake and were undoubtedly perplexed at how it had been served for lunch. Charmaine grinned and slipped into the crowd.

It wasn't long until it was time to line up for the parade. Charmaine joined the parents who were getting their children ready. Diana and Burdy were there, and both thanked her profusely for the favor she'd done them in seeing to this project on their behalf. Diana pulled a small box from her skirt pocket and handed it to Charmaine.

"I don't want a gift," Charmaine told her. "You're family, and I like to help."

"That's why you deserve this," Diana said. "Take it or you'll hurt my feelings."

Charmaine accepted the box and opened it to find a silver pair of pearl-encrusted hair combs. "They're lovely," she said in surprise.

"They reminded me of you. They'll be so pretty in your hair."

Charmaine hugged her and tucked the gift into her pocket. "I do love them. I'm sure I'll wear them often. Thank you."

The parents had the arrangement of the floats handled, so Charmaine wasn't needed. She was able to sneak her first look at the competition, however, and decided theirs was still the best.

She found a spot on Main Street, where she'd be shaded by the overhang of the ice-cream parlor, and waited as others lined the street in anticipation.

Her parents found her, Uncle Eldon and Aunt Mildred accompanying them. Before long the rest of the family joined them, and the parade began.

The little schoolhouse, bell clanging and children waving, caused a stir in the crowd as horses drew the wagon forward. Will and Daniel, seated together on the side, waved as the wagon rolled by. Burdy, holding Margaret on his shoulders, ran out to give all the children a peppermint stick. He walked alongside for a while to get them all gifted, then came back, a broad smile on his face.

He slid his arm around Diana and she tucked up against him,

her hand on Margaret's back. Burdy turned to Charmaine then and grinned. "Thanks!"

She waved in return.

The parade moved on, and some of the crowd followed along, others went back to their booths and games. "Care to join us at our house for tea?" her aunt Mildred asked.

"Thank you," she replied. "But I have something I want to do."

Her parents and aunt and uncle moved on and Charmaine entered the ice-cream parlor. Miss Marples wasn't present, Charmaine had seen her in the crowd at the picnic, but two girls of about sixteen were taking orders and serving. She took a seat and asked for a dish of peppermint ice cream.

It tasted as good as she remembered, with crushed peppermint sticks making each bite crunchy.

"I would love a cup of tea," she told the young lady who came for her empty dish.

The tea was hot and tasted strong after that candy ice cream. She was enjoying her outing immensely when the bell over the door rang. She looked up to discover Wayne making his way toward her.

He paused behind the opposite chair. "May I join you?"

"Certainly."

"Tea, please," he told the waitress.

Charmaine observed as he added sugar and sipped. He'd never escorted her here. All of their outings had been to social events and church functions. There had been a time when she'd imagined it would be romantic to have a young man invite her here and to sit sipping tea together. Now she thought it odd that he actually preferred tea when all the men she knew drank coffee.

"Your float was exceptional," he told her.

"Oh, it wasn't mine. I only helped."

"It was the hit of the day, nonetheless. There's a blue ribbon hanging from the corner of the roof."

The news was good. She smiled.

Wayne leaned forward. "Do you think we could speak somewhere alone?"

She glanced around. There weren't any other customers except a small family at the table near the front window. "Isn't this private enough?"

His cheeks darkened with color, and he glanced at their surroundings, then back at her.

"I can't imagine what we have to say that's too personal for here," she added.

"Well." He adjusted the string tie at his throat and simultaneously raised his chin in a nervous gesture. He rested both hands on the table. "I've been thinking," he said, "that I've become entirely too comfortable with things the way they are."

She folded her hands and listened, unable to guess what he was getting to.

"What I mean to say is that, well, we've been attending functions together for quite some time now."

"Four years," she supplied.

"Truly? I hadn't realized. In that time I don't believe I've strictly been courting-minded. It's no reflection on you, Charmaine. You're lovely, and I enjoy your company."

Hadn't been courting-minded? "I don't understand. You've been calling on me. I thought we were…a couple."

"We were. I mean we are. I want us to be. I'm doing this all wrong." He reached across the table and took her hands. "What I'm trying to say is that I think it's time to make a commitment. To each other."

She blinked in surprise. "Oh!"

He squeezed her fingers gently. "I'm asking you to marry me."

Chapter Eleven

"**O**h!" She almost snatched her fingers from Wayne's, but caught herself. Her head swam for a moment, and when it cleared she focused on him. With his fair hair and blue eyes, he was classically handsome. She'd always imagined they made a striking couple. She'd anticipated the day that he would propose marriage to her.

Charmaine had even rehearsed her reaction and her answer in front of her mirror. She would blush prettily, fan herself with her hankie or her gloves and press her hand against her bosom as though she were speechless with joy.

She was probably blushing, if the pulse at her throat was any indication. Her gloves and hankie were tucked away in her handbag. She did press her hand to her chest, but it was because she thought her heart might be breaking from the tide of disappointment that washed over her.

How long had she waited for that? Yearned and dreamed? How much had she built up the moment in her foolish mind? Nothing could have compared to the fantasy. No words or proposal could have been as romantic as she'd wished for. She was a dreamer coping in the real world.

This was the best she could ever hope for.

"This is so unexpected," she said finally, realizing that what was truly unexpected was her reaction. Or lack of.

"So will you marry me, Charmaine?"

Until recently she would have shouted yes and jumped up from the table to hug him and shout the news to the town. Until recently she'd been convinced that this was what she wanted.

But her thinking had been changing.

She could say yes and they could rush out to announce their engagement to their friends and family. She could agree and she would finally be able to use all the things in her dowry trunks. The image of her elaborate gauze and seed-pearl veil floated across her mind, followed by those satin nightgowns and the lacy lingerie.

She did take her hands away from his then. Thoughts of Wayne and her wedding trousseau were incompatible. She didn't want to wear those things for him. Another man's face had replaced the faceless groom's in her dreams. A man with dark hair and eyes, a man whose appearance and nearness stole her breath and made her heart race. A man who had shown her she'd never be satisfied with what Wayne had to offer.

"If you'd asked me a year ago…or even a month ago, I'd have said yes without hesitation," she told Wayne. "And who knows? Maybe I wouldn't have been sorry. Maybe we would have had a nice life together."

His brows drew together.

"I don't want to spend the rest of my life knowing you weren't courting-minded until you felt somehow challenged or that it was expected of you."

"I thought we were…I thought we would…" He couldn't seem to form the words.

"So did I," she said. "And I don't regret our outings. We enjoyed each other's company. But if you look around, you'll see we never had what we should have. Look at your sister and brother-in-law. Watch the Carpenters or the Cutters, and you'll know what's missing between us. That's what I want. And even if I never have it, I just can't settle for less."

His look of surprise and indignation told her he didn't understand. But he nodded. "Very well then."

"Thank you for doing what you felt was right," she said. "What you thought I expected."

"Is it him? Is it that Easton fellow who's muddled your thinking?"

"My thinking is more clear than it's ever been," she assured him. "And maybe meeting him made the difference. If so, then I'm glad. I couldn't live with regrets."

"I hope you don't have to," he told her.

There wasn't a doubt in Charmaine's head that she'd made the right decision. She knew it as soundly as she knew night from day, right from wrong. This was right.

When the two of them exited the ice-cream parlor a few minutes later, nothing had changed, but *everything* had changed. Charmaine was no longer the same wistful girl with fanciful dreams in her head. She had accepted her ordinary self.

She didn't want what had happened today to hinder a friendship with Wayne. Living in Copper Creek they would see each other often. "Let's go see who won the cake contest."

She slipped her arm through his and they headed for the picnic area. The women were gathering their dishes and belongings and Charmaine called out that she'd join them in a moment.

Flora Sample's Yankee ginger cake sported a blue ribbon, and Flora stood within a group of ladies, smiling for all she was worth.

The contest cakes were being cut and served, and though she was full, Charmaine sampled a smidgeon of the ginger cake. It was indeed delicious. Kate and Annie joined them. "Sampling the blue-ribbon winner?" Kate asked.

"I am, and it is undoubtedly the best on the table."

"There must have been a mix-up," Annie said suspiciously. "Your walnut cake wasn't among the cakes being tasted."

"No mistake," Charmaine replied.

"There was nothing wrong with it. I know, we shared a piece," Kate said.

"No, it was perfect."

Her cousin released an exasperated sigh. "What happened then?"

"Nothing. I just changed my mind. There's no law against that, is there?"

"Your cousin is in a mind-changing mood, it seems," Wayne said. "If you'll excuse me ladies. Have a good evening." He left them gathered at the contest table.

Charmaine headed for her belongings.

"What did he mean by that?" Annie asked, limping slightly as she walked alongside.

"Are you tired?" Charmaine asked.

"A little. It's been a long day. Don't make me chase you. Tell me what Wayne meant by that."

Charmaine stopped. "Where's Luke? He can come get you."

"Not until you tell me what's going on."

"He asked me to marry him."

Kate's face crinkled into a smile, but Annie looked more skeptical. The two women glanced at each other, then Annie grabbed Charmaine's forearm. "What happened?"

"I said no."

"What?" both women echoed.

"I told him no. I don't want to marry him."

Annie released her arm and lifted both hands in a question. "Since when?"

"It's just like you said. I don't want a man who has dragged his feet for so long. I don't want a husband who wasn't eager to wed. If I can't have what you have—both of you—then I won't settle."

"Oh, dear heart," Annie said. "What a difficult and brave thing you did."

"Not so much really. I just did what my heart told me to do."

Annie hugged her.

Over her shoulder, Charmaine smiled at the tears in Kate's eyes. "Those had better not be for me." She pulled away. "I'm going to find your husband to see you home," she said to her cousin. "You stay right here."

Much later, her father pulled the wagon into their dooryard, and she and her mother climbed down. When her father left to put up the horses, she told her mother about Wayne's proposal and her answer.

"Just like that without taking time to think about it?" Vera asked. She set a crate on the kitchen table and looked at her daughter with concern. "Are you certain it's what you want?"

"You told me love would happen on its own, without forcing it. I tried to force it, but it never happened. I know that now. I was just getting…scared. I've been afraid for a long time."

"Of not having a husband?"

Charmaine nodded. "And not having what others have."

Her mother pulled her into a soft hug. "Oh, my precious girl." She took Charmaine's shoulders and held her away. "It's Jack, isn't it? You're confused because of him."

"Actually, I'm less confused. I'm absolutely sure that I don't want a life married to Wayne. I was kidding myself. Pretending."

"I'm relieved to hear you say these things."

While her mother put dishes away, Charmaine put the dish towels in a kettle on the stove to soak. Mort came in and told them he was done in and heading for bed.

Half an hour later, the sound of a wagon alerted the women, and Charmaine went out on the back porch. It was her father's wagon, the one they'd used for the float, and Jack was leading it with horses she recognized as his.

"I've returned the wagon," he said.

"Where's Daniel?"

"Sound asleep in back."

She walked around to the gate. "Poor guy." She looked up. "My father's gone to bed."

"I'll put up the horses."

"Carry Daniel inside and lay him on the sofa in the living room. You'll have to wake him when you go, but he can sleep for now."

Jack picked up the child and followed her through the kitchen to the darkened room, where she guided him with a hand on his arm to the sofa.

Charmaine removed his shoes and set them aside.

"Mama. Daniel's asleep on the sofa," she told her mother who was returning from the pantry.

Vera glanced from Charmaine to Jack. "I'll check on him in case he wakes."

"I'll help Jack get the wagon into the barn."

"You can probably leave it in the yard for tonight," her mother said.

"Mr. Renlow would have to hitch up a team in the morning to pull it inside," Jack told her. "I can do it right now while my team is in the traces. Won't take a minute."

"He keeps it in the far barn," Charmaine told him as they hurried back out into the night. "I'll go open the doors for you."

She went ahead, opening the barn doors, finding a lantern and striking a match to light the interior. Jack guided the horses and wagon inside, bringing them to a halt. He jumped down and unfastened the traces from the wagon. "There's a saddlebag under the seat," he told her. "Will you roll the straps and tuck them inside, please?"

The leather was all top quality, well seasoned and pliable. She followed his directions and packed the harnesses and reins.

"Heard all the talk about your cake today. Ran right over and had myself a slice before it was gone."

"Did you like it?"

"I did. It would've won, you know."

"I know."

"Why'd you do it? Take it out of the contest."

"Guess it just didn't matter anymore what other people

thought of me. I was happy with it and that was good enough. I don't have to be perfect all the time."

"Nobody's perfect."

"I know. I was trying to prove something all the time."

"What did you have to prove?"

"That I was special."

Damned if the woman didn't just mess with his heart with every admission and thought that came out of her mouth. How could she not see how special she was? "You really don't think you're special?"

She turned away from him and carried his saddlebag to his roan, which, once loose, had ambled over to a bucket and was prodding the rim with its nose. She studied the saddlebag, and then attempted to lift it over the horse's rump.

"Let me do that." He strode forward and took it from her, easily resting it behind his saddle. Doing so placed him right beside her. The lilac-water scent that defined her rose to titillate his senses. "You really don't know, do you?"

"Know what?" she asked, and attempted to take a step back, but her heel caught on a bump on the hard-packed earth floor.

Jack steadied her with both hands on her upper arms. "That you're the prettiest young woman in any crowd. That you're smart—knowledgeable about things I wouldn't have guessed—and kind. I was wrong about asking you to back away from Daniel. He's fond of you and you've been nothing but generous."

She blinked in surprise. "Tha-thank you."

"You're good at everything you set your mind to. Baking, painting, sewing pretty clothes. I've seen how you are with your family. Warm. All natural. They're crazy about you. Seeing how you are with them, well, that was the first time I ever really saw what I was missing."

"What do you mean?"

He collected his thoughts for the best way to explain what he was feeling. "You touch your father when you bring 'im coffee. You don't even think about it. You just rest your hand on his shoulder in a way that says everything's right with the world. Your father has what every man wants. A wife who loves him. A child who appreciates him."

Her blue eyes were shining in the lantern light when she looked up at him. "You want a family like my father's?"

He nodded. "Who wouldn't?"

"I know just what you mean," she told him, a yearning he'd never heard in her voice. Her hand crept to the front of his shirt, and he didn't think she was aware she'd done it. "I want what Annie has. Is that so wrong?"

He covered her hand with his. "What is it you want?"

"Someone who looks at me like the sun and moon are in my eyes."

He lowered his head toward her. "That's not wrong. Not wrong at all."

She was only a breath away. "But unlikely."

"Not unlikely either."

"How can you say that?"

He flicked his gaze over her face, studied her eyes in the lantern light. "Because the sun and moon *are* in your eyes."

Her laughter was like music to his ears. "No one's ever said anything like that to me before."

"If I thought I could make you happy, Charmaine, I'd tell you that every day for the rest of my life. If I thought for a minute that you could be satisfied with a man like me, I wouldn't waste a minute before asking you to belong to me."

An expression of surprise crossed her features, and a fine trembling shook her shoulders where he held her. "What are you saying?"

"I'm saying that if I was that fool Brookover, I'd ask you to marry me."

"He asked me today."

The air was sucked from his lungs that instant. He released her and took a step back, not wanting to breathe and feel the pain.

She met his gaze squarely. "I said no."

The rush of blood to his head nearly obscured her words. "What did you say?"

"I turned him down."

"Why?"

Behind her, his roan shook its head and took a few steps. "Because I couldn't see his face when I pictured my husband," she replied.

He'd probably never understand that one.

"Over the years, when I sewed veils and dish towels and nightgowns and crocheted doilies, I had a fuzzy image of who the man I shared all those things with would be. I couldn't see him clearly. I guess..." She closed her eyes as though finding the words to explain, then opened them. "I guess I just knew how he made me feel."

The air in the barn fairly crackled with anticipation. "And now you know it wasn't Wayne?"

"Now I know."

Jack had never felt so vulnerable in his life as he did at that moment while a question rose up inside and burned to be asked. He wasn't anybody's dream come true. "Could it be me?"

His voice hadn't even sounded like his own.

"I don't know," she said. "Ask me."

The world skidded to a halt. "Can you see me as your husband?"

Her lids swept down to cover her eyes, and his insides quivered as the seconds passed by. He became aware of the sound of each horse's breathing, as well as his own.

The corners of her lips swept up in a smile, and after an agonizing minute, she opened her eyes. "Yes."

Tension drained from his body, and hope swelled. He could breathe again. "You would marry me, Charmaine?"

"Yes."

"I'm a simple man. I don't set store by the same things you do, and we'd have to wash our differences."

"Yes," she agreed.

"I have a boy you'd have to mother, and neither of us are used to havin' a female around."

"Are you trying to convince me to change my answer?" she asked.

He stepped toward her and she met him. "I'm just trying to believe it."

She tucked herself against him and he pulled her close, joining their lips in a kiss that proved it was real. She felt so good, so right in his arms. Kissing her was the best thing that had ever happened to him.

He parted their lips. "I can't wait," he told her. "Let's get married tomorrow."

"What did you say?"

"I said tomorrow. We can wake up the preacher and then let everyone know."

"No, the other part. What you said first."

"I can't wait?"

"That part." She wrapped her arm around his neck and kissed him so well, he considered going for the preacher tonight.

Several minutes later, a shove from behind brought Jack back to earth. He steadied them both and turned. The roan had wandered the center aisle of the barn and come up behind him.

"So," he said. "Tomorrow?"

Charmaine smiled up into his eyes. "We'll need a little more planning than that. Nothing fancy, though. But I do want to invite all my friends and family. And we'll need to figure out a few things. Could you wait a month?"

"Charmaine," he said. "I love you."

Her gaze softened. "All right. A week," she agreed. "I love you."

"Let's go talk to your folks…and wake up Dan."

* * *

They were married the following Saturday in a simple ceremony on the Sweetwater's lush green lawn. After the preacher pronounced them man and wife, Jack raised the voluminous seed-pearl veil and kissed her to the accompaniment of clapping and murmurs of appreciation.

Hugs and kisses abounded as they were congratulated.

With a broad smile, she turned to her cousin Annie. "You told me the next too-good-to-be-true man was mine." Charmaine looked up at the man she had dreamed of, thankful that not all her dreams had been foolish. This one had come true. "And I got him."

Jack snagged her around the waist and swept her aside, where he touched her cheek and gazed into her eyes. "So, Mrs. Easton. How long do we have to stay?"

"What's your hurry?" she teased.

He placed his lips against her ear and whispered his next words.

Charmaine dropped her gaze to his mesmerizing mouth and smiled. "We can eat cake anytime."

Dear Reader,

When my editor at Harlequin invited me to join this anthology, I was very flattered. She told me that my tale should include a Western bride. That left the horizon wide open for my hero and heroine to burst onto the scene.

I picked a setting I love. Cripple Creek, Colorado, once called Colorado City, was the gateway to the goldfields. While doing research, I discovered that several owners of the more scandalous establishments in this boomtown constructed tunnels beneath the street so their patrons would not be seen crossing Colorado Avenue to the forbidden Southside. I found this odd historical footnote irresistible, and I am happy it found a place in this tale.

While writing this story, I got to thinking about my own wedding. I was a happy bride. But that is not always the case. Many marriages are forged out of necessity, and so it is for Clara and Nate Justice. He has a promise to keep and she a daughter to protect. But this is romance, and bad beginnings only add spice to the sauce. Thankfully, Clara knows how to cook and she's not bad in the kitchen either.

So it is my honor to invite you to a Western wedding. No, you do not need to bring your shotgun.

Visit my Web site, www.jennakernan.com, for information on receiving a **free** set of limited edition collector bookmarks.

Happy reading,

Jenna Kernan

HIS BROTHER'S BRIDE

Jenna Kernan

This book is dedicated to all those women who have promised to stick with a man come hell or high water. Remember, marriage isn't all it's cracked up to be—sometimes it's better.

Chapter One

Colorado City, Colorado, 1859

As Nate Justice saw it, he had a choice between two equally bad alternatives. Either he could ignore his brother's last request, or he could marry his widow.

Jacob would have done it for him and expected Nate to be capable of the same kind of selflessness. He rubbed a hand over his brow. He had no notion of how to be a husband, let alone husband to a woman as proper as Clara.

Only his love for his older brother could have induced him to make a proposal so contrary to his nature. Nate wanted to do the right thing, but this didn't feel right. What was a respectable lady going to do in a rough-and-tumble mining camp where the only women within a hundred miles are whores?

Lord help him.

From his seat at an empty table in his saloon, Nate searched for answers in the worst of places—a liquor bottle. He spotted the old hypocrite who called himself "Reverend" headed his way. Just what he needed—a sermon from a drunk. The padre spouted verse like a whale spouts seawater, but only as a means to achieve his goal; in this case he had his eye fixed on the half-empty bottle of whiskey on the table. The man drank, whored and gambled most of his waking hours, making him no different from the miners. The reverend always absolved himself, and anyone else who needed it after a binge with some verse about man's weakness and God's mercy.

"I was told you abstained from spirits," said the reverend, taking a seat without invitation.

"On any other day you'd be right."

"Then perhaps you would feel inclined toward company."

Nate pushed the bottle at the man who did not wait for a glass. When he finished a long pull, he wiped his mouth with his sleeve and made a sound of pure satisfaction. He maintained control of the bottle, gripping the glass neck as if it was a sinner in need of redemption.

"Bless you, son."

"Oh, I'm just brimming with blessings."

The reverend gave a wary smile. "So I have heard."

Nate glared at Charley, who'd obviously been gossiping again. His barkeep took up a glass and began polishing.

The reverend continued without noticing the exchange. "Perhaps I can do you a service in the near future." The man nodded conspiratorially. "'Go in unto thy brother's wife and marry her,' sayeth the Lord."

He had Nate's attention.

"To marry your brother's widow," said the reverend, nodding his approval. "It's the honorable thing."

"Well, there's a first time for everything." Nate regained custody of his bottle with a forceful tug and took a swallow.

"You are modest, sir. I know for a fact you have a soft heart."

The reverend leaned in, whispering, "I've seen you."

Several possibilities ran through Nate's mind, and he scowled. Hitting a minister would certainly not hurt his reputation, but he resisted.

The man continued, unaware of his peril. "You feed a stray cat out back."

"How in hell do you know that?"

"I've slept in that alley a time or two."

"That enough to get me into heaven, you think—feeding a cat?"

"Well, my son, that's a fair question. Do you have anything on your conscience?"

Nate gave a wry laugh, and then pushed back his hat. "I don't have that kind of time."

His new friend reached for the bottle, his fingers creeping forward like a spider.

"Try me."

"Well then let's stick to the present. I'm thinking of backing out. What do you say to that?"

"You run the largest saloon in Colorado City, so I'd say you do not shirk from responsibility, nor lack the funds to adequately provide for a woman. I know you enjoy female company on occasion, but keep no steady woman." He took another slug from the whiskey. "So this must be personal. Does she have buck teeth?"

"I've never seen her. All I know of her comes from my brother's letters. He loved her and in his eyes she was singular to her gender—a woman of virtue. Now I'm dragging her to a dirty mining town where the only minister is drunk every day before noon. She deserves better than a saloonkeeper for her husband, don't you think?"

The minister sat back, dragging the bottle to his side. "A valid point. She undoubtedly will be the only female in town not inclined to charge by the hour." He eyed Nate. "You could pull up stakes."

"Location won't solve my inadequacies." Nate stared at the man. "Any chance you'll remember this conversation tomorrow?"

The reverend shook his head. "Doubtful."

Nate reclaimed his liquor bottle.

"I got her acceptance right here." Nate pulled the letters from his breast pocket, splaying them as if they were a deck of cards. He drew out the first. "This one is from my brother asking me to see to his family." He slapped an envelope on the table before him as if discarding. "This here is from her saying my brother passed." Another discard.

Nate paused to draw in a breath. The lump remained lodged in his throat as he again fought the overwhelming sense of loss. Word reached him seven months past and still he couldn't get his mind around the truth.

Jacob had been gone over a year.

His older brother had loved him and with his passing, Nate had lost the only person in this world he cared about.

"And that one?" prompted the reverend.

"From her. She asks my help. My brother's death left her without means, and she has a young daughter."

"A child—here?"

Nate propped his elbow on the table and rested his chin on his fist. "Can't account for my own stupidity."

"Overwhelmed by grief no doubt."

"Never thought she'd have me. She must know of me from my brother. Only shows her desperation because yesterday I received her reply. She's coming. Why, I cannot fathom."

The reverend's bushy brow lifted. "Perhaps she has no other option."

"That's true. If she did, she'd have taken it."

The reverend pointed at the final correspondence, asking a question without words.

"This?" Nate held up the final letter. "Evidence of my low character."

He lay the envelope upon the others.

"My withdrawal of the only honorable proposal I ever made to a woman."

His drinking partner pointed a bony finger at the damning evidence. "You haven't sent it."

"Not yet."

The reverend's smile did not comfort. "Did you include funds with your original communiqué?"

"Of course."

"Then I suggest you resign yourself, my son—for she has likely already crossed the Mississippi."

The whiskey rolled in Nate's stomach as the truth of the words struck him in the gut.

"Now, now, my son. A woman will bring order to your chaos."

"From what I've seen, women generally have the opposite influence."

"Do not judge all women by the ones who have wronged you. Just remember your mother's love"

"She's the one I was thinking on."

Nate saw the surprise on the man's face and wished he could take it back. Not that it wasn't true; his mother was coldhearted, the perfect match for his father with his exacting standards of morality. Damn and damn again. He remembered too late why he quit drinking. Any notion that struck his mind popped out of his lips like a soap bubble rising from a washtub.

Nate stood. "Keep the bottle, Reverend."

"Bless you, my son. And remember, the Lord works in mysterious ways."

A boy skidded into the saloon, eyes searching as he blinked in the dim light of The Lucky Strike. "There's a lady at the station. Everyone's there. Where's my pa? He'll want to see this."

Clara Justice took charge of her carpetbag and trunk from the stage driver. Her six-year-old daughter bounced up and down in excitement at their arrival. Clara's first inclination that something was amiss came when Kitty stilled. She glanced up to see a circle of men forming about them.

Kitty huddled in her mother's skirts until she all but disappeared. "What do they want, Mama?"

Clara didn't know, but their owl-like stares and utter silence lifted the hairs on the back of her neck. She glanced from one dirty face to the next. Their menacing continence and growing numbers caused her to retreat toward the stage until her backside bumped up against the wheel.

One of the lot stepped forward, dragging his ragged felt hat from his greasy hair.

"I'll give you five penny weight if I can touch your hair."

Her eye's widened in alarm as she saw other men drawing out little sacks and glass bottles filled with gold nuggets. Her daughter's fingers dug into her thigh as she tightened her grip.

Clara straightened her shoulders, preparing to defend them. "You will do no such thing."

The man frowned, but did not retreat. "What about a sniff?"

"Nor a sniff either. Instead you will tell me where I may find Mr. Nathaniel Justice."

A murmur rippled through the assembly.

"She means Nate," said someone to her left.

"You his sister?" asked a man with a beard streaked with gray.

These were miners, so she thought it best to establish Nathaniel's claim upon her immediately.

"He is my betrothed."

Jaws dropped in astonishment, and she heard several groans. She swallowed her mortification. Here she was, engaged to a man she knew of, but had never met. Jacob said he was a good man. His father likened him to the devil. Who was right?

Clara did not think her breathing could be any more rapid, but now it came in frantic little pants. She closed her mouth in an effort to tamp down her panic.

"If you're looking for a husband, you could do better. Man's got the temper of a riled buffalo, ma'am, if you don't mind me saying. Nearly shot my partner yesterday."

The distinctive click of a trigger drew complete silence.

"And I'll shoot *you* today if you don't step aside."

The topic of conversation appeared. She stared at the scowling face of a man who did not resemble her late husband in any way. The dark stubble on his chin added to his imposing demeanor as he spoke to the crowd.

"Disperse before I lay someone out in the street."

The men stepped back a few paces, widening the circle. She longed to go to this imposing man. But the very quality that sent the crowd into retreat also kept her from moving toward her protector. His dark hair seemed a counterpoint to the light blond of his older brother. She stared into his eyes, expecting a familiar warm brown and saw instead cold steel-blue. This man stood tall and solid as a chestnut tree, glaring at her like the devil himself. What had she done?

She swallowed back her apprehension, remembering her purpose. Jacob left her with nothing but fond memories. The good people of Catskill, New York, knew of her past. There were no proper proposals from any men there, though she had already fielded several improper ones. After her husband's death, his parish wasted no time in reclaiming her home. Nathaniel's proposal gave her a choice between turning to the life she narrowly escaped or marrying a stranger. When forced to pick, she chose the devil she did not know.

Nathaniel Justice.

She turned her attention on her future husband.

It appeared that Nathaniel did not like the speed with which the mob complied with his order to disperse, so he aimed his cocked pistol at the nearest man. It was then she noticed Nathaniel's companion. He was smaller and slighter with worried eyes that darted about the crowd.

"Gentlemen," he began, raising his voice to be heard, "a free round to the first twenty men in The Lucky Strike."

There was a hoot and a cry as men charged down the street and disappeared into a saloon.

Nate watched them go and then holstered his pistol. "Should have let me shoot Kingston. The man is nothing but trouble."

"And you'd be an expert on that," said his companion, who then turned to Clara. "Pleased to meet you, Mrs. Justice. I'm Harvey Winkelman, Nate's partner at the hardware store. Welcome to Colorado City."

She reached to accept his hand and found hers shaking.

"A pleasure," she murmured.

"And you know Nate, of course."

She was about to shake her head when she considered that her brother-in-law might not have told this man of the circumstances of their arrangement. Did he even know she was widowed? The image of her husband rose in her mind. How could it be a year already since she'd last heard his laughter? She knew she would never find a man with a kinder heart. Jacob forgave her for her past and offered her a chance at respectability.

Clara glanced at Nathaniel. He looked as if forgiveness was in short supply as he watched the last of the crowd enter the large cabin with the false front. She took the opportunity to study his profile as she tried to still her quaking. Clara had always thought Jacob had a pleasant face. His younger brother could only be described as imposing. If not for his scowl, she was certain he would easily be the most handsome man she had ever seen. An unaccustomed flutter erupted within her. She straightened, surprised at her reaction to him.

Harvey noticed her daughter then and squatted down before her. "Hello, darling. Aren't you prettier than a bug's ear?"

Clara glanced from Harvey's smiling face to Nate's dark glower and wished their roles were reversed.

"What's your name, darling?"

Her daughter knew her manners, but instead of giving Harvey

a curtsey, she turned to hide her face in her mother's skirts. Clara could hardly blame her. She felt inclined to do the same.

"This is Katherine. We call her Kitty," Clara said, just then remembering that there was no longer a "we."

"Well, I'm happy to meet you both."

Her daughter continued to cower behind her and Clara felt the hairs on her neck raise. She turned to find Nate pinning her with a cold stare.

His assessment of her person sent a shiver down her spine. At first she thought it was fear that caused her reaction, but as the skin on her arms began to pucker like gooseflesh she could not account for her emotions. He stepped closer and leaned in her direction. She bit her bottom lip as she waited for his first words.

They struck her with the unmistakable odor of whiskey.

"I have a reverend waiting at my store. If you aim to get married, you best make it quick. I drank enough to put down a bull elk."

Her eyes widened in astonishment as he listed and then righted himself. Was he actually proposing to wed her in his present condition? Memories assaulted her. Bickerfield drank. He drank hard and then beat her. Her eyes narrowed in suspicion. She was desperate, but not so desperate that she would give herself to another beast. She would be better off on the streets of Colorado City.

She thought of the crowd of men and shuddered. Perhaps not.

From somewhere deep within she found the courage to confront him. "Mr. Justice, I have some knowledge of spirits. If you are a drunkard, please say so."

Harvey sprang to his partner's defense. "No, ma'am. I actually never saw him drink before today."

Her brow knit in confusion, but she would not be distracted. "Judging from the encounter I witnessed, you are a man who tends toward violence. Is that correct?"

"When necessary."

She drew a breath and plunged ahead, ignoring the hammering of her heart. "Do you find it necessary where women and children are concerned, Nathaniel?"

Nate looked thunderstruck. She did not think it possible for him to look more angry until he spoke. His words spat out at her like a curse, "You must think very little of me to even ask such a thing."

Somehow she held her ground. "Still, I ask it."

Harvey shifted uncomfortably and then busied himself with her trunk, hauling it through the nearest door.

"I don't beat women." He glared at Kitty. "Or girls."

She gauged his answer for sarcasm, but found none. Could he be trusted? Jacob believed so. His father did not. He so despised his youngest child that when he'd passed five years ago, he'd left Nate nothing. She glanced at Nathaniel's fine coat. It did not appear that he'd suffered from the lack.

The stage pulled away, leaving her with this stranger. Her daughter's hand gripped hers as Clara debated her narrowing choices.

"You'd best decide," he said.

"I'm afraid," she admitted.

His eyes widened as if this shocked him. And then he shocked her by smiling.

Her breath caught as she stared. The smile transformed his face, making him seem momentarily kind. She leaned forward in wonder.

"Me, too," he admitted.

She straightened. Him, too? He was afraid—of what—her? Impossible. No one could be less intimidating.

"I don't understand."

His smile changed into a roguish grin. "Why do you think I'm drunk?"

"I don't know."

"Because I'd never have the guts to marry you sober. So if you've a mind to, you best marry me quick. I can only stay this drunk so long. Sooner or later I'm bound to pass out."

"But you didn't know to expect me today."

He reached into his breast pocket. "Just got your acceptance."

She stared at the familiar envelope she had mailed three weeks prior to her departure.

"Mercy."

"Not for me there isn't."

Still she hesitated. He stared down at her, his face now vacant of his earlier anger.

"My brother asked me to look after you both. I mean to do just that."

Yes, that was right. This was what Jacob thought best. She had always put her faith in him.

She knew she hadn't deserved Jacob, for certainly a fallen woman had no business marrying a minister. Perhaps that was why God had taken him from her. Possibly, she did not even deserve this drunken grizzly bear of a man before her. But her daughter deserved a chance at a better life than the one her mother had endured. She glanced downward at her child. Jacob's daughter was worth any sacrifice.

Nathaniel offered his arm.

She drew a deep breath and clasped his elbow. The hard bulge of his bicep sent her stomach fluttering again. Never in her life had a man so rattled her composure. The butterflies in her stomach increased in number as she stood between her daughter and Nathaniel Justice.

Doubts trailed her footsteps. What if this was not the man Jacob remembered? People changed and it had been years since their parting. Her mouth went dry and she paused.

He glanced down. "Reverend's waiting."

Chapter Two

Her little hand rested in the crook of his arm. Nate could feel her heat clear through the fabric of his coat, and he trapped her fingers next to his body. Over the stink of mud and manure on the street came the unexpected scent of lilac. He thought of the ancient shrub laden with clusters of tiny purple blossoms back in Catskill. As a child he'd hidden in those branches. There in a place of beauty and peace, where the world smelled sweet and the petals rained down about him, he was safe.

Clara smelled of lilacs. He leaned toward her and breathed in the fragrance. It suited her. She cast him a nervous glance, but continued marching beside him like a good little soldier.

What did she think of him, this respectable little lady? Had Jacob told her of his childhood as the family's whipping boy? His father had seen his spirit as the devil's seed and had missed no opportunity to punish him. Jacob's only beatings had come when he had tried to intervene. Between his livid father and stubborn little brother had lain dangerous ground. But Jacob often had placed himself on that very spot and afterward tried to understand why his little brother could not back down.

Jacob had loved him.

And now he was gone and all that was left of him on this earth was the child. He glanced down to study the girl. She had her father's fair complexion and blond hair. His heart squeezed with remorse and he stiffened with conviction.

I'll take care of them for you, Jacob.

Kitty skipped along, heedless of his attention, tethered to her mother by their clasped hands. On that side, Clara held her arm relaxed, allowing for the movement of her offspring. On his side, the hand clasping his arm felt as stiff as a corpse. He sighed.

"This is my place," he said.

Together they crossed the threshold of the hardware store he had begun just four months after opening the saloon. Situated on the north side of Colorado Avenue, it stood on the respectable part of the street. His saloon lay on the other side with the gambling halls and brothels. No decent woman crossed the street to the south. 'Course, up until today, the only one here that fit that description was Lucy Maggard who owned the boardinghouse, also on the north. But Gunn's wife was expected any day and others would follow.

Soon the town would have a church, and he'd be thinking about moving on. He knew in his head that all folks who attended church weren't like his father. Jacob had been proof of that. But his heart remained wary of such places, preferring the rowdy reality of the goldfields to the quiet hypocrisy of churches.

His brother had chosen the opposite path as a minister in Catskill. Nate should have seen that coming. Jacob had loved peace and order and always had a charitable heart toward people. He'd seen a kind of goodness in the world that Nate never found. They had been different in all ways but one—their love for one another. How he missed him.

Nate searched the room's interior for the reverend, finding him waiting by the counter, his hat beside him. Dust coated his jacket, showing prominently on the black fabric. In his hand he held a small leather Bible. Just the sight of that book turned Nate's stomach. His father had used the words first and then the leather spine in a vain effort to beat righteousness into Nate's thick skull. He squinted at the black book. Jacob had found meaning in it.

The dusty black crow motioned them forward, and Nate was impressed at the way he held his whiskey. The preacher neither wobbled nor swayed, but stood solid as the Rock of Gibraltar. Came from much dedicated practice, he supposed.

"This here the bride?" he asked.

Nate scowled. "Well, the other one is a might small, don't you think?"

The reverend frowned. Needing little excuse for a fight, Nate accepted the challenge, lowering his chin and silently daring this man to object.

The padre cleared his throat. "You are here, Madame, with the intention to wed this man?"

"I am."

"Then come forward and be joined in God's name."

Nate felt sick to his stomach as the reverend began the ceremony from memory. What was she doing marrying him? Couldn't she see he wasn't good enough, never would be good enough, for the likes of her?

The low ceiling of the log cabin pressed in upon him as the alcohol in his belly migrated to his bloodstream. His vision dimmed, and he fought to remain vertical.

Beside him, his bride stood stiff as a fire poker. He glanced her way.

Dressed in gray, like a mourning dove, she faced the reverend with her chin raised. Jacob had told him everything about her. He knew she could read and write thanks to Jacob's teachings. Her favorite flower was honeysuckle, and she had named her daughter after a beloved grandmother.

What he didn't know was why she had agreed to marry him.

He staggered back a step before catching his balance and thought he could not have made a worse impression. He was certain she found him as appealing as a slug on a rose petal.

Unshaven, dressed in dirty clothes and stinking of whiskey, he made quite the bridegroom. How disappointed she must be.

He glanced at her again.

Why hadn't Jacob mentioned how beautiful she was? Her perfect skin glowed pink with good health. Jacob had told him that her hair was ash-brown, but not that the strands escaped her pins coiled at the nape of neck and fluttered when she walked. Her form surprised him most of all. He thought a minister's wife would be thin and rigid with piety. Instead, Clara had a figure for sin. Standing with shoulders back only accentuated her full bosom and flaring hips. She must have sorely tempted the males in her husband's congregation with impure thoughts.

Another surprise was her youth. Since Jacob was eight years his senior, he had assumed Clara would be of a similar age. Now he judged her to be several years his junior. Old enough to bear a child, he reminded himself, though barely more than a child herself.

No, she was a woman. Her chest rose and fell faster than a person at ease, making her full breasts strain at the hook-and-eye closure of her dress. He swallowed back the lust that surged though him at the picture she made. His brother's bride—now his.

He would not fall upon her as if she resided on the south side of Colorado Avenue. She deserved respect. But with a body like that, respect would sorely press the limits of his sense of duty. That was a shallow pool.

Jacob obviously had not married her for her figure, though it was reason enough in Nate's mind. His brother had seen deeper than the woman's stunning shape. How often had he written of her kind and gentle heart?

Nate knew if he had sent his final letter she would not be standing beside him, clutching his arm. He vacillated between wanting her gone and wanting to nuzzle the soft skin at the base of her neck. Would she now look to him for support? He hoped so. He wanted to care for her and the child. He just feared his own limitations. Fatherhood, he shook his head in dismay.

He swallowed at the sour taste in his mouth.

"Do you have a ring?" asked the reverend.

He exchanged looks with his partner. Harvey shook his head. Why hadn't he thought of a ring?

She stared up at him with worried gray eyes. "It doesn't matter," she said.

The reverend belched. "Skip that part. Do you, Nathaniel Justice, take this woman to be your lawful wife? Will you—"

"I do," said Nate.

"I ain't finished yet. So hush up."

Nate felt his face heat and lifted his free hand to throttle the minister for embarrassing him before Clara. Then he saw her eyes widened in shock. His hand fell to his side.

"Go on then," said Nate.

"Will you love and honor her in sickness and health and, forsaking all others, cleave only to her until death do you part?"

Nate waited. Images of cleaving unto her set his blood racing. He stared down at Clara, who seemed to be holding her breath.

"Now you say it," prompted the reverend.

His vision blurred again. He should have drunk beer instead of jumping into the eighty proof.

"'I do,'" prompted the preacher. "You do, don't you?"

"I already said so, didn't I?"

"Close enough."

He turned to Clara. "And do you—ah, what's your name, child?"

"Clara Stanton Justice."

"Do you, Clara Stanton Justice, take this man to be your husband? Will you care for him in good times and bad and promise to love, honor and obey him, forsaking all others until death do you part?"

"I do," she breathed the words like a kiss.

Nate swayed, closing one eye to keep the room from spinning.

"By the power vested in me by God Almighty, I pronounce you man and wife."

Nate couldn't keep the room from swimming. He felt Clara pushing at his arm to keep him propped up.

"You may kiss your bride."

Could he? He stared down at Clara's beautiful, worried face and reached. He dragged her to him, feeling her lush curves against the plains of his chest. He threaded his hand through her soft hair and breathed the scent of lilacs as he lowered his lips to hers.

She gasped at the contact, and he took full advantage, stroking her tongue with his. She pushed at his shoulders in an effort to escape, but he did not withdraw, and in a moment she was tugging at his neck. He trailed kisses down her soft cheek to the slim column of her throat and heard her soft sigh.

His hand settled on her hip and then moved north toward her full breast.

Before he reached his goal, he felt someone pulling at him. He broke away from Clara to punch whatever fool interrupted him and saw his partner shaking his head. What was he saying?

Nate didn't know because his words were drowned by a rushing sound like a waterfall. He lurched over the edge into blackness.

Clara felt him listing and had the foresight to step aside. He toppled like a rotten tree, landing hard upon the packed floor. The ground beneath her feet shuddered, and she winced. Like Goliath, Nathaniel Justice had fallen to earth.

Her lips tingled from his kiss. Never in her life had a man kissed her like that. Her mortification had quickly vanished in a warm sea of desire. Now the shame returned in full measure. She had kissed him like that in front of the reverend, Nathaniel's partner and, Clara gasped, her innocent daughter. She had fallen prey to feral lust. She pressed her hands to her cheeks, trying to hide the burning flesh.

To respond to him in that fashion confirmed all her worst fears. Had her time with Jacob gained her nothing? Even at his side she had often felt like a hypocrite, playing at the part of minister's wife. She grew faint and retrieved her handkerchief, patting the moisture from her clammy brow. What must these men think of her? She lowered her gaze as humiliation burned her to the bone.

This, of course, gave her a fine view of the object of her desires, snoring at her feet.

"He's drunk, ma'am, or I swear he never would have done such a thing."

Clara squatted beside her new husband, drawing her daughter in tight.

"Is he asleep, Mama?"

That was one way of saying it. "Yes."

Kitty curled beneath her arm. "I want to go home."

Clara's stomach churned. There were some things from which she could not protect her daughter. The home they had known was gone forever. But she had saved her from the worst of it. Because of Nathaniel, they were not turned out onto the street.

"We *are* home, Kitty."

Kitty looked around the cabin filled with picks and shovels. Traps hung from the ceiling by menacing chains, making the room seem like a house of torture.

"We're gonna live here?" The despair in her daughter's voice broke Clara's heart.

Harvey stepped in. "No, sweetheart. Your new daddy has a house with planed wood floors and glass windows, and he's got a bed just for you. I'll bring you over and then come back for Nate. Reverend, you stay here."

The reverend smiled.

"And in case you forget that stealing is a sin, I'll tell you, I have an inventory down to the last bottle and recall to your mind the horse thief the town just hung."

The bright gleam of anticipation vanished from the reverend's eyes. "Point taken."

Harvey motioned to the door and Clara lifted her child to her hip.

They walked north one block and then east until they came to a one-story square box with a shingled roof. The hewn boards were rough, but it was the only building she had seen of such construction. Even the businesses on the main street made only their storefronts of planking, disguising the log construction behind. She lowered Kitty to the street and stared at her new home. The two windows and a front door made it appear to be staring back at her.

"Gonna build another room in short order," Harvey said as he opened the front door.

Clara crossed the threshold and waited. Harvey did not enter. "I'll be back directly." He left her there.

She spotted her trunk and sat upon the only familiar thing in her new world. Kitty snuggled in her lap, and Clara stroked her daughter's pale hair as the afternoon shadows grew long. Opposite her lay his bed, constructed of logs lashed together and covered with a faded quilt. A smaller bed of new logs, topped with a Hudson Bay blanket, stood against the adjoining wall. Flour sacks had been tacked to the ceiling with horseshoe nails to provide a rough curtain between the beds.

Clara had suffered many hardships in her life, but never had she seen such rough surroundings. Nothing Jacob had told her had prepared her for a home without a pump, sink, fireplace or cook stove. She glanced around. There was not even a table on which to make her bread, nor a Dutch oven in which to cook it. Her gaze fixed on the small cast iron box stove. Upon its blackened surface sat one dirty pot. This, apparently, was the source of heat and only means to cook a meal.

Tears burned in her throat, but she held back the sobs, continuing to stroke her daughter's silky hair. Kitty would not know of her mother's uncertainty. Clara's own mother told her everything, leaving no shield between her and the terrors of the world. They had a roof above them, after all, and her new husband owned a store and a saloon. That was something.

Kitty snored and Clara lifted her. The rough mountain roads had made sleeping impossible. She lay her daughter in the strange bed, grateful for this safe place for Kitty to rest.

Her glance strayed to the other bed. Her place would not be safe. Nate's kiss made it obvious what he intended in that regard. She pressed her hand to her lips, admitting that he had shaken the ground beneath her. One minute she'd resisted and the next she'd thrown herself into his arms. The memory of his scalding kiss sent a shaft of heat through her breasts, bringing her nipples to hard points. Shame washed her.

The words of her tormentor rose in her memory. "You like it, Clara, were born for it, and men will pay anything to have that body. You'll make me a fortune in the goldfields."

She shuddered. Ten years ago, and the memories of Carl Bickerfield haunted her still. How could she have trusted him? She had been young, so young that she had let him sweep her off the street with false promises of marriage. Stupid, naive and green as grass—that was what she had been. Her mother had been happy to let her go. One less mouth to feed. Carl had paid her mother ten dollars in silver. At the time Clara considered the money a gift to a woman in need. But now she saw it for what it was, the price of a fifteen-year-old's innocence. For that sum, the man had bought her mother's silence.

Clara's blood ran cold, and her gaze flew to the form of her sleeping daughter. She'd kill any man who touched Kitty.

A thump outside the door brought her to her feet. Curses followed and then a gentle rapping.

"Mrs. Justice, I have Nate here."

She opened the door to find her husband slung between Harvey and another man, his limp arms about their shoulders and his head drooping to his chest.

She stepped aside. "Bring him in."

The men hustled forward, panting under the weight of their burden. At the bed, they released him, and he toppled face-first onto the quilt. The ropes beneath him groaned in protest as he came to rest.

Harvey stood over him a moment, then turned to her.

"Is there anything else you need?" he asked.

"No, Mr. Winkleman. I thank you for your efforts."

Harvey reddened. "Mrs. Justice, don't judge him harshly. He's rough, I'll admit, but a good man."

"So his brother told me. Still, I do credit my own eyes."

Her husband's partner lowered a satchel from his shoulder. "He asked me to give you this."

He held out the bag. Inside she found fragrant soaps, men's hair tonic and a silver toothpick.

She eyed Harvey with suspicion. "These are from you."

He dropped his gaze and patches of color stained his cheeks.

"Do you spend all your time cleaning up his messes?" she asked.

His eyes met hers. "I wouldn't if he wasn't worth the effort."

She smiled at that. Jacob said much the same, as she recalled. "I see. Thank you, Mr. Winkelman."

He hesitated and then withdrew. She bolted the door behind him then went to check the box stove, rousing embers hidden in the ash. She found a pot and skillet, coffee, oats, honey, flour, salt, soda, bacon and beans.

Kitty awoke, and Clara cooked them biscuits and bacon. She hoped that Nathaniel would rouse to the smell of supper but he remained motionless. After their meal, Clara heated water and bathed her daughter in a washtub. Clean of the dusty road, she dressed Kitty for bed and tucked her beneath the new blanket before singing her a lullaby.

The traveling had been hard on them both, and her daughter's eyelids grew heavy as she struggled in vain to stay awake. Her breathing told Clara she slept so she rose from the tiny bed, feeling suddenly exhausted.

She stretched her aching back muscles and went to fill the bucket from the rain barrel beside the front door. As the water heated, she removed her dress, washed and quickly changed into her nightgown. She glanced toward his bed that would be large enough for two if he did not lay squarely in its center. She removed his muddy boots and set them by the stove to dry. She lit a lamp to chase away the shadows as the day rolled into night.

They would share this bed, and he would have rights to her person. That was the bargain she'd struck when she agreed to be his wife. A small price to pay for all he offered. An unexpected quiver of excitement stirred in her belly as she remembered his lusty embrace. There was no denying the effect he had upon her. She had never experienced so strong an initial attraction.

She folded her arms about herself, shamed by her reaction. What would Jacob think of her now?

"But he wanted this," she whispered. "He insisted. Made me promise to go to him whether he agreed to take us or not."

What was it he had said? *Go to him. He needs you now.*

From what she saw, the man required nothing she could provide. Need her? She would be well satisfied if he merely tolerated her and was kind to her daughter.

Regardless of his present state, this man had taken her when no one else would. Gratitude filled her. In slumber, he did not seem menacing. She took a step closer. Was this what Jacob had seen when he'd looked at his younger brother?

In his state of unconsciousness he slept peacefully. She studied his face, becoming familiar with the sharp angle of his jaw, the square chin and faint lines etched at the corners of his eyes.

Feeling tender, she leaned forward to whisper in his ear, "I'll be a good wife to you, Nathaniel, and make this house a home."

She straightened, waiting for some flicker of acknowledgment. Receiving none, she glanced about the rough plank walls and sighed. The task would be difficult. This place was so wild. She turned to Nathaniel once more. The surroundings suited him. He seemed half-wild and as imposing as the Rocky Mountains.

She lifted a hand and stroked the rough skin of his cheek. Jacob had told her he had a restless heart, never staying in one place for long. What was he searching for?

Could she help him find it?

She wondered if she should remove his clothing and then decided she couldn't manage that. She sighed. His boots would have to do.

The way he sprawled facedown upon the bed made it impossible for her to squeeze beside him. Tapping did no good. Nudging or shaking gained her no reaction.

She studied his position, then grasped his shoulder and tugged, succeeding in lifting him only a few inches from the mattress before releasing him. Her second attempt failed as well. At last she rested his near arm up over his head and this time managed to roll him toward her. She fell panting upon his chest and, as he stirred not at all, she allowed herself to rest there a moment, enjoying the steady beat of his heart.

She felt hopeful for the first time since Jacob's passing. Perhaps he did know best. This was his brother, after all, no matter how different in appearance. And if he was half the man her late husband had been, she would be lucky indeed.

A crackling sound beneath her caused her to draw back.

Letters spilled from his coat onto the quilt between them. She recognized the writing, and her breathing caught. Jacob's last letter—the one he'd written when he was so ill. She ran a finger over the uneven scrawl. He had struggled with the pen and with his words, refusing to let her perform this final task for him. The envelopes propped against Nathaniel's side were both addressed in her hand. Her chest constricted as she recalled composing those dreadful messages. The trapped, desperate feeling returned, and she forced a long breath as she collected herself. Then she noted a final letter peeking from his breast pocket. She inched closer.

It was addressed to her.

Chapter Three

Clara reached for the letter with trembling fingers. She recognized Nathaniel's hand by his tight even letters. The arrival of such an envelope had brought great joy to Jacob, who loved to read about his brother's adventures in the cavalry and later in the California goldfields. But this letter was addressed to her. He appeared to have used pencil rather than pen for this particular correspondence.

She sat beside him upon the bed and lifted the slim envelope from his pocket, tilting it toward the lamplight.

He had not sealed the flap.

She drew out the folded page and scanned the date, written just two days past. She glanced at the formal greeting as her gaze galloped over the words and then came screeching to a halt. She released her grip upon the page and the letter fluttered to the floor.

A mistake. That was what he called it. He promised sufficient funds for their support, but did not wish to marry her.

But he had. She balled her fist and thrust it into her mouth to keep from screaming as the truth of her situation rained down upon her like hailstones.

He didn't want her.

What had he said to her earlier? *I'd never have the guts to marry you sober.*

Out of duty to his brother or pity for his child, he had married her. But he had second thoughts strong enough to ask her not to come. She lifted the letter and read his words again.

Sorry to have made such a rash offer.

Jacob must have told him. This letter removed all doubt.

No wonder he needed to get drunk to meet her at the altar. It was the only way he could stomach saying his vows. The kiss he gave her told her plainer than words what he thought of her. No man with an ounce of respect for his bride would kiss her in such a scandalous manner, unless he thought her a prostitute. A man could kiss that kind of woman any way he liked.

Deep in her heart, she had never believed the words that Jacob had said to her, that she was good and pure and that she was not responsible for what had happened but merely the victim of a lecherous, evil man. Now that he was no longer here to reassure her, she listened to the other voices, the ones that whispered in her ear that no amount of learning or starch could change what she was. She knew it, and her new husband knew it as well.

Nate woke to the sound of singing and wondered where he was. His head ached and he reeked of alcohol. He squeezed his eyes closed against the sunlight and rolled to his side. His gut heaved.

For the next several moments he remained motionless, trying to convince his stomach not to release its contents. The song came again, sweet and high, followed by a woman's voice telling her to hush.

"Your daddy is sleeping."

Daddy? He opened one eye and found a blond child staring at him, her lip thrust out in a pout.

"*That's* not my daddy. My daddy died of fever."

Why did his pillow smell of lilacs?

A looming sense of dread rose with the contents of his stomach. He hurtled to his feet and charged across the floor. The little girl screamed, running to her mother as Nate cleared the steps and vomited into the street.

He stood with one hand propped against the rough exterior wall, sweating and panting and then heaved again, releasing the bile wrung from his guts.

Finished at last, he sank to the stone step. He covered his eyes with the pads of his fingers, trying to stop the pulsing pain behind his eyeballs. Remembrance crept into his foggy brain.

Clara had arrived. He recalled her standing in the street surrounded by the scent of lilacs. Harvey had been there and the preacher.

Oh lord, no. He had done it.

He released the pressure on his eyes, surprised his skull did not crack open like an eggshell. He patted his chest. He didn't feel married—just hungover.

But he was married. God help her, she'd said "I do." How dire must her situation be that she would marry a slobbering drunk? His hand went to his clammy forehead as another memory emerged. He'd kissed her. Not just kissed her, he'd—he'd…

He rubbed his head and groaned. What must she think of him?

Then he stiffened as another possibility struck him. What else had he done to her?

Nate searched his mind, but he couldn't remember a thing after that kiss. *That* he'd remember until they put him in a box. He had kissed his brother's widow as if she worked in a brothel. Embarrassment filled him, and his head sunk another notch.

He had no right to wed this woman. He could think of hundreds of men more deserving, men with honor and morals who would know how to treat a lady.

But Jacob hadn't asked some other man. He'd asked his brother. He believed Nate was capable of being a proper husband. Lord help him, he didn't have the first clue.

And he'd certainly made a grand start.

He heard the swish of her skirt on the planking as she came to him and wished he could crawl under the stone step he'd laid with the help of a winch and ox. Instead, he turned his gaze upon her only to see her bearing down upon him with a full bucket of water drawn back like a notched arrow. Instinctively, he ducked as she hurled the water. It sailed past him and into the street, eliminating evidence of his disgrace. She returned the way she had come. He breathed a sigh of relief that he had not been the target of her assault, though it was no more than he deserved after yesterday.

He closed his eyes a moment and when he blinked them open, he found her standing beside him with his coffeepot in one hand and a tin cup in the other. He accepted the cup, and she leaned forward to pour.

Oh, she had a fine figure, prettier than he remembered from yesterday. She wore a deep blue dress today. His heartbeat accelerated as she stooped before him. He could smell her again and breathed deep.

Suddenly he was glad he had not mailed that letter.

"Thank you," he said.

She nodded and stepped back.

"Will you be joining us for breakfast, Nathaniel?"

No one called him that but his parents. He didn't like the sound of his full name, since it often foretold of his catching hell for some damn thing or another.

"Call me Nate."

"If you like."

She stood beside him, waiting. He glanced up and saw her red, swollen eyes. He blinked as understanding crashed down upon him. She'd been weeping.

Of course she had and why not? She'd married a drunk who kissed her like he owned her and then passed out. He groaned again.

He opened his mouth to apologize and then shut it. Where to begin?

"Breakfast?" she asked again.

He tried to judge if there were other signs of damage. Her lips did not look swollen. She moved without apparent discomfort.

"Clara, did I, that is to say, did we…"

The woman did not make it easy on him. Her eyes and her silence accused him.

He stood and reached out a hand toward her and she stepped back.

"If I've hurt you, I am sorry for it."

"You have not hurt me in that way."

His shoulders slumped in relief. He was so thankful he had not molested her that it was not until she had returned to the house that he wondered what she meant.

He stood staring after her as she pressed dough into biscuits on a small board that rested on a wide plank placed over two barrels. Over half of this plank, she had spread a white linen cloth embroidered with bluebells. He blinked in disbelief. The cloth looked as out of place in his cabin as snow in July.

He stripped off his coat and shirt, leaving them on the step as he walked to the creek and dunked his head, wishing he could drown himself rather than face her again. After a moment he righted himself and then shook like a dog. Returning to the cabin, he dressed once more. He retrieved his cup from the step and downed his coffee like a shot of whiskey. Then he gathered wood from the woodpile, delaying his return to her as long as possible.

Somehow the smell of biscuits, the tablecloth and cutlery she furnished transformed his cabin, making it now seem more hers than his.

He stood before the table as if it were an altar. Nate fingered the raised pattern on an unfamiliar spoon and then drew his hand back as she turned. The child sat silent before him with watchful eyes.

"Did you wash your hands?" Clara asked.

He hesitated only a moment before lying. "Yes."

She looked surprised. "I was speaking to Kitty."

He nodded, grateful for the child's name. For the life of him he could not conjure it from his befuddled mind.

"Yes, Mama," said the girl showing clean palms to her mother.

She turned to her daughter and mopped her face with a wet cloth as if she were polishing a teakettle. He hoped he would not receive similar treatment.

"Sit," she ordered, and he did so.

The meal stretched on for centuries. Glaciers moved with greater speed. The scrape and squeak of cutlery on tin offered the only respite from the silence. If this was married life, he planned to start work on a new cabin forthwith.

"I'm finished, Mama," said the child.

She received another mopping before being released like a trout to the stream.

"Go sit on the step with Rebecca."

He wondered who Rebecca might be as the girl whirled across the floor as if dancing with some invisible partner. Did the woman have a baby he had not seen? Dread filled him at that possibility, and he craned his neck to watch the girl.

Kitty went to the small bed he had completed before deciding he could not go through with this farce. She grasped the arm of a doll with porcelain head.

Rebecca, he decided as relief flooded him.

"Stay on the step, Kitty."

The child sat in the doorway, chattering to her doll as she pointed toward the street.

Nate turned his attention back to the woman. He gave himself a little shake—not the woman, his wife. A sense of pride he knew he did not deserve grew within him. She was a woman to make any man proud. He planned to start this morning and make things right with her. He'd care for her the best he could and look after the child.

She laid something on the table before him. His stomach dropped as he recognized the page. It was the letter he had never sent.

Chapter Four

He stared at the damning evidence and understood the accusation in her eyes. She knew.

His ears tingled with heat as if he'd been caught in some crime. But he had written it for her own good. This town was no place for the likes of her. They had no churches and no schools. He met her gaze. She'd be better off elsewhere.

She drew a breath and then began, "I know you do not want us and that you only married me out of duty to your brother. I am sorry to be an imposition upon your sense of honor. No doubt you deserve better than me."

What did that mean, better than me? According to Jacob there was no better woman in all of New York State. Before he could say so, she was speaking again.

"Regardless of what you may think of me, I would not have married you had I known your feelings on the matter. I do have some pride."

Shame and sorrow curled within him like smoke. How could he tell her that he did not find *her* lacking—that the fault lay with him? He had not the first notion of how to be a husband, let alone a father to a little girl. And he couldn't be the kind of husband

Jacob had been. Even knowing it was wrong for Clara and the girl, he had done as his brother wished.

Now this good and trusting woman stood before him, offering herself. Pearls before swine, that's what his father would say, and he had gobbled them up.

He cleared his throat. "I've come to know you through Jacob's eyes, Clara, and now I behold you with my own. Any man would be lucky to have you." He was about to tell her the reason he wrote that damn letter, but he stopped short.

No. He had his pride as well. He stared into her gray eyes, watching them fill with tears.

"Yet you asked me not to come."

Nate could not deny it.

"If not for Kitty, I would leave on the very next stage. But on her account, I cannot. Jacob thought it best we come and I respected his wisdom. I ask that you do not fault my daughter for the foolishness of her parents. It is for her sake and in deference to my husband that I will stay and honor the contract of our marriage."

She shouldn't have to. "I don't expect you to have relations with me, Clara."

Her brow wrinkled in confusion as he drew a breath and prepared to save face.

"I give you my protection and will be a father to Kitty. But I will see to my needs elsewhere."

Why did her mouth swing open like a gate? She looked more upset now than a moment ago. He thought she would be glad not to suffer his attentions and appreciate his sacrifice. Instead she pressed a hand to her mouth.

"What have I done that you despise me so?" she asked.

Despise her? What he wanted to do was draw her into his arms and stroke her until she cried out his name, and it might come to that if he stayed here another minute looking into those soulful gray eyes. Instead he rose to his feet. He did not think himself a coward.

He'd faced many foes in his lifetime, but this battle he did not understand. He could not fight a woman, so he sought retreat.

"I have work."

She did not withdraw. Instead she stepped before him, blocking his path.

"I am your wife now."

"Are you? A moment ago you said you were here at your husband's request. Now suddenly you recall that you are mine. I see you buried your heart with my brother."

She dropped her gaze, and he knew he had scored a coup. She still loved Jacob, would always love him. He could never compete with Jacob in life. What chance did he have in death?

"I would be *your* wife," she whispered.

"Only because Jacob willed it."

"Is it not because of him that you agreed to wed with me?"

He couldn't deny it, so he said nothing.

"Is that why you will not have me, because you have seen me through Jacob's eyes?"

He did not understand why she wrung her hands as she stood before him.

Best tell her the truth in this. "You have the way of it. Jacob told me everything about you."

She gasped and stumbled to her seat.

He went to his precious box, opened the lid and drew out his brother's letters. He had carried them with him for all the thirteen years of his absence. He lifted the two bundles tied with twine and laid them before her upon the makeshift table.

Then he left her. Kitty rose to her feet as he crossed the threshold and he paused a moment to lay his hand upon her head, feeling the sun's warmth collected in her hair. There was a child to care for. The terror of that realization sent him into motion again. He did not pause until he reached the sanctuary of his hardware store.

Harvey stood behind the counter tallying the ledger. At Nate's approach, he laid his pen aside.

"How's the head?"

"Splitting."

"Your bride?"

Nate leaned upon the counter.

"What have I done, Harvey?"

"I don't know. You tell me?"

"She found the letter."

"*The* letter?"

Nate nodded and Harvey gave a low whistle.

"She thinks I don't want her."

"Logical conclusion, considering you told her not to come. Did you explain why you wrote it?"

Nate glared and gave an angry shake of his head. "Nor shall I. I told her she needn't worry about me molesting her either."

Harvey's brow lifted. "How did that go over?"

"She cried."

Harvey grimaced.

"I thought she'd be happy about it. That was the honorable thing, seeing how she doesn't want me. She told me to my face she wouldn't have married me if she didn't have to see to the girl's welfare."

"You thought that after sending her a letter saying you don't want her and then telling her you also don't want to have relations with her either, that she'd be happy. Is that it?"

Nate rubbed his neck. "Well, when you say it that way…"

"So she threw you out?"

"I walked out—ran, really."

"Shall I make a bed for you in the back?"

Nate snorted. "I suppose you could have done better."

"I sure would love to try. Unfortunately, she married you."

"Exactly." He fidgeted with his gun belt buckle. "So what do I do?"

"Go back and tell her you're an ignorant mutton-head without an ounce of good sense. And then take what she offers. If you don't, you're a bigger fool than I always took you for."

Nate's scowl darkened.

"Don't you take this out on me. I'm not the one you're mad at and besides I'll just bleed all over the ledgers."

"Well, I can't punch myself in the jaw."

"Might be what you deserve. Now listen. You're going to do this right. You took a bad start is all. How you finish is what matters."

"I ought to send her east."

"And I might as well slap you in the head with a shovel. Good advice is just wasted on you."

"That's what my father always said." Nate turned toward the door. "I'll be at the saloon."

"Wait. We finished the tunnel. Just in time, too. Gunn's wife and daughters are waiting on him in Denver. Soon this will be a real town."

"God help us," said Nate, but he returned the way he came and then paused. "Don't you think Gunn's wife might wonder why he spends hours in the hardware store?"

"Set up a checkerboard."

Nate pressed a hand to the counter and leaned in. "Or why he comes home stinking drunk."

"Respectable women don't care what their husbands do, so much as what folk will say if they see them at it. That's why we need a tunnel."

With that Nate lifted the buffalo robe and descended the ladder into darkness. At the bottom he struck a match and lit a lantern. The smell of fresh earth surrounded him as he made his way under the sturdy beams. He popped up like a gopher in the near corner of the Lucky Strike.

Charley's eyes widened at the sight of him.

"Do I look that bad?" he asked.

"Just didn't expect to see you this morning."

"Because of the whiskey or the woman?"

Charley gave a grin. "Either one would have been enough for me."

"You aren't me."

"That's a fact."

Nate needed a messenger and glanced about for the boy. He tried to keep him off the street with odd jobs. His bar wasn't the best place to grow up, but it seemed preferable to the whorehouse where his mother worked.

"Send Randy to my office when you get hold of him."

He made it to his chair and lay his head on his desk, dozing until the knock brought him awake. The boy stepped in, his eyes nervous as a weasel's.

"Go over to Harvey and tell him to gather the dry goods a woman would need to set up a kitchen. I also need a table and two more chairs. Get them from the saloon, then go by Van Dykes and order a replacement."

"The cat's back," said Randy.

Nate's gaze flicked toward his back door. He figured it for a goner after going missing for three days.

"She's got kittens."

"Kittens! I thought she was just getting fat. How many?"

"Only two that's living. I think a coon got after the others."

Nate frowned. "Put the cat and her litter in a box with some rags and bring them here."

In a few minutes he sat before a crate. Inside the black mama cat licked her wiggling blind offspring. There was a pink one and one whose skin showed black spots.

Nate stroked the mother's glossy head and ragged ear, thinking of the girl in his cabin.

"Kitty's getting a kitty, or rather two."

Clara lowered Jacob's final letter in astonishment. He'd said not one word about her past. He'd told Nate of their first meeting, but not the circumstances. He didn't mention her split lip or broken ribs. He didn't tell Nate that he'd had to break Bickerfield's nose and threaten to have him arrested to win her freedom and even then he'd come back. Their marriage had given Bickerfield no recourse.

But here in his letters he was lucky to have her. She exhaled in wonder. *He* lucky to have *her.* The absurdity of the notion forced a mirthless laugh from her. If not for Jacob, she would have been a soiled dove in some miserable brothel in California.

Jacob had taught her to read and write and speak like a lady. He'd fashioned her into an illusion until at times she forgot who and what she was—the first of seven daughters of a widowed laundress in Albany. Snotty-nosed and dressed in rags, living on the streets and foraging in refuse for something to eat.

An easy mark for the likes of Bickerfield. He'd seen past the dirt to notice a face and figure of value and sought to exploit her. He's succeeded, too. Still she was lucky to get clear of him before he'd given her to other men. When Jacob took charge of her, only Bickerfield had bedded her.

She wondered about Marie then. She had not escaped him. Likely he'd taken his wrath out upon her. When he'd brought Marie home, Clara's illusions had shattered. He'd made it clear he did not intend a wedding, but rather a stable of girls on which to make his fortune. When she'd tried to run, he'd taken his fists to her.

She hunched at the memory.

Confusion wrinkled her brow. If Nate did not know of her past, then why did he want a marriage in name only? And then she understood. Rather than not being good enough, Jacob's letters had led Nate to believe just the opposite. Nate thought her the perfect lady.

Should she tell Nate the truth? Surely he deserved to know. Clara stood and glanced out the door. Her gaze settled on her daughter carefully dressing her doll.

She sank back into the chair, suppressing a shiver. He might put her out. Many men would. Then what would become of Kitty?

No, she must never tell him. Not ever.

Throughout the day, supplies arrived, carried by a skinny boy hovering on the brink of manhood. He had fuzz on his chin and his voice wobbled between songbird and toad.

Foodstuffs, a table, a rocking chair and fabric. Clara set to work making curtains for the windows. She cooked a thick stew for supper, but her new husband did not return by the time she put Kitty to bed.

She dragged the rocking chair outside and sat beside the door trying out the red yarn Randy left. Her wooden needles clicked as she knitted and rocked. Easy work, honest work. Gratitude settled in her. Here was a home for them both, if she were wise enough to keep it. But first she must make amends with Nate.

The man was a puzzle, and she did not have all the pieces. She would tell him some of her past in hopes he would confide some hidden part of himself as well. She knew from Jacob that Nate's early years were also hard. A middle ground then, something they both shared.

She saw him heading up the street and knew the moment he spotted her, for his steady step faltered. He resumed his brisk pace until he stood before her, holding a crate.

"Welcome home. I made a stew from the pronghorn shank and potatoes. Are you hungry?"

He nodded. Devilishly hard to converse with, she decided as she rose to her feet.

"Thank you for the supplies."

He said nothing as he shifted the box beneath one hand and lifted the rocker in the other, carrying them within.

She ladled a bowl of stew and placed it before him with a cup of coffee and then she settled in the opposite chair.

"I read Jacob's letters."

Nate glanced up from his meal.

"He wasn't honest with you."

One brow quirked.

"I am not the paragon of virtue he described."

Nate gave her a look of skepticism.

"I once threw a cup at him."

"Sure he deserved it."

"I thought so at the time. The point is, he did not mention any of my faults. I have them, you know. Everyone does."

Nate smiled indulgently and lifted his coffee to his lips.

Her stomach gave a flutter. She pressed her damp palms upon the table, stretching the cloth between them. "Why did you write that letter?"

He scowled.

"What I mean to say is—do you wish me to go?"

Nate pushed his empty bowl aside.

"I don't. But I can't see you being happy here and if what you say is true, I'm thinking that Jacob didn't tell you all about me either. If he had, you wouldn't be sitting there."

"Are you so terrible?"

"I don't live a respectable life, like Jacob. I live wild. First as an army scout and then in the goldfields."

"In the cavalry, Jacob told me."

"I own a saloon at the mouth of the only pass to the diggings, located to snatch the gold from thirsty miners. Know how I got the money for start-up? I sold canvas in California at six times the cost. I got the land in town for free because the men who formed this fair city couldn't defend their stake without my gun. Are you getting a clear picture?"

"Jacob didn't mention my childhood. I wanted to tell you it was difficult as well. My mother raised us alone. We had little money. Though she never beat me, I did work hard, helping with my brothers and sisters while she worked."

"Where was your father?"

"He left us. My mother took in laundry. Often she had to choose between food and rent. It was a hard time."

He gazed at her with disbelief but as he studied her she saw him nod his acceptance of this part of her.

"We have something in common then. I had enough food, but a child needs other things as well."

Like love? she wondered.

"Jacob told me that you struggled with your parents in your early years."

"Struggled? That's one way to say it."

"And that you could be stubborn—a quality that your father disliked. Stubbornness can be admirable, especially in business."

"My father hated everything about me."

She knew the reason. He sat before her looking troubled and sad. Didn't he deserve to know why he could never earn his father's love? She could give him that, at least. "He was very fair-skinned."

Nate nodded.

"Like Jacob and your mother."

Chapter Five

The implication struck him hard in the gut, like a sucker punch. He scowled at her and then slapped his palm upon the table with enough force to send his bowl crashing to the floor.

At Nate's display of anger, Clara leaped back and away from the table. She moved as if her skirts were afire. He reached for her in astonishment, hands outstretched to see what was amiss, but she sank against the cabin wall whimpering.

Realization dawned. He had never hit a woman but it was painfully obvious that someone had struck this one.

"Who has hit you?" Surely not Jacob. Please, don't let that be so. His father, perhaps. Their parents lived in Jacob's house. But his brother would never have allowed the man to strike his adored wife. Even as a boy he'd intervened for Nate. As a man, he would not have permitted such treatment.

Who then?

He sank to his bed as another realization struck him, seeming to press the air from his lungs.

She knew the truth—the family's shameful little secret.

"He hated me because I wasn't his son."

She stared up mutely with wide frightened eyes.

"He never forgave Mother. Used to beat her as well." He turned to Clara. "When did you know?"

He drew her up beside him on the bed and she sat stiff as a fence post.

"Don't hit me," she whispered.

"I don't hit women."

The tension drained out of her, and her shoulders dropped as she exhaled the breath she held. She believed him.

"It's clear as dawn. You are unlike your father in almost every feature and your mother was fair, like Jacob."

As a child, he'd heard the whispers from adults and lived with the taunts of his fellows. When he'd asked his mother, she'd slapped him hard enough to make his ear bleed. But she needn't have said a word. The truth was written right there on his face.

He had not learned the identity of his real father.

With his parents both gone, he'd never know. The weight of that pressed upon him and he sighed, lost in his own thoughts for a moment. She shifted, bringing his attention back to her once more. She sat small and hunched with her hands balled in her lap as if trying to disappear. Nate could easily put a bullet in the black heart of the man who had struck his woman. It was because of him that Clara flinched at Nate's raised voice. He gritted his teeth and cautioned himself to speak gently to her.

"I'm sorry for all you've suffered," she said.

He rested a gentle hand on her shoulders. "You've suffered as well. Will you tell me about it?"

She shook her head, dropping her gaze to her lap. Clara didn't trust him yet. And why should she? They were still strangers.

"I have lived with only bad examples. I don't know how to make a home for you and your little girl. But I swear I'll never strike you."

Clara's eyes focused on something across the room and a tentative smile curled her lips.

"If you are such a wicked man, such a dangerous man, why then did you bring us a crate of kittens?"

He turned to see the mother cat carrying a wiggling baby from her box in search of a new home. She deposited her offspring behind a sack of flour in the corner.

"There are only two."

"Kitty will be delighted. Thank you." She leaned forward, bringing the sweet scent of springtime with her and kissed him on the cheek. His body quickened with desire.

When she tried to draw back he captured her, bringing her near.

"I'm sorry for how I kissed you yesterday."

Her face flushed. Was he frightening her again? He told himself to release her, but could not seem to do it.

"It was no way to kiss a lady," he said.

She lowered her lashes.

"But it is how I want to kiss again."

Clara gasped, and her gaze snapped to his. He saw then why she'd lowered her eyes. She didn't want him to see the yearning there. She wanted his kiss. He could see it clearly by her high color and quickening breath. He swallowed hard and waited for her consent.

In answer, Clara placed a hand upon his chest.

He swooped like a hawk, kissing her hard and deep. Her grip upon him tightened and she pressed her body to his. All he need do was lean backward and he could take her to his bed. She clutched his coat, tugging at him as she moaned.

It was his undoing. He lay her down, trailing kisses over her cheek and neck. She writhed beneath him, making him hard with wanting. He took her earlobe in his mouth and sucked.

She arched up against him. The room seemed filled with lilacs as Clara's hand snaked down his chest to find the bulge at his groin. Nimble fingers stroked him. The animal rush of need brought him rearing up to gather her skirts. He stared down at her flushed and panting, seeing the marks his passion had left upon her pale neck and shame doused his lust.

He drew back. This was a good woman, not some whore.

He pushed her to arm's length.

"I'm sorry, Clara."

She struggled to a sitting position, confusion etched her brow. Her heavy breathing made it impossible for Nate not to glance at her full breasts. He gritted his teeth and resisted the urge to bed her.

"I can't," he said.

"But why?"

"You were Jacob's bride. He loved you with all his heart."

"And I loved him."

There, she had said it, cutting to the truth of the matter. She still loved his brother.

"But he never made me feel the way you do."

His breathing caught as he struggled not to reach for her again. Then he realized what she meant.

Lust. This is the emotion he raised in a noble woman, the baser urge of rutting animals. He felt Jacob's ghost staring down at them from heaven.

He stood. "I'll sleep elsewhere."

"But this is your home."

"And you are Jacob's woman. He brings us together and he holds us apart. I don't blame you for your feelings. He was the better man."

Nate crossed the room and reached for the latch. Her hand fell upon his arm, staying him. He could not face her, so he stood waiting, his insides still trembling with need.

"Nate, if you leave, then others will know. Do not shame me."

Harvey's words of earlier in the day returned to him. *Respectable women don't care what their husbands do, so much as what folk will say.*

He turned to her. "I'm *going* so I *don't* shame you."

"But a good wife sees to her husband's needs. All his needs. If you leave it makes me a poor wife—married just two days and already my husband seeks out the company of other women."

"I'll sleep in the store."

"It amounts to the same thing. I've driven you from your home. I'll not have it. If you've any respect for me, you will not do this."

He did not have the courage to stay, but he did not wish to bring her more sorrow. The black cat weaved about his legs, purring. He released the knob.

"Where will I sleep?"

"In your bed."

He faced her. She seemed so calm now, so sure.

"And you?"

"Beside my husband."

"No." He shook his head.

"Yes."

He relented, knowing this for the grand mistake it would be. "All right, Clara. I'll stay."

"And in the morning you will eat your breakfast here and come home for supper, too."

He nodded, ready to agree to anything if only she would release his arm and step away.

"If need be, you can return to your work after your meal, but you must eat, after all."

He nodded his consent and she released him. He felt branded by her touch. Awkward silence followed. Clara shifted her feet. "Are you ready to retire?"

He was ready to bay at the moon. Somehow he nodded.

"Shall I snuff the lamp?"

He sat on the bed, waiting. She laid a white cotton gown over the chair and placed a brush upon the table. Her fingers worked at the pins behind her head, removing them one by one. He gripped his knees with enough force to make his fingers ache.

The brush drew down her thick hair making it shimmer like a waterfall in the lamplight. His breath caught.

This was what Jacob had seen every night before retiring. Did he know how lucky he had been?

She sat and released the laces of her boots, then rolled her high socks down over her knees as he devoured the glimpse of soft flesh. With one hand on the closure of her dress and the other on the lamp she gazed his way.

Her eyes questioned and he nodded. The room went dark as the lamp winked out.

He hung his gunbelt on the headboard and stripped out of his boots and britches, then drew away his shirt, leaving him in his long johns. From the center of the room came the rustle of fabric. He pictured her there naked just beyond his reach and then saw her emerge from the night as his eyes adjusted to the dark. Moonlight stole through the window.

He made her out, cast in blue as she dropped her petticoat. She gave him her back, as his gaze measured the narrow waist and flaring hips. His breathing came in ragged gasps now as he fought to remain on the bed.

She turned, reaching for her nightgown. His breathing stopped as he stared at the full orb of her breast cast in moonlight. Quickly now she drew on the gown, popping her head through the middle and pulling at the hem. Her long legs vanished in a cloud of white.

He breathed again.

Clara shuffled toward him, tangling in his discarded breeches and stumbling toward the bed. He was on his feet and catching her before she fell.

She steadied herself on his forearms and then stepped back.

"Which side do you prefer?" she asked. Her whispered voice exposed some of her disquiet.

He did not trust himself to speak. Clearing his throat he tried to pretend that he wasn't hard as a chunk of cord wood and randy as a goat.

"Which what?" His words were gravel.

"Side of the bed—the wall or the room side?"

Pick the easy getaway.

"Room side."

She stepped past him and slipped beneath the covers. He stood there a moment, not daring to lie down beside her. No man should face such temptation.

He groaned and threw back the covers, then changed his mind and lay on the top.

Clara rested still and rigid beside him. He drummed his fingers on his chest and tried to banish the image of Clara cast in silvery light.

He lay beside her a long while arguing with himself. The fire in the stove no longer heated the room. He shivered in his underwear. Beside him, Clara's breathing told him she slept.

At last he drew down the covers and eased beneath the sheets warmed by Clara's body. He closed his eyes, courting sleep, but his mind played tricks, sending him dreams of loving her. He woke trembling, bathed in sweat. This would not do. He could not rest. This fever for her poisoned his blood; his jaw ached from clenching his teeth.

Enough of this, he thought, throwing back the covers. Clara's hand reached out, clutching his arm.

"Where are you going?" Her voice sounded husky from sleep. The intimate whispered question struck him like another arrow to the groin.

"Outhouse," he lied.

Her hand slipped away and he ventured into the night. The cat joined him on the step. He rubbed its head, feeling the purr vibrate through his palm.

"She makes me crazy as an elk in rut," he told her.

The cat circled around, rubbing his hand. Clara's hair was softer.

He shook his head in misery. "I can't go to the whorehouse in my underwear and I can't sit on this step all night."

Already the cold stone numbed his seat.

"I ought to jump in the creek."

The cat wandered off, leaving him with his thoughts.

It took some time for the cold to steal the fever from him. Shivering, he headed back inside and stoked the stove, adding more wood. Finally he returned to his bed, staring down at his wife. She lay curled in his spot on the mattress. As he sat upon the edge she moved over. When he lay beside her, wrapped in the sheets warmed by her body, she settled against him, hugging his arm as a child hugs a doll.

He sighed as his body came to full attention once more.

How long he stared at the ceiling, he did not know, but he watched the moonlight recede until there was nothing but darkness and the warm, inviting scent of her body and the feel of her embrace.

A screech brought him from his bed. He reached for the holster hanging from his headboard. He had not cleared leather when he noted the sun shone brightly through the open door. Another shriek brought him around to see a small backside, swathed in pale blue skirts, emerging from behind the sack of flour.

"Mama, I found them! Two, Mama, two!"

Nate holstered his revolver.

"Hush now," Clara said and then turned toward him. Her shoulders slumped. "I'm sorry she woke you. She is so excited about the kittens."

Kitty ran across the room to him. "She made a nest of your shirt for her babies."

Nate sank to the bed blinking at the child. What should he say to her?

Kitty grasped his hand and pulled. "Come and see the kitties!"

He let her steer him to the creatures.

"See? See? Can I keep them?"

She stared up with wide hopeful eyes. Her hands were clasped and she bounced up and down like an Indian rubber ball.

"Yes. They're yours."

Kitty squealed again and he grimaced at the ear-splitting sound. Then she threw her arms around his legs and hugged him.

"The mama cat is under your bed. She won't come out."

"I know just how she feels."

"But her babies are crying."

Clara intervened. "Come to the table now, Kitty."

The child looked to him for help. "Do I have to?"

"Do as your mother says."

He did not need to raise his voice for the girl stomped to the table and sat, shoveling oatmeal into her mouth without seeming to swallow. Her gaze remained focused on the bed.

Nate slipped into his trousers and a new shirt and then headed for the outhouse. He grabbed the bucket from the step on the way by and went to the creek to wash. Returning, he found his breakfast waiting. No oatmeal for him. He had gravy and biscuits. He smiled. Maybe there was something to be said for a full-time woman.

"How did you sleep?" she asked.

He nearly laughed. His ears buzzed from fatigue.

"Fine," he lied.

Kitty straightened and pointed with her spoon, then slid from her seat with the agility of an eel. Nate turned to see the cat carrying one of her kittens in her mouth as she hurried toward the bed and disappeared beneath.

He grasped the girl's arm, holding her before him as they watched the cat return for her second kitten.

Kitty wriggled. "I want to see."

Nate drew her back and the girl turned her attention from the bed to Nate.

"That cat needs peace to feed her kittens. If you bother her, she'll leave them and they'll die."

Kitty's eyes widened. For the first time she stood absolutely still. Her mouth dropped open, she drew a breath and then emitted an ear-splitting wail.

Nate flinched as if struck. What in tarnation?

Kitty bawled as panic washed Nate like an ice bath.

"It's all right now. I brought them home for you to care for. But that mama needs time with her litter."

Had she heard him past her wailing? Fat tears streamed down Kitty's cheeks. He grabbed his napkin and brushed them aside. This was why children made him edgy. They were unpredictable as wolverines. Quiet one moment and howling the next and they fell down all the time and dropped things.

He puffed a breath and tried again. "It's all right. They won't die if you let her care for them."

Kitty closed her mouth and sniffled.

He patted her shoulder in a move that felt awkward as writing with his left hand. "You understand? She moved them because you made her feel her babies were not safe behind the flour sack. So you mustn't crawl under the bed. Give the cat peace to care for them and when she comes out, you can pet her and feed her."

Kitty rubbed her eye.

"It's all right now. But you must let her be."

"I promise." Kitty nodded her seriousness and solemnly returned to her place, resuming control of her spoon.

He exhaled his relief and returned to his meal, but paused, feeling Clara's gaze upon him.

She stared at him now with a loving smile upon her lips. He blinked in wonder. What had he done to receive such a gift?

She brought him coffee. He returned her smile as he accepted the cup.

Her gaze raked him pausing on his face. A prickling awareness crackled between them. She stood close as he felt the tension building between them once more.

She gave him a conspiratorial smile. "I couldn't sleep either."

Chapter Six

Nate had little experience with respectable women such as a minister's widow. Jacob had always been better with sporting fine manners. No matter how he shook it around his brain, he just couldn't get past his shortcomings. He wanted to make Clara happy. But the hows of it flummoxed him.

Last night she'd been worried about appearances. He never would have thought of that. Even Harvey understood it, and his partner had never been married. Seemed every man knew these secrets but him. So he stayed to please her, straining not to do something to offend her and as a consequence he'd dozed off twice so far this morning. This last time he upset the inkpot, staining his finger and thumb bright blue.

He stood to shake off the lethargy and thought of his bed. He should build her a better house, something with rooms and a kitchen. He fiddled with the frayed cuff of his favorite shirt as he returned to his desk. And he'd better buy himself some new clothes so that didn't embarrass her as well.

He sat back down in frustration. The clothes didn't change the man inside them. Putting on airs. That's what his father had said.

But the man wasn't his father. Nate felt sure Clara was right. She was so smart, too clever for the likes of him.

He rubbed his tired eyes and focused on the books again. But his eyelids grew heavy and he rested his head on his arm allowing himself to rest—just for a minute.

Charley's voice intruded into his dreams. He was dancing with Clara, swinging her round and round.

"Nate, you best get out here now!" Charley stood at the door motioning for him to hurry.

Nate startled to his feet, came around his desk and stumbled out into the bar. The quiet stopped him. Every miner in the place stared toward the entrance.

There stood Clara, wide-eyed and staring. Did the woman have no common sense? If she worried about what people would think, she shouldn't venture into a bar like a common whore. Nate crossed to her in angry strides, captured her elbow and steered her out to the wooden walkway.

"What the devil are you doing on the south side of the street?"

"You have to come home."

"What?"

"Home. I need you at home."

Only then he recalled his promise to return for supper. He glanced up to see the summer sky turning toward twilight. Had she waited all this time for his return? No one had ever checked up on him before. He didn't know if he should be flattered or angry.

"Clara, the only kind of women you'll find on the south side of Colorado Avenue are the working girls. You need to go."

"I'm sorry. I didn't know what else to do." Her head dropped and she clasped her palms together. Then her shoulders slumped, and she began to cry.

He gathered her into his arms. "Oh, it's all right. No harm done. I'm sorry I missed your supper."

"I've shamed you."

"No, you haven't. You couldn't."

"I could. You don't know me."

"I know you, Clara. You're good as gold."

Her sobs came faster now, so he held her tight as she nestled against him, sorry for her pain, but not the excuse to comfort her.

Clara clutched the rough fabric of Nate's lapels wondering how to tell him? She wasn't good as gold. She was a fraud. Instead she came to the reason she'd tracked him here. Urgency pressed her to speak.

"Nate, you must come home."

"I'm not hungry."

The door behind him opened, and light splashed across the wooden slats.

"Is this your wife, Justice?"

Clara stiffened at the familiar voice. Memories she could never forget leaped upon her like a wild beast. Impossible. He could not be here. He had been bound for California.

"Kingston," said Nate by way of a greeting. He drew Clara to his side.

She resisted the urge to hide behind him.

"I wanted to express my congratulations to your bride."

Her blood turned to ice, as certainty settled over her like a shroud. It was him.

She wanted to run or burrow beneath Nate's coat. Instead she lifted her chin. Dread congealed in her belly like cold lard as she realized what had happened. He had recognized her in the saloon and hunted her down.

Nate's hand went about her back. "Clara, this is Carl Kingston. He runs a—er—a business on the south side of Colorado Avenue."

She knew what kind of evil business he ran.

Clara glared at the leering face of Carl Bickerfield.

"So happy to meet you, Mrs. Justice. Welcome to the gold-fields."

There was not the least question that he knew her. She could see it in the triumphant glimmer of his eyes. She waited for him to expose her, feeling the dread build in her like steam in a tea kettle. Instead, he tipped his hat in farewell and headed down Colorado Avenue.

"Stay away from that one," said Nate.

Yes, she would. She remembered his fist pounding at her breasts and belly. How she hated and feared him.

She tracked Bickerfield with her gaze until he disappeared into the following building. So he had done it. He had his whore-house, minus one whore.

"Come now, I'll walk you home."

The word home shook her from her musings to the purpose of her journey. "Kitty is sick."

He faltered and turned to her. "What?"

"A fever."

He gripped her elbow as he made for home. His stride lengthened as he reached the street, and she had to run to keep up with him. When they arrived at the stone step, he released her and she dashed inside. All four lamps blazed, filling the room with light.

Kitty sat against the cabin wall clutching her doll. She wailed at seeing her mother. Clara reached her in a moment, taking her daughter into her arms. Nate leaned down and pressed his hand to Kitty's forehead.

"Warm," he said. "How do you feel?"

Kitty cried. Big fat tears spilled from her eyes, breaking Clara's heart. Fear choked her as all the possibilities rolled through her mind. Please don't let it be typhoid fever.

"My throat hurts."

"Hmm," he said. "How about your tummy?"

"It doesn't hurt. Just here." She stroked her neck.

"Clara, why don't you make some tea with honey?"

Kitty's gaze turned hopeful. "I like honey on biscuits."

"You'll have that tomorrow," he promised.

Clara felt so relieved to have someone take charge. Just having a task to do helped calm her frayed nerves. When she found Kitty was ill, all she could think to do was find Nate and she went right out to seek him. He stroked Kitty's head and asked her about her doll as Clara heated the water.

Kitty yawned as she told him that Rebecca didn't like big dogs or men who shouted.

"Does she know anyone who shouts?"

"My grampa John use to holler at Rebecca sometimes. She spills her milk."

Clara glanced at Nate and saw his jaw muscle clenching.

"I'm sure Rebecca didn't do it on purpose. Sometimes people are so angry inside that they yell at everyone around them."

"He was mean. I walked around him on tiptoes so I didn't make a ruckus and he said 'stop sneaking about!'"

"That was my father. I mean, the man that raised me."

Kitty's eyes widened. "Was he mean to you?"

Nate nodded.

Kitty leaned forward and whispered. "I'm glad you aren't mean and shoutie."

Nate palmed the top of Kitty's head. "Me, too."

"He died before my daddy. Now he's gone to heaven."

Nate's smile bore no humor. "Not if there is any justice in the world."

Clara and he exchanged a look. She pitied the child he had been. Perhaps Nate read her feelings in her expression for his eyes glittered dangerously. She swallowed and found her voice.

"Here is your tea, Kitty." She held out the cup. "Two hands."

Kitty slurped from her cup and then asked for a story. Clara began one of her daughter's favorites but Kitty interrupted.

"No, I want my new daddy to tell it."

Nate turned to Clara as his jaw dropped in astonishment. He recovered in a moment and Clara warmed to see him grinning with pride. Then his brow wrinkled and he cast her a glance that seemed to beg for rescue.

"I don't know her favorite story," he said.

"Just tell me one with a princess," said Kitty.

Nate scratched the dark shadow of a beard beneath his jaw and thought for few moments and then launched into an odd version of the princess and the pea where the princess discovers a litter of kittens under her mattress, which she delivered to local children with the help of the cavalry. Clara admired the way he tackled this task, which was unfamiliar to him as panning for gold would be to her.

He finished his tale and waited for Kitty's judgment.

She nodded her approval. "I like kittens."

"Do you want another story?" he asked.

"No, just a tuck-in."

Nate looked to Clara for help. She smiled as memories that once made her so sad now blended the joy and sorrow in equal measures.

"Jacob used to tuck the blankets in tight and then kiss her on the forehead."

Nate started to comply and then hesitated. "You know, second daddies do things differently than firsts."

He had Kitty's attention.

"For example, we fluff pillows and we give kisses on both cheeks. You think that will be all right?"

Kitty thought a moment and then nodded. Clara's heart squeezed with a tender joy. How could she ever thank him enough for his kindness to her child?

He took Kitty's pillow and gave it several good punches before replacing it beneath her head. Then he leaned in and kissed her on both cheeks. How wise of him to make his own ritual with her daughter, one that allowed Kitty to feel secure, but did not try to replace her father. She thought that she could fall in love with this man, if he would only give her a chance.

Kitty settled and closed her eyes. Clara smiled and waited for Nate to meet her gaze. When he did, she could see him struggling with something. His expression looked troubled.

She waited.

When he spoke his voice choked with emotion.

"I love her already."

His words hit Clara like an arrow in the heart. Tears sprang to her eyes and she hugged him tight. His arms came around her and they sat there upon Kitty's small bed, supported by each other's embrace.

"Thank you," she whispered.

"It was only a story."

Clara pulled backward. "No, it was much more. I was so worried." She dared not say more in case Kitty was still awake.

"We'll take good care of her."

Clara stood and stared down at her little girl. Her flushed face brought a crease to her brow. She needed to keep a close watch on that fever.

Nate lifted one end of his bed and dragged until it lay parallel to Kitty's, with mere inches between the frames. Clara glanced at him.

"So you can see to her during the night."

She smiled at him and stillness filled the room.

"I was afraid to come here. Did you know that? This seems such a wild place. But Jacob said you would care for us. I'm so glad I listened."

She lifted onto her toes and kissed him on the lips. He flinched and tried to draw back, but she persisted, trying to overcome that wall he erected between them. He stilled. She kissed him with affection and tenderness, trying to show her gratitude. But then he pulled her into his arms and the grateful kiss changed to a slow burn, heating her from within.

Kitty coughed and she stiffened. He stepped away instantly as they both watched the sleeping child.

"I'll go wash up," he said and left her alone for a long while. She snuffed all the lamps but one, which burned low on the table. Crawling into bed, she waited, knowing she shouldn't anticipate his return, but she did. No doubt she was wicked to want him to kiss her again. He thought her a lady, but these emotions he stirred made her feel scandalous. Oh, how she wanted this man.

He entered silent as a night shadow and snuffed the lamp. The bed sagged as the ropes absorbed his weight. Her breathing betrayed her as she waited for him to slide in beside her.

"Good night, Clara," he said and gave her his back.

Disappointment landed on her chest like a millstone. She pressed her lips together to keep herself from asking for a goodnight kiss and shocked at how much she had anticipated it.

Kitty was ill. Of course he would not kiss her now. She touched her daughter's forehead, absorbing the heat of her fever and finding it no worse. She rolled to her back.

He loved her daughter but he did not want her. But their kiss—surely she didn't imagine the fire between them. She tried to understand why he kept avoiding her touch.

Jacob had loved her and she wanted that love again.

If she was honest with herself, she would admit that her love for Jacob stemmed from gratitude. She had been faithful to him, but he'd never made her ache with longing like this strange, brooding man beside her.

He wasn't asleep. She knew it because he lay as rigid as a corpse. Without any encouragement from him, her body quivered with need. She pressed a hand to her trembling belly. Waiting was so hard.

He felt it, too—this desire between them. She knew it from his kiss. But he did not see her as his wife, rather the wife of his dead brother. Somehow she needed to make him believe she was his.

She must think of something other than this or she would not be able to resist the call of his body to hers.

The image of a cruel man sprung into her mind. Bickerfield.

Her eyelids popped open. She recalled the flash of recognition in his eyes, followed by his evil grin. Clara's breath caught. Why hadn't he exposed her?

She feared the answer. The frightened part of her brain told her to run—to gather her daughter and leave before he could harm them. But she had nowhere to go, no money, no family. Involuntarily, she drew closer to her new husband. Nate would protect them. But would he ever forgive her for her deceit?

Chapter Seven

Nate opened his eyes at the gentle rocking of his shoulder. His gaze focused on Clara's worried expression. He slept light so he knew she'd been up half the night checking her daughter.

"Kitty's fever is higher."

He rolled to a seat, squinting in the morning light, then turned to the child. No, his daughter now. In the gray before dawn, he could see little, so he reached past Clara and pressed a palm to Kitty's forehead. Heat radiated back to him.

"How do you feel, Sweet-pea?"

She lifted a hand to her throat. "Hurts."

Nate felt her neck and the swollen glands below her jaw.

"Thirsty?"

She nodded.

"Clara, make some more tea and honey."

He stood and drew on his britches as she lit the lamp.

"She must have a doctor," Clara's worried voice barely hid her alarm.

He tugged on his boot and turned to her.

"There is no doctor here."

"No doctor." Her anxious, frightened voice pulled at his heart.

"It was one of the reasons I thought you should not come."

She stoked the fire and added more wood. He found her accusing gaze upon him.

"And what were the other reasons?"

That I'd be second to Jacob in your regard. His mother and father had never loved him. He understood why. But it didn't soften the pain. He didn't want a wife who wed him only from necessity. And he could see little other reason to wed with him, though he'd had offers. All the women who tried to tie him down had one thing in common, a longing for the money he made.

Better to be alone.

"Well?" she asked, filling a pot and lifting it to the stove.

"We have no other children here, no school or church."

She whirled, sending her braid off her back for a moment. Her cheeks grew pink as she glared at him.

"You did not write that letter because of schools and churches. You didn't want me."

His eyes narrowed.

"Don't be silly."

"Why then?"

"Maybe I like my privacy."

That stopped her, and he breathed a sigh of relief. Funny that she would think he didn't want her.

Not a man alive would not want Clara. She was beautiful, kind, a good mother and a righteous woman. She also had the body of Eve, to tempt a man to follow her, whichever way she led. She offered him the apple. How long could he resist?

To remove her from his sight, he found the honey and rested it on the new table that Randy had brought. Clara poured the tea and then began cooking oatmeal, setting the cup aside to cool.

Nate stirred the contents and blew away the rising steam. Kitty sat up to receive the tea. After drinking it, she wiggled in her bed.

"Rebecca has to use the outhouse."

"You can use the chamberpot," Nate offered.

She shook her head.

Clara, still in her white nightgown, extended her hand.

"I'll take her," said Nate.

Kitty did not object, so he scooped her into his arms and carried her out the door, depositing her within the outhouse. When she finished, he lifted her again. Kitty scratched at her arms as he walked toward the house. Then she scratched at her legs.

The hem of her nightgown lifted. It was then he saw the raised red rash. He quickened his step and brought her back to her bed.

Clara must have read trouble in his expression, for she rushed to them.

"What is it?"

"She has a rash."

Clara snatched the gown from her daughter, revealing Kitty's pale skin, thin limbs and a chest and belly covered with small red spots.

Clara sank to the bed. Her breath came in a low whisper, like a prayer. "Lord in heaven, is it typhus? Oh, no, please not smallpox."

Nate looked at Kitty, who now lay mute, with big round eyes looking to him for answers. Clara clasped her hands and regarded him as well. He grit his teeth and turned his attention to the rash.

He had seen typhus on the trail and in California. There was a rash, but it didn't look like this. He rubbed his cheek and thought. His mind cast back to the Indians he'd seen riddled with smallpox sores. Poor devils. It was a wretched death. He tamped down the fear for his child. How quickly she had wheedled into his heart. He leaned forward to study the marks.

"Do they itch?"

Kitty nodded.

Nate turned to her mother. "Looks like measles to me."

"Measles?" Her gaze went back to her daughter and she touched a raised red mark. When she spoke again, her voice rang with relief. "Measles. Oh, thank God—thank God."

"I'm not going to die?" asked Kitty.

Nate stroked her head. "No, Sweet-pea. But you are going to have to resist scratching. Those little sores leave a scar. See?"

He pointed to the spot on his forehead between his brows where a pox had marked him. Kitty stared and nodded gravely.

"The doc at Fort Henry used a paste of baking soda to bring down the itch," he said.

"Do you have any?" asked Clara.

"No, but they have it at the dry goods. I'll be back in a bit."

Nate finished dressing and headed out. Clara stood in the doorway, watching him make his way up the street.

He turned back and waved and she returned his salute before attending Kitty. She washed her skin and dressed her in her nightgown once more. A few minutes later there came a knock at the door.

Why did he knock, she wondered as she lifted the latch and drew back the solid wood planking. Perhaps his hands were full with supplies.

"That was quick," she said. The smile fell from her lips.

There on her doorstep stood Carl Bickerfield.

"You," she snarled, recoiling as if he were a rattlesnake.

"Good morning, Clara, my dear. It is good to see you thriving."

"Get off my step."

"Not just yet, I'm afraid. We have business to attend."

At the store, Nate learned that Gunn's wife had arrived with two daughters in tow. One was near an adult but the other, still a girl. That would mean Clara and Kitty might find female companionship, of the right sort.

On his return, he came across the owner of the Colorado Rest Home. Ridiculous name for a whorehouse, thought Nate. Kingston's establishment was the only two-story structure in Colorado City and he lived upstairs.

So why was he headed up Second, coming from the direction of Nate's home?

Kingston tried to get by with a tip of his hat, but Nate side-stepped him.

"What are you doing on the north end?"

"Looking for you."

"That so? I didn't see you slowing down."

"My mind was elsewhere, I'm afraid."

"You see my wife?"

"Briefly. She informed me you were not at home."

"Kingston, you stay on the south side where you belong and stay the hell away from my home and my wife."

"I meant no offense. I merely wanted to ask you if you would consider extending your tunnel. Several of my clientele would make use of it, now that the wives are beginning to arrive."

"Build your own damn tunnel."

"I just thought to inquire. I could give you free service."

Nate had seen the way this man conducted his business. He was all smiles and good manners in public, but he beat his whores. Nate disliked a hypocrite, so he leaned forward and placed a finger in the man's face.

"Let me make something clear. You want to talk business, you see me at the saloon. Because the next time I catch you near my house, you'll be whistling through a new gap in your front teeth."

Clara cursed the luck that brought Bickersfield to this boom-town. Here at the gateway to Ute pass, all miners must stop—the perfect place to set up his vile business.

He wanted money and she had none, so why not go directly to Nate? Perhaps this was her punishment for leaving him. She must face the humiliation of confessing to her new husband that once Carl Bickerfield, the one Nate called Kingston, had used her again and again before she could escape.

Shame burned, making her cheeks hot. How she hated the man. Even before he turned up at her doorstep, she had never truly been free of him. He haunted her thoughts like a ghost. Not a day passed when she didn't remember. He was the reason she had never been good enough for Jacob, why she could never hold her head high when walking beside him. People knew, people talked. Here she thought to make a fresh start, away from the gossips. It seemed that the outer reaches of this new territory were not far enough to escape the demons that pursued her, for she carried them in her heart. And now she faced her nemesis in person.

She heard a footstep beyond the door as someone stomped and then lifted the latch. Her breathing caught. She released it as Nate filled the entrance.

"I have the soda," he said lifting a crate. "Also saw Mr. Gunn. He owns the feed and flour store. His wife and daughters have arrived and are anxious to meet you."

Not for long they won't be, thought Clara. No respectable woman would speak to her once Bickerfield told them of her past. She did not believe that a bribe would buy his silence, though if she'd had the money she would certainly have paid him. She felt in her heart that the man wanted his pound of flesh. What better way to extract it than to expose her in this new place?

"I hope you told him my daughter is ill."

"No, I told him *our* daughter is ill."

Her eyes rounded. Here she tried to build a family and then excluded him at every turn.

"I'm sorry, Nate. Of course you are her father now."

"I also saw Kingston."

She stiffened.

He waited for her to speak. She lowered her gaze as terror made her ears buzz as if she fled a hive of wasps. Stinging humiliation pricked her.

"Did he trouble you?"

"I don't like him." Her voice came breathless. He'd know or guess. Did he know already? She sank into a chair. Why couldn't she tell him? Her gaze went to her daughter. Here was the reason for her silence. Kitty needed a home. She could not bear to bring shame on her daughter and if Nate abandoned them—what then?

Would Nate accept them if he knew?

No. He was not his brother. This man was impulsive, brooding and held a grudge. He would not forgive such deceit.

"I told him to keep clear of you. If he bothers you again, I want to know."

"Yes, Nathaniel."

He handed her a sack of baking powder and she set to work making a paste for Kitty's measles.

Over the next four days she did not mention Bickerfield or the reason for his call. Kitty's measles wept and itched but her fever had gone, and she now scrambled about beneath the bed with the kittens whose eyes had opened.

A pattern established between Clara and Nate. He ate breakfast with them, but not lunch. He returned midafternoon to play with Kitty while Clara cooked their evening meal. Often she felt his gaze upon her. When she turned she found him watching with a focused intent that quickened her blood. His silence seemed laced with need. When she served him, she noted how his muscles tensed. He hurried through his meal and then returned to the saloon until after she retired. Each night in the darkness he lay down beside her like an enchanted prince in some fairy tale; she longed to touch him but knew that a lady would wait for him to come to her. Why would he not touch her?

Suspicion and dread haunted her dreams.

She waited in misery for the day that Bickerfield revealed her secret. What would Nate do with her then?

By the eighth day, Kitty's measles had dried and the scabs began to fall away. She seemed back to herself again and eager for visitors. Mrs. Gunn and her two daughters, Lydia, age sixteen, and Katherine, age eleven, came to call. She was thankful that Nate had warned her of the impending guests so she had Kitty up and dressed.

"Such a pleasure to meet you at last, Mrs. Justice. We are so grateful to find civility here in the wilderness." Mrs. Gunn held her hand a moment, and Clara noted the white gloves and lacy cuff.

"Welcome to you and your girls. Please come in."

Nate had provided five chairs from the saloon for the visit. Clara disguised the knife cuts on the table with a linen cloth. Her silver teapot already waited beside five china cups.

"Do you take sugar?" Clara asked, feeling like an imposter once more. Just like her life in Catskill, only there the women did not call. They treated her with a begrudging civility and secret loathing that revealed itself immediately after her husband's death.

Clara managed the pouring and distribution of the tea and opened the box of shortbread from England that Nate had provided for this special occasion.

Mrs. Gunn sipped her tea. "I understand you are recently arrived from Catskill on the Hudson River."

Clara stiffened wondering what else this woman knew?

"That's correct."

"We hail from Philadelphia. My girls were in private school. I am chagrined to learn that we do not yet have a school or church in Colorado City. I have spoken to my husband about the lack and do hope you will do the same."

The door banged open, and all the women jumped. Katherine sloshed tea upon the white linen and Mrs. Gunn scowled at her child.

Clara's heart nearly stopped as she imagined Bickerfield leaping forward to expose her deceit. Instead Nate strode into the room.

"Forgot my hat." He grasped the brim and stilled as he noted the company.

Clara rose, still recovering from her fright. "Mrs. Gunn, Lydia, Katherine, this is my husband, Nathaniel."

Nate stood like a frightened deer ready to bound away. His eyes strayed toward the door with an expression of longing, but he inched forward.

"My apologies, ladies. I'll just be leaving."

Mrs. Gunn rose and offered her hand, palm down. Nate reached and then noted the gloves. He showed a filthy palm. "I'm sorry, I just been picking the horse's feet."

Mrs. Gunn's nose wrinkled, and she withdrew her offer. "Well, I am very happy to meet you in any case. My husband informs me that you run the hardware store."

"And the saloon."

Her mouth twisted, as if she sucked a lemon. "Oh, how unfortunate. We don't approve of spirits. They are the devil's tools."

Clara wished to sink through the floor. Nate must have felt the same, for he backed up. She had never seen him look so uncertain. Suddenly Clara grew angry. It was one thing for the "good" women of Catskill to whisper behind *her* back, but it was quite another to stand here and insult her husband.

She stepped before Nate, shielding him from the scornful glance of their guest. "My husband's businesses provide us a roof over our heads."

"A roof forged with the suffering of others," said Mrs. Gunn, stiffening her spine.

Clara felt her control snap. "Yet you accept our hospitality and then find fault with the way in which it is provided. I will not hear my husband criticized in this house. I wish you all a good day."

The woman looked positively shocked. "Mrs. Justice, surely you do not approve of your husband's venture."

"On the contrary, I hold him in the highest regard."

Mrs. Gunn flounced her skirts as if shaking off the crumbs from the shortbread she had consumed. "Well, I am only glad that since *my husband* abstains from strong drink, he will not be counted among your husband's clientele."

"It must be very comforting, Mrs. Gunn, to be so superior to the rest of us. I do hope that our children may yet be friends."

Mrs. Gunn gathered her daughters. "This is a wild place, Mrs. Justice. I had wished to find female companionship here."

"I shall not choose it over the companionship of my husband. I'm certain you understand."

"Well, good day then, Mrs. Justice." The three sailed out of the cabin, without acknowledging Nate, who stood slack-jawed.

Clara crossed the room and slammed the door.

"What the Sam Hill did you just do?" he asked.

"I believe I offended her while I defended you."

Nate leaned back against the cabin wall. "I never saw the like."

Clara felt her temper drain away leaving only a sickness in her stomach at her outrageous display of temper. "Are you ashamed of me?"

He clasped his hands about her waist. "Ashamed? I'm so proud, I could bust a button. Only person in this world ever stood up for me was…"

She gazed up into his eyes. "Jacob."

He nodded.

She wrapped her arms about him, and he pulled her to the warm comfort of his embrace. "We both miss him. He was such a good man."

Above her head, she felt Nate nod.

Clara drew back. "But that woman insulted us. I'll not take that kind of treatment from anyone again. I'm through with turning the other cheek."

"Well, she was right about one thing. Her husband abstains from strong drink." Nate grinned. "I only ever saw him drink beer—lots of beer."

Clara gaped and then covered her mouth as the laughter shook her. "Why didn't you tell her?"

"And lose one of my best customers?"

"Oh, you have more restraint than I. I would certainly have hurled *that* into her face."

"No, you wouldn't." He hesitated and then released her. "I built a tunnel from the hardware store to the saloon so he can come and go without his wife seeing him cross the street.

They live behind the dry goods store, and I hear she watches him like a hawk."

"A tunnel!"

Her laughter was contagious. He joined her with a rich booming baritone laugh. Kitty scampered over, laughing at a joke she did not understand and he lifted her into his arms. He held her on his hip and pressed Clara to his side. She felt happy for the first time since their arrival.

"Thank you," said Nate.

Clara waved a dismissive hand. "She's a…well, I can't say what she is." She swept her head meaningfully in the direction of her daughter.

"She's a what, Mama? A what?"

Clara hesitated and then said, "An uncharitable woman."

"She's also one of the only respectable women here in Colorado City."

"Then I shall do without respectability until it arrives with tolerance."

He gave her a squeeze. "Mighty unexpected. But you may have made an enemy today."

Clara lifted her chin. "Not my first."

He smiled. "I don't believe that."

"And why not?"

"You never did a bad thing in your life Clara. What kind of enemy could you possibly have?"

She thought of Bickerfield and suppressed a shudder.

Chapter Eight

❧∾◦∽❧

The guilt was eating her alive. Clara could barely meet his gaze any longer. He thought her pure and good and without fault. He'd witnessed her very unbecoming fit of temper and still he made excuses, thinking she'd only tried to protect his honor. Perhaps that was part of it. But she was far, far from the paragon of virtue he believed her to be.

She could never live up to his expectations. She had tried with Jacob, but at least he knew of her past.

Clara tucked her daughter into bed and told her the story of Rose Red, while Nate sat quietly by the fire nodding and smiling.

She joined him there after Kitty had dropped off to sleep.

"You're a good mother," he said.

Pride swelled in her chest and then deflated like punched bread dough as she realized his opinion of her was jaded.

"Did you learn the stories from your mother?"

She shifted uncomfortably, thinking the time was right to broach the subject of her past. She feared telling him the truth nearly as much as letting this wall of lies between them stand.

"I read them in a book Jacob gave me. He was such a good father."

He gave her a look of such longing it took her breath away.

"I'd like to be a good father, too. I've always wanted to feel a part of a family. But I didn't know how to go about it. Now Jacob has provided me with even that."

"And he has given me a fine husband."

He snorted waving away the compliment. He opened his mouth to speak and then hesitated. "I know you loved him, Clara."

How could one not love Jacob? He was dear and kind, if somewhat naive in his always believing the best in people.

"Yes, I did."

Nate's eyes fixed on the mica window in the stove, staring at the orange glow beyond.

"After loving him, could you—I mean, could you ever love another man?"

She smiled at him. "A woman's heart is a marvelous thing. It has unlimited capacity for love. When Kitty was born, I thought my heart would burst from the love I held for her. But it did not diminish the tenderness I felt for my husband."

His gaze returned to her again, cast in the soft glow from the stove.

"Loving one man does not mean I cannot love another."

Was that hope she saw in his eyes? It vanished so quickly she was not certain.

"You have feelings for me, Clara?"

She nodded. "There is a force between us that never existed between Jacob and me. Surely you feel it?"

He did. And he knew exactly what it was—desire. He stared at her lovely mouth. Each night was like torture, lying beside her, listening to her soft breathing, inhaling her scent.

Never did he expect to find such attraction with a lady. In his experience, respectable females were about as warm as an ice house in January. But Clara proved him wrong. My God, she'd even defended him against that Gunn woman.

She was a contradiction and she fascinated him.

The fire crackled between them, and it had nothing to do with the stove. She'd lie with him if he asked. Still he hesitated because if it were only lust, if she felt none of the love and desire she stirred in him, the pain might kill him. Somehow he had already fallen in love with her.

Jacob had been right. No one who knew Clara could not love her.

She broke the silence. "Nate, I want to tell you something about myself. Something personal."

He turned, giving her his full attention. "Go on then."

"I told you I was poor in my youth. Nate, I used to have to beg on the street."

He couldn't mask his surprise.

"We were desperate, destitute. Our situation could not have been more grave. One day a man took me from that life. He was well dressed and handsome. He promised me marriage."

Nate felt his stomach clench. Somehow he just couldn't abide another singing of Jacob's praises. He stood and she followed him, her hands clasped before her in tight knots.

"I thought he was my rescuer but—"

He silenced her in the only way he knew how, by pressing his lips to hers. She stiffened in surprise and then softened against him, swaying until his chest met the wonderful curves of her bosom. Her kisses told him what she wanted.

Nate knew how to please a woman. He just didn't know how to make one love him. If only she could love him just a little. He drew her into his arms, deepening the kiss as she clung to him. In a moment he had her up on the sturdy chopping block he had brought her. Her legs splayed to allow him to press himself to the juncture of her legs. She made soft moaning sounds that roused him to near madness.

Up went her skirts as he located the slit in her pantaloons, finding the soft silk of her inner thigh. She whimpered and leaned back as he trailed kisses along her throat, feeling her blood pulse in the great vessel there.

He caressed her, searching the soft folds of female flesh to find the bud at her center. He stroked with his thumb as his fingers danced along her sensitive flesh, finding her wet with wanting.

Her breathing became more frantic and she grasped at his clothing in desperation. Her eyes opened wide as she approached her pleasure.

"Please, Nate, please take me now."

He held back, determined to resist. She only needed what he could give her—not him. She didn't want him.

His kiss silenced her pleas as his fingers did their work. She arched and stiffened. His mouth absorbed her cry of release.

He held her as she trembled and gasped, lowering her skirts back to her ankles.

"Why?" she whispered. "Why would you not take me?"

"You're still Jacob's wife."

She thumped her open palms upon his chest in a blow that surprised him. "I am *your* wife."

"Not by choice, but from circumstance merely. I won't take advantage of you."

"I need you. Why do you push me away?"

He turned from her, trying to ignore the pulsing want she raised in him. "I have given you what you need."

She gasped, and her eyes widened with shock. He offended her and perhaps that was best. When her eyes misted, he backed away, fleeing the cabin like the coward he was.

Clara slid her feet to the floor, following him. She stopped at the front step as he disappeared into the night, then she sat on the cold stone.

He didn't believe she needed him. Could he not see she was desperate for his touch? Still he held himself in check. How did this happen? One moment she was determined to confess all and the next she was sitting on the chopping block.

She closed her eyes to savor the sweet sensations still rippling through her. How could she convince him that she could love him if he would only let her?

A family—that was what he'd said. He wanted to be part of a family. Clara could give him children, but first she would need him in her bed.

She had half a mind to march over to that bar and insist. Then she remembered Bickerfield and trembled. He wanted money.

Sweet Jesus, what was she to do?

She sat a long time on that rock until she had a plan. In the morning she rose to find Nate had not returned. She went to the hardware store but found only his partner, Harvey Winkelman.

"I need to speak to the reverend," she said.

Harvey looked surprised. "Well, I can stir him up, if you don't mind watching the shop."

"Certainly."

It took longer than she expected. In the meantime Kitty played checkers with Katherine, who spotted them on the main street and joined them at the store. Clara sold a pick to a miner with a broken tooth. Harvey returned at last with the man she requested, whose bloodshot eyes told of a long sleepless night.

"How is the happy bride?" he asked.

"I have some concerns. May we speak in private?"

Harvey stepped into the supply room, giving them some privacy as Clara lowered her voice to explain her dilemma. The reverend recovered from his initial shock and vowed to speak to Nate about his responsibilities.

Clara returned home and waited on pins and needles as the afternoon wore on into evening. Her only visitor was Katherine Gunn, who came after lunch to ask if Kitty might like to come to her house to play. At first reluctant, Clara then decided it was best if Kitty had a friend. She walked her child to the Gunns'.

Mrs. Gunn greeted her at the door.

"I am regretful we got off on the wrong foot. Please accept my apologies," said Mrs. Gunn.

Clara did not admit her surprise, but studied the woman for signs of sarcasm. Finding none she nodded. "Certainly."

"We must stick together, you and me. There are so few women here."

Clara knew there were many women, but they resided on the south side, safely away from Mrs. Gunn's delicate sensibilities.

"Is it all right if Kitty plays with Katherine?"

"Of course. I'll walk her home before supper, shall I?"

Clara departed pausing on Colorado Avenue when she heard a familiar voice raised in anger. The reverend backed out of the saloon with Nate in pursuit. Her husband held a raised gun pointed at the reverend's nose.

The preacher fell in the mud.

"Don't you tell me my business again," shouted Nate.

He holstered his gun and then chanced to glance in her direction. The look he aimed sent her into motion. He stalked toward her as she hurried toward home. She made it to within sight of her front door before he captured her elbow.

He growled at her through gritted teeth. "I got your message."

She said nothing as he hustled her toward the house that she now realized held no refuge. She did not think he would strike her, but still she held some doubt. She thanked God her daughter was safely away.

He did not speak until thrusting her within and closing the latch behind her.

"Where is Kitty?" he asked.

"At the Gunns'."

His scowl deepened as he stalked forward. "So you told the reverend I haven't slept with you. 'My duties' he called them."

She backed away but he reached out, capturing her wrist.

"You want me that bad? You got me."

The fierce embrace did not injure, but left no doubt who was in command. His kiss showed less control as he took her mouth with a possessiveness that heated her blood.

She wrapped her arms about him and tugged him toward the bed. He set her aside and she tried not to whimper in disappointment. He would not reject her again, she prayed, not after seeking her out.

He released the buckle of his gun belt, and then the cord about his thigh. He reached for her, expertly stripping away her clothing until he left her naked before him. She covered herself with her hands.

"Don't," he ordered. "You wanted this and, by God, you'll have it."

He tugged his shirt over his head, throwing it aside before grasping his boots. These he hurled across the room so they crashed against the wall.

Nate turned to her, panting. His eyes fixed on her like prey and she did not know if his expression indicated fury or desire. She dared a step of retreat, but he hauled her up against him and then carried her backward to the bed.

She trembled at the delicious warmth of his naked chest as he pressed her to the mattress, letting her feel his arousal through the coarse denim of his trousers. He released the buttons shoving aside this last barrier.

She opened her thighs to him, wanting him to join them with a need that stole her words. He cupped her breasts. She closed her eyes at the delight of his kisses on her sensitive skin and the wonderful pressure of his hands upon her flesh. When he sucked at her nipple she moaned at the pleasure he drew from her and rocked her hips in invitation. His hands shifted, holding her down as his gaze pinned her. He slid forward to join them.

She gasped as he filled her. His possessive gaze never left her, as her breath caught at the fierce desire she saw blazing in his eyes.

"You're mine," he said.

"Yes," she whispered.

Now he moved, quick and deep as he captured her hips, bringing her up to meet each powerful thrust. Her insides quickened as the rising tide of pleasure carrying her upward toward her release. With a swiftness that shocked and overwhelmed, she reached her summit, crying out her joy. His stroke quickened as he drove into her again and again. She wrapped her legs about his waist to bring him deeper within her. He arched and cried out her name as he spilled his seed.

At last, she thought, *he has made me his own.* She had never expected to find such pleasure in coupling. Her first experiences were embarrassing and painful. Jacob's lovemaking was always gentle and sweet. Neither had prepared her for this rushing torrent of delight.

This man was a good father and an excellent provider. Either of those would have been enough to satisfy her. But these things he did to her took her breath away. She was the luckiest woman in the world.

She stroked his head as he lay damp and panting upon her replete body. He was like her, full of fears and flaws, but inside he tried, perhaps too hard, to please. Here was a man she could love.

No—not a man she *could* love, she realized. A man she *did* love. She had fallen in love with him the day he called Kitty his own. She leaned close to his ear and whispered. "I love you, Nathaniel."

He groaned and rolled away, throwing his arm across his eyes as if he could not stand the sight of her.

The first inkling of worry nipped at her. "What is it?"

Nate lifted his arm and met her gaze. Her stomach tightened at the obvious suffering written in each line of his face.

"Love me? I just used you like a… Clara, my God, you should have a husband who can control his anger and his lust. You deserve a gentle hand."

"I prefer your hand." She lifted up upon her elbow and drew his palm to her breast, gasping at the shaft of pleasure that drew her nipple to a point. "Nate, I am not a fragile violet to be crushed by your embrace. I am stronger than you think."

He drew back his hand, adjusting himself and fastening his trousers.

"You should not have to suffer my lustful urges." His hands knit in his hair and balled into fists. "My God, did I hurt you?"

She laughed, but his face stayed fixed in a look of repentance. He slid from the bed, grasping his shirt and gunbelt before retrieving his boots.

"Where are you going?" she asked, drawing the sheet up to cover her nakedness.

"I should be whipped."

He shrugged into his shirt and latched on his gun.

"You're not leaving me."

He did just that, and in such a hurry, he went out in his stocking feet, carrying his boots in his arms. By the time Clara was up and dressed, he was long gone.

She sank into a chair. Why did he think her so fragile?

And then she knew. Jacob's letters, again. He had created a lady to be worshipped instead of loved—someone untouchable when Clara longed for Nathaniel's touch. Now she was trapped by this lie.

He would hear the truth. All of it. If he understood that she had made mistakes, terrible mistakes and done things of which she was not proud, then perhaps he could understand that she was like him.

If anyone could sympathize, it should be Nate.

Dared she take the risk? She gambled with her daughter's life as well. Doubts filled her mind. He was stubborn and unforgiving. What if he blamed her for her deceit? What if he could not find it in his heart to forgive?

He had not forgiven his father. She bit her lip and considered what she had to lose.

Could she risk Kitty's new home on her selfish desire to win his love?

She rested her elbows upon the table and her cheeks upon her hands. She must tell him. With nothing but lies between them, what chance did they have to become a family?

Chapter Nine

Nate stood behind the bar staring at the street. He thought he could do as Jacob asked but he couldn't. He'd never make a proper husband—didn't have it in him.

Jacob had asked him to look after his family. Nate had thought that marrying his widow would be the surest way to offer his protection.

But who would protect Clara from him?

He didn't deserve to walk on the same side of the street with her, let alone share her bed.

He groaned at the memory. He'd tossed her down like a doxy and showed not the least restraint as he'd used her. He'd wanted her to see the beast he kept locked away, all because she had hurt his pride. If any other man had touched her the way he just had, he'd see him lynched.

And the saddest part of all was that he loved her. Who could not love her? Clara was gentle and kind. But she wasn't for him. Too damn perfect for his sorry hide.

What had happened between them would happen again. He knew that for sure. It was why he'd tried so hard to keep his hands from her. Now he'd tasted that apple and, Lord help him, he'd never have his fill. She was without equal, just as Jacob had said, singular to her gender.

He'd told her she was his. Now he knew she never would be.

Nate pressed his palms flat to the mahogany bar he'd had shipped from Illinois. He knew what had to be done and it broke his heart. Even though their time together had been difficult, he had never been happier. He loved Kitty and Clara and knew his life would be poorer without them.

But Kitty needed a father to be proud of, not some savage saloon keeper, and Clara deserved a gentleman like Jacob.

Things had been better off before their arrival, when he was alone, because then he did not know what he missed. Certainly he recognized something was lacking but now he knew just what that something was and that he could not keep them. For love, he would do what was best for Clara and Kitty.

He'd leave her enough money to buy the damn town. He'd sell the saloon and leave his share of the store to Clara. Maybe in time she'd forgive him, but he didn't deserve it.

They were finding gold in Montana. Plenty of fools there waiting be separated from their nuggets. He'd be happy to oblige.

Now that he'd decided, he couldn't put it off. Best to tell her right away.

He found Clara at the washtub, scrubbing his shirts. He felt guilty for bringing her to this place.

She straightened and brushed a damp curl of hair from her face. Then noticing him, she gave a tentative smile. It died there upon her lips.

Clara held up a palm, which was pink and raw from the lye in the soap. "Let me speak first, please."

She dried her hands upon her white apron and stepped closer.

"I have been burdened with something, a lie that needs correcting. I want to apologize for making you think I am other than what I am."

What was this nonsense?

"I tried to tell you yesterday about the man who took me from the streets."

"Jacob," he said.

Her eyes widened. "No. His name was Carl Bickerfield. He was a libertine, who promised me marriage. It wasn't until much later, after he had his way with me, that I learned his true intentions. He planned to make me a prostitute in the goldfields."

"Bickerfield? Where did you hear his name?"

"He was the man who seduced me."

He knew of the man, had read about him in the newspaper. He had beaten two whores to death in Bakersfield and was wanted for hanging. Why she would choose this name for her outlandish tale escaped him.

"Clara, what are you talking about?"

"I am trying to tell you that I am not the proper lady you believe me to be. I have a past of which I am ashamed and am unworthy of you."

"Unworthy? You—of me?" It was all he could do not to laugh out loud. Then he saw what this was. She'd grasped his feelings and taken steps to stop him. Somehow she knew what he intended, perhaps even before he did. This was some female trick to make herself seem more suitable.

"Nate, I love you and pray that you will forgive me."

As if he had any right to judge her. Even if it was true, which it wasn't, he'd not be distracted from his purpose. He'd fulfill his promise to Jacob and be gone.

"Clara, I've come to tell you something as well."

She gazed up with large hopeful eyes. He reminded himself of what he'd done to her. It was all the reason he needed to do what was right.

"I'm leaving. You'll get the house, my share of the hardware store and all the profits from the saloon. It is more than enough to provide for you and Kitty. In a few years you can claim abandonment and marry a respectable man. I'm sure there'll be a line around the block to fill that post."

"You're leaving?" The sorrow in her voice nearly broke his heart.

"I am."

"Please stay."

"This is best."

She cried as he stood rigidly before her, chewing the inside of his cheek bloody.

Both Clara and Kitty were waiting on the step when he came to say farewell. He hugged the child and felt the tug of regret for that which he would never have.

"Be good and listen to your ma," he said and released her.

Kitty cried and clutched his leg.

Clara pulled her off and lifted the weeping child to her hip.

"Will you reconsider?" she asked.

He shook his head, not trusting his words. Getting on his horse was the hardest feat he'd ever pulled. Riding away took more courage than facing the Apache.

As he rode, he chewed on his regrets. He wished he could have been the man she deserved, but that man was dead and buried.

Clara needed a decent husband, like a banker or grocer. Up until today he'd acted as assayer and unofficial banker in town, and owned the biggest saloon and gaming hall in Colorado City. But no longer. He didn't own a thing that wasn't respectable now.

He drew up on the reins.

An idea rose in his mind, like a tiny bubble in a glass of beer. No, it couldn't work. He only conceived it out of the desperate sorrow caused by losing Clara.

But what if he could?

He let the idea grow with possibilities. He wouldn't need a tunnel to sneak people in and out of this business. He'd have a line of work more suited to a family man.

Hardware and banking. He knew he could pull off the business part of it. He'd never had any trouble making money. It was the one thing at which he excelled.

He felt himself flush. Well, one of the things.

But what about the other half?

Could he be a gentleman? Just acting like one didn't make it so. His father would say you can't make a silk purse out of a sow's ear.

Nate spat in the dirt. Well, the hell with him. How long was he going to let that bastard tell him what he could and couldn't do?

He was his own man now. And if he wasn't fit for the likes of Clara Justice, he'd just have to make himself fit. That's what he'd do—he'd become the man she deserved.

He wheeled his horse around just short of the town of Burns and headed back toward Colorado City. Now that he'd decided, he was anxious to find Clara and see if she'd be willing to take him back.

The horse moved from a trot to a lope as Nate grew impatient to see her again. For the first time since her arrival, he had hope that he might make this work.

His horse was lathered when he arrived, and he knew he should take him to the livery, but instead he steered for home at an impatient walk, so as not to kick up too much dust.

He found his front door open and saw a man standing within his cabin. His senses on alert, he swung down and headed in.

Clara's eyes widened at his entrance, but it took her only an instant to run to his side. Before him, stood Carl Kingston.

"Ah, Mr. Justice, just the man I seek."

Nate pushed Clara behind him and squared his shoulders. Clara pressed herself to him so he could feel her trembling.

Nate gripped the handle of his pistol. "Why are you here?"

"Business, my friend. I thought your wife would have told you. We are old acquaintances, she and I." He leered in Clara's direction.

Nate's hands curled into fists.

"I see she has not and you are in the dark. Let me enlighten you. I found your precious bride begging on the docks in Albany. Filthy as she was, I saw she had qualities that could be turned to coin. But the little vixen bewitched your brother before I had a chance to change my investment into profit. I mean to correct that now."

Nate's jaw dropped. She had told him the truth and he had not believed one word.

"I see I have shocked you. Others will be shocked as well. For the good people to learn that your wife was once a member of my stables, well, I think you will agree, it wouldn't do.

"But you are well off and I am a man of business. My silence can be bought."

Nate cocked his fist and punched the man in the face. Kingston hit the ground on all fours, blood running from his mouth. Between his hands lay his two front teeth.

"I told you what would happen if you came round my house again."

He took a step forward and Kingston retreated on all fours, scuttling backward like a crab.

Nate hauled Kingston to his feet. "And you can tell everyone you meet about Clara and it won't change my love for her. But it will change how many teeth you have in your head."

Kingston whimpered and lifted a hand in supplication. Nate grabbed him by the collar and hauled him out into the street. Clara hovered in the door, wringing her hands.

"This here's Carl Bickerfield?" he asked her.

She nodded, biting her lower lip. He turned attention back to the vermin in his grip. Resisting the urge to throttle this man was hard, but he did it for her sake.

"Wait here," he ordered and then dragged Bickerfield to Colorado Avenue. The man struggled as Nate threw open a door, coming to a halt before Sheriff Dagget's desk.

"This here is Carl Bickerfield. Wanted in California for murdering two women." Nate released his quarry.

The man dropped to the ground, still spitting blood.

"What?" said Dagget, rising to peer over the desk at the wreckage Nate left before him. "How do you know?"

"Later." Nate spun on his heels, returning the way he had come. He had business to attend and not even this murderer would keep him from Clara one second longer than necessary.

As he crossed before the jail's front window, he saw Dagget pulling Bickersfield toward an open cell.

Nate still wanted to kill the man for what he'd done to Clara, but knew a noose was in the fellow's future as soon as the sheriff in Bakersfield confirmed Nate's story. Bickerfield wouldn't be abusing any more women—that much was certain.

Nate had to keep himself from running back to Clara.

He found her right where he had left her. She moved back into the house as he mounted the front steps.

Clara gripped his arm as he cleared the doorframe. "You came back. You rescued me."

He nodded. "He'll trouble us no longer."

Her sigh of relief was audible.

He stood staring at her as if he had never seen her before in his life. For in fact, he had not. He had seen only what he chose to see.

He turned to face his wife. His images of her as flawless shattered against the truth. She was imperfect, fallible, human—like him. She made mistakes and carried the scars of her life, just as he did. He had not seen it, had not believed it even when she told him the truth. His own stubborn misconceptions nearly caused him to throw away the only woman he'd ever loved and, if she was to be believed, the only woman who'd ever loved him. What a great fool he was.

"Can you forgive me?" they asked in unison.

Her eyes widened. "Forgive you? You saved me from that horrible man. You've given me so much."

"Except my trust. I should have believed you when you came to me."

"I'm so ashamed." Her chin sunk to her chest.

"I still don't think I deserve you, but I'm a step closer to thinking this can work."

Her head snapped up. "What?"

"Clara, I could never live up to my brother's standards."

Her words came on a whispered breath. "Neither could I."

He laughed.

She clasped his hands. "I do have a temper, among other faults. It was terribly difficult for me to be the minister's wife. I am sorry I am not the woman you expected."

"I thank God for it, because I expected a rail-thin schoolmarm with crooked teeth, staunch morals and no feminine allure."

She gasped. "You did?"

He gave a quick nod. "You're the woman for me, Clara Stanton Justice. Jacob knew it all along. It just took me a while to come around to the same conclusion. I'll be forever grateful to him for having faith in me."

She smiled and wrapped her arms about his waist.

"Jacob said something to me. I didn't understand it at the time but I think he was right."

Nate's brow rose in question.

"He said that you needed me."

He smiled. "I sure do. I can't live without you."

"I love you, Nathaniel."

"I couldn't believe it before. Now I can't believe my luck. I love you, too, Clara. Now and always."

She rested her head upon his chest.

"Why did you come back?"

"I decided I was a damn fool and I'd give it another shot."

Their gazes met and he saw the love she held for him.

"Where's Kitty?" he asked.

"At the Gunns' again. They have a stereoscope." An inviting sparkle glittered in her eyes and he felt himself rising to her unspoken invitation.

She drew back to link her arm with his. "I've been thinking as well."

"Oh, yes?"

She nodded, giving him a coy smile as she closed the door and led him toward their bed.

"I have plans to create the family you deserve."

His heart squeezed as the sweetness of her words struck him.

"That is, if you're willing."

He pulled her close.

"More than willing."

She unfastened the top button of his shirt. "Then I suggest we begin right away."

* * * * *

Paying the Playboy's Price

(Silhouette Desire #1732)

by

EMILIE ROSE

Juliana Alden is determined to have her last—
her only—fling before settling down. And she's
found the perfect candidate: bachelor Rex Tanner.
He's pure playboy charm...but can she afford
his price?

Trust Fund Affairs: They've just spent a fortune—
the bachelors had better be worth it.

Don't miss the other titles in this series:

EXPOSING THE EXECUTIVE'S SECRETS (July)
BENDING TO THE BACHELOR'S WILL (August)

On sale this June from Silhouette Desire.

*Available wherever books are sold, including most
bookstores, supermarkets, discount stores and drugstores.*

HOTEL MARCHAND

**Four sisters.
A family legacy.
And someone is out to destroy it.**

**A captivating new limited
continuity, launching June 2006**

The most beautiful hotel in New Orleans,
and someone is out to destroy it. But mystery,
danger and some surprising family revelations
and discoveries won't stop the Marchand sisters
from protecting their birthright…
and finding love along the way.

**Hidden in the secrets of antiquity,
lies the unimagined truth...**

Introducing

**ROGUE
ANGEL**™

a brand-new line filled with mystery
and suspense, action and adventure,
and a fascinating look into history.

And it all begins with DESTINY.

In a sealed crypt in
France, where the
terrifying legend of
the beast of Gevaudan
begins to unravel,
Annja Creed discovers
a stunning artifact
that will seal her destiny.

*Available every other
month starting
July 2006, wherever
you buy books.*

GOLD
EAGLE ®

GRA1

Page-turning drama...

Exotic, glamorous locations...

Intense emotion and passionate seduction...

Sheikhs, princes and billionaire tycoons...

This summer, may we suggest:

THE SHEIKH'S DISOBEDIENT BRIDE
by Jane Porter

On sale June.

AT THE GREEK TYCOON'S BIDDING
by Cathy Williams

On sale July.

THE ITALIAN MILLIONAIRE'S VIRGIN WIFE

On sale August.

With new titles to choose from every month,
discover a world of romance in our books written
by internationally bestselling authors.

It's the ultimate in quality romance!

Available wherever Harlequin books are sold.

www.eHarlequin.com

HPGEN06

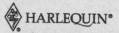

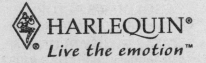